T3-BVR-751

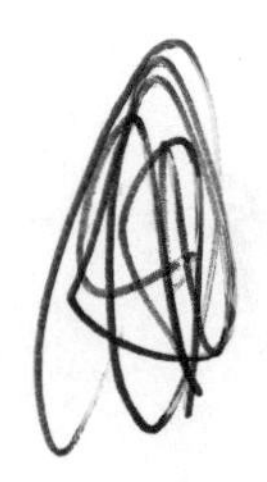

R.S.V.P. MURDER

Also by Mignon G. Eberhart in Large Print:

Alpine Condo Crossfire
Another Woman's House
Casa Madrone
A Fighting Chance
Five Passengers from Lisbon
Melora
Murder by an Aristocrat
Next of Kin
The Patient in Room 18
Three Days for Emeralds
Two Little Rich Girls
Unidentified Woman
The White Cockatoo

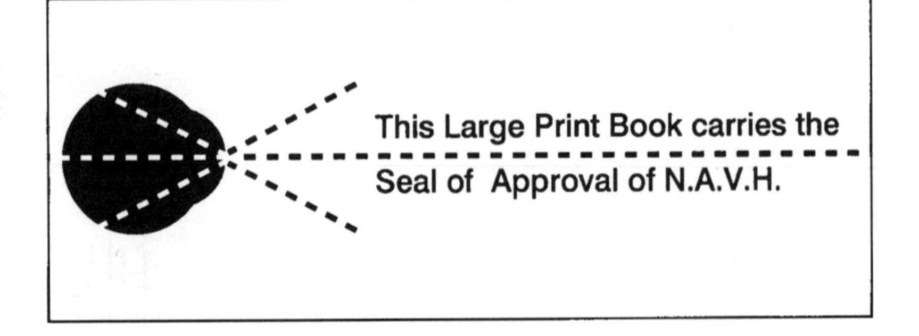

R.S.V.P.
MURDER

Mignon G. Eberhart

Thorndike Press • Waterville, Maine

Published in 2001 by arrangement with
Brandt & Brandt Literary Agents, Inc.

Thorndike Press Large Print Romance Series.

The tree indicium is a trademark of Thorndike Press.

The text of this Large Print edition is unabridged.
Other aspects of the book may vary from the original edition.

Set in 16 pt. Plantin by Al Chase.

Printed in the United States on permanent paper.

Library of Congress Cataloging-in-Publication Data

Eberhart, Mignon Good, 1899–
R.S.V.P. murder / Mignon G. Eberhart.
p. cm.
ISBN 0-7862-3516-0 (lg. print : hc : alk. paper)
1. Rich people — Fiction. 2. New York (N.Y.) — Fiction.
3. Large type books. I. Title: RSVP murder. II. Title.
PS3509.B453 R18 2001
813′.52—dc21 2001034745

R.S.V.P.
MURDER

1

Both houses have been sold.

The house near Gramercy Park was sold to a club. I have wondered whether or not anyone has shied a hat at the marble curls of the Venus who stood in the hall, or if anyone has dropped an overcoat over her white nudity. I don't think so. It is a very sedate club.

I wonder, too, if a certain room in that house is ever quite warm.

Richard said once, "A plague on both our houses." He laughed when he said it but he had little humor in his eyes.

The trial is a thing of the past. Perhaps its conclusion might have been foreseen.

Tonight is again New Year's Eve. The sun has been golden all day and the sea very blue but growing purple as the sun drops down. On the Promenade I saw a man and woman who reminded me of Lord and Lady Tweed but when I hurried to catch up with them, I was mistaken; they turned blank, polite faces to me.

Tonight there will be festive dinners, everywhere. Tonight at midnight the dance orchestras will pause; for a moment the lights will be put out and everyone will kiss everybody else and then with a burst the lights will go on and the New Year will come in.

Perhaps it was inevitable in its way, this return to Nice. Nothing really started here; the beginnings were obscure, only gathered together all at once and coming to a climax at the same time. But for me the beginning was in Nice.

That was Christmas Day a year ago and all the bells sang, Noël, Noël. The Cathedral bell alone sent forth a solemn dong, dong, dong, which set up respondent vibrations along the streets with their gray houses and bougainvillaea-draped walls and sunny balconies.

In New York the skies were leaden and, as it happened, a violent snowstorm was in the making. In New York, I recalled, Christmas wreaths hung in the elevators of the great apartment houses. I wondered how the Plaza and Rockefeller Center were decorated for the Christmas season; I thought of the Christmas-trimmed windows of the Fifth Avenue stores. I thought of the Santa Clauses at every street corner with their red suits and padded stomachs and white hair and beards. But this was Christmas Day. I wondered what happened to them, once Christmas was over; did they take off their red suits and wigs and padding, and disappear? New York seemed a long way from Nice and I was in Nice.

I went to the service in the Cathedral; the floor was stone and cold, the air had an age-old stillness, the service was grave and beautiful. I then walked over to the Promenade des Anglais. I had no notion whatever that I was being followed.

It was one of those gold and blue days in Nice, with the Mediterranean looking as if it had distilled all the blues in the world and thus produced its own, almost unearthly blue. There were other strollers on the Promenade. There was the usual young French family: Papa very proud and conscious of his responsibility, Mama concerned with her hat and her offspring, the whole little family with their hands joined. There were the usual English, looking rather stuffed, as if they had on whole layers of woolies below their tweeds, striding along at the grimly determined pace of their grim constitutionals. A bus discharged a load of Bedouins, I guessed, clad in flowing white burnooses. The contrast of costume and conveyance amused and diverted me for a moment. Then I knew that someone had approached quite near me, as if he had been on the watch for a moment when I was not looking and had sprung from ambush. He was dapper, dark and smiling. He said, "Miss Hilliard."

He then took off his dapper hat, disclosing black hair as shiny as his shoes, and said, "I wish to speak to you. Your father's affairs —"

A wave of heavy perfume drifted out in a cloud all around me. He smiled but his eyes didn't smile; in fact, I didn't like the look in them at all. I particularly didn't like his perfume.

It seemed likely, however, that there was some tag end of business — some bill, perhaps, concerned with my father's illness and death — which I had not paid — and I had a wave of dismay, for my sheaf of traveler's checks had grown very thin. Before I could question him he said, "My name is Benni—" I couldn't hear the rest of the name — Bennivici, Bennedetto, I didn't know what. He looked at me slyly, however, as if I should recognize his name.

I said, "Is it a bill I haven't paid?"

His eyes flickered exactly like the shutter of a camera clicking. "No, no. That is — your father — business — a little talk with you — one of his clients —"

My father had been a lawyer, a trial lawyer, what is called a criminal lawyer. Still I didn't think it likely that Mr. Benni had been the type of client my father accepted.

It then struck me rather sharply that I had no idea at all of what the type of client my father accepted could possibly be. That part of his life had always been shut away from me. I said, "I don't know anything about my father's affairs. His office is in New York —"

Mr. Benni's dark eyes were very nasty indeed and very skeptical. I couldn't have failed to see that.

He said after a pause, "You might wish to know that the account will be settled. I think a talk with you would be of some benefit. Terms — all that. I have my car here, perhaps a ride in this so nice day —"

Well, I wouldn't have gone for a ride with him. I don't think either that if he had walked along the Promenade with me or even stood for another moment or two talking, he would have slipped a knife through my beautiful Chanel suit and into me, not there in the sunny daylight and full view of other strollers. In any event he didn't have the chance, for at that instant Lord and Lady Tweed bore down upon us.

That was not their name; I never knew their name; they lived at the hotel and it was the name my fancy had given them. Lady Tweed said, "How ja do?" and looked remote and embarrassed by her own action. Lord Tweed cleared his throat, looked out over the Mediterranean, mumbled, "— back to the hotel — might join us —" and looked even more embarrassed than his wife, but determined.

I didn't clutch at them but felt like it. "Thank you," I said, and to Mr. Benni, whose eyes looked very cold and very ugly at this development, "If you'll write to my father's office — I really know nothing of his affairs —"

"The receipt," Mr. Benni said. I had a notion that he wanted to seize me by the arm. "I — that is, terms and the — the receipt —"

"I'm sorry — his office — good morning —" It was jumbled up. I marched off between the Tweeds and didn't look back, but I had the absurd feeling that Mr. Benni was standing perfectly still, watching me with that ugly look which I could almost feel sticking into my back.

"Wrong un," Lord Tweed said presently.

"Young gel like you," Lady Tweed said.

I understood both of them as if they had

uttered long speeches and said again, "Thank you."

Lord Tweed muttered something about feller should see solicitors, not annoy gel.

We parted at the door of the dining room in the hotel. Lord Tweed coughed and said, "Heard about your father. Sorry. Pity." Lady Tweed unexpectedly and firmly shook hands with me. I never saw them again. I have never forgotten them.

I did forget them though for a few hours, as I forgot lunch and forgot the perfumed Mr. Benni, for the desk clerk, in spite of its being Christmas Day, had a registered letter for me; it was a long envelope with the return address of Mr. Hatever, who had shared my father's offices for many years.

The letter had been a long time coming and had been preceded by one or two formalities; I had cabled Mr. Hatever about my father's illness and death. I had also asked his advice about my father's estate for a simple reason; I was rapidly running out of money and had none to draw on. Mr. Hatever had replied with regrets and told me that he should have a limited power of attorney in order to act for me; I had immediately sent this on to him by way of the first *avocat's* office I encountered near the hotel. He had acknowledged its receipt and then there was a silence until that day and this letter.

I hurried up to the suite which my father had extravagantly taken and which I, as extravagantly, had retained, although I had given up my father's bedroom after his death and had moved his baggage and clothing into a closet of my room. I read the letter in the living room of that suite and in ten minutes began to wonder how I was going to pay for it. I wondered how I was going to pay my way home, too. There were many things for me to think about, for my safe and secure if rather odd world had been swept away. Mr. Hatever's letter was regretful, kind and perfectly clear.

My father had been a lawyer. He had left no will. He had thus died intestate. That hadn't made any difference, Mr. Hatever explained, for I was his only heir, but the fact was, there was nothing to inherit. There was almost no estate to leave to anybody.

Mr. Hatever had induced the inheritance tax appraisers to do their chore promptly, and it appeared to be a wasted effort on everybody's part. There was no life insurance. There was one bank account, which was overdrawn, and another in which there was a total deposit of one hundred and thirty-three dollars. There was no safe deposit box, too clearly because there was nothing to put in it. There was the house at Ninety Pennyroyal Street. This is a short street forgotten by all but old-time New Yorkers, wedged into the otherwise orderly and numbered streets and avenues surrounding Gramercy Park. It appeared that my father, just before our unexpected trip abroad, had increased the already heavy mortgage on the house. And that was all. Mr. Hatever sent his sympathy and best wishes, and I thought, I'll need them.

I know that I read the letter over and over, though after the first shock I not only believed Mr. Hatever but I also knew that the situation was perfectly consistent with my father's character.

He had earned money; he had earned some very large fees indeed; he had also spent money. He lived in a flamboyant way; he did everything in the grand style. Perhaps it was a theatrical temper, perhaps it was a requirement of the façade he showed the world. In any event, it was his style.

And he had died at exactly the right time. It is not so given to every man. His professional sun must have been setting for some time, and he was too astute not to know it. I was then sure that the increased mortgage on the house near Gramercy Park had supplied the money for this trip abroad. I think I knew, too, that while my father had denied ever having had a heart attack preceding the attack which resulted in his short and merciful illness and death, almost certainly he had lied. He had been perfectly aware of his own condition and that was why he had taken me out of school so suddenly; he had tried in his own way to make up for the years during which we had seen little of each other.

This school, by the way, was one of many schools in New York, in Paris, in Switzerland. I had sensed long ago that my father really didn't know what to do with me, and schools seemed the answer, at least while I was very young. I neither liked nor disliked the procession of schools; in self-defense I chose a special study, modern languages, but cannot say that I became an expert. However, I had resolved to call a halt to this peripatetic educational process. I was twenty and I was going to tell my father, in the coming summer, that I'd had enough and I wanted to come home to stay.

But then he came for me; the latest school had been in Switzerland, which was convenient. We had gone to Paris and then to the Riviera, and in Nice, on a rambling way to Rome, he became ill.

I remembered looking down at my Chanel suit and white blouse; even I was not so naïve as not to know that name. My father had made me buy clothes in Paris; he had selected them. He had said crossly, eyeing my polo coat and beret, that he did not intend to travel with a schoolgirl frump.

All those clothes, I now thought, on borrowed money. And that very short but lavish trip, the best of everything, everywhere, not only on borrowed money but on what he must have known was borrowed time.

Yet that was the whole point of it. He had desperately desired to establish our relationship of father and daughter; he had, in his own way perhaps, clung to me as his child; we were beginning to get acquainted.

As Lord Tweed had said, in that sense, it was a pity.

When the telephone rang I was vaguely surprised to discover that the room was dusky; outside the long windows and the railed balcony the Mediterranean stretched, infinitely blue and purple. In the sky I could see an evening star. I picked up the telephone and the desk clerk said that a Mr. Richard Amberly wished to see me.

"Amberly!"

"Yes, Mees. Meester Reechaire Amberlee."

I said to ask Mr. Amberly to come up to my suite. After a surprised second or two I ran into my bedroom, brushed up my hair, dabbed on lipstick and straightened my white blouse. I couldn't remember Richard Amberly very clearly; I must have seen him now and again when I was a child, for Stella, his sister, and I had been schoolmates for a time, in one of my early sojourns at a school in New York. Stella was a few years older than I; we had gone to the same children's parties. The Amberlys were friends, although I didn't think close friends, of my father.

But I remembered the newspapers. I remembered the dreadful headlines of three — no, not two years back, about a year and a half. I had been then, of course, in another school — in Paris this time — and the headlines had been in the Paris editions of the New York papers.

Even then, fleetingly, I had wondered how anybody I knew could have lived through those headlines and all that they represented. Such events must have left their mark upon Richard Amberly and upon everybody connected with them, even stolid, friendly Stella.

But now obviously Richard had heard of my father's death; he was in the vicinity and thus, I thought, making a friendly visit of condolence. It occurred to me that I needed a friend just then and the doorbell tinkled. I ran to open the door and was instantly thankful for the moment or two I had spent at the mirror; it was a purely instinctive feminine reaction.

He didn't look like Stella; I remembered her perfectly, stocky, fair and freckled. Richard was tall, dark-haired and undeniably attractive, although he looked rather older than I would have expected. I thought swiftly that perhaps the tragedy he had experienced accounted for the fine-drawn look in his face. He did not smile. Rather oddly he ignored my outstretched hand but came into the room as I spoke, closed the door behind him and then just stood there in the dusky light from the darkening windows, holding his proper black homburg in his hands and looking at me in a way which struck me even then as out of place. There was no smile; there was no word of sympathy.

He said, "I had your letter."

"My — *what?*" I had written him no letter.

"I should say your father's letter. I was in Paris on business. The letter had gone to New York and was then sent back to me in Paris." He was speaking in a rather jerky and not at all friendly way.

This was a peculiar impression. I said, "Do sit down. It's kind of you to call. I didn't know that my father had written to you."

I sat down in one of the gilded, pink-upholstered armchairs; he did not sit down. I looked up. His gaze had reached my feet and stopped there with the slightest look of perplexity and I knew why. I had worn my scuffy schoolday loafers to church because I knew I was going to walk later, and was still wearing them. I wished that I had changed to high heels.

He said, "Somehow I didn't expect you to be so young. Stella seems quite settled and — perhaps that accounts for it. But your father must have gone out of his head."

"I — really —" I got my breath. "I don't know what you're talking about. My father was perfectly clear in his mind right up to his death. That is" — for the sake of truth, I had to hedge a little — "that is, as clear in his mind as a very sick man can be —"

"He couldn't have been clear in his mind!" Richard Amberly turned toward the window, looked out on the purple sea very hard as if he could see all the way to Africa, then turned back to me. "There's no sense in beating around the bush, Miss Hilliard."

Miss Hilliard, I thought; it would have seemed more natural if he had called me Fran or even Frances, although only my father had called me Frances.

He went on. "I told you, I had the letter. I came to tell you, first, that I do not intend to be blackmailed."

"You — *what* —" I stood up, grasping the arms of the chair.

"I was wrong. I made a mistake. Your father advised me. Wilbur advised me. But it was my decision. I was wrong."

I said feebly, "Wilbur —"

He made an impatient gesture. "Stella's husband. Wilbur Cullen. Banker. Able man."

"Oh. Yes." I had received an invitation to Stella's marriage.

Richard sat down and deposited his black homburg on the floor. "In a way I ought to be thankful to you. It's decided a course of action for me. I've known all along, of course, that what I did was stupid. Yet I hoped that it was all done, over with. That was a mistake, too. It isn't done and over with. I'm going back to New York and go straight to the police and tell them the whole truth. But first I've got to have that diary."

"That — did you say *diary?*"

He gave me a look of searing contempt. "It's no good. I'll not pay blackmail. I'm going to the police with the whole story myself so there's nothing you can blackmail me about —"

"You've got to tell me what you're talking about!"

He eyed me for a second; then he dug into a pocket, took out a folded piece of paper, rose and handed it to me. I recognized the hotel stationery.

"Refresh your mind," he said.

It seemed to be a day of unutterably shocking letters. That was my second.

The letter was in my father's handwriting, although a little shaky. It read: "My dear Richard: I have had a bad heart attack. It is not the first. The doctors are lying to me. I know that I'll not get well. I am leaving my dear daughter Frances to your special care. She will need care, I am sorry to say, but I know that I can depend upon you. Almost the only thing she has in the way of an inheritance is my diary. With my gratitude in the measure that I have had your gratitude in the past."

The letter was signed, a little more firmly than the rest of it, Orle Hilliard. It was dated three days before his death, two weeks and three days ago. He had thoughtfully, far too thoughtfully, put the name of his bank below his signature. It happened to be the bank where there was an overdraft.

Perhaps an emotional crisis of some kind hones the perception to a sharp edge. In ordinary circumstances I don't think the truth would have so much as trembled on the outskirts of my knowledge. But I knew then, immediately, what my father had intended in that letter and why he intended it. Perhaps the very obvious statement of a quid pro quo in the ending convinced me.

The threat was too lightly veiled; even the name of his bank, while it might appear to be merely an address for letters which would be forwarded to him, meant, I saw at once, that he had intended money to be paid into his account, without my knowledge. *Repondez s'il vous plait,* I thought strangely, but this demanded a response of money. My father would never have wanted me to know of his action or of the source of the money.

I folded the letter with fingers that surprised me vaguely because they were steady. I said, quite steadily too, "I don't want any help from you."

"So you admit it's a blackmail letter?"

I said dully, "I don't see what else it could be. I know nothing of it. I don't suppose you'll believe that. I don't have any diary. I never saw a diary. I don't want your money."

"It's a very dangerous game, you know. For one thing, there's a law against it. No court looks kindly upon extortion or blackmail. For another thing — well, I'm not going to kill you but another kind of man might."

I thrust the letter at him and sat down again because I began to feel a little unsteady.

"Am I the only string to your bow?" he asked.

I didn't exactly understand that. He said, "Did your father write some other letters?"

And he had. I remembered them. Several days before his death my father had given me a little sheaf of envelopes and said, with an emphasis which I now remembered rather sickly, that he wanted me to mail them myself. I had gone out to the nearest post office so I could tell my father that they were actually in the post office.

Richard Amberly said in a queer voice, "I see that he did. How many?"

I knew exactly how many. I had counted to make sure that I didn't lose one of them. "Five."

"Good God," said Richard Amberly.

I thought I couldn't speak but then I did, although huskily. "They may not have been letters like — like yours."

There was another silence. Then he said, slowly, "Are you perfectly sure that you do not have this diary?"

"I don't have it. I never saw it. I knew nothing of it."

He eyed me, thinking hard, not really seeing me. "Then where is it?"

"I don't know."

"I've got to have it."

"I tell you I know nothing about it."

He took a turn up and down the room, his head bent; finally he came back and stood before me. "Your father obviously believed that what he knew of me, if it was known by the police, would expose me to a charge of murder — as I expect it will."

"Murder —"

"Your father was a trial lawyer, a well-known criminal lawyer, a brilliant and, possibly, ruthless man. He may have known or guessed some dangerous secrets concerning other people. As dangerous as the secret he knew about me. I take it that he wrote all those letters here in Nice."

"Y-yes. Only a few days before he died."

"My letter was written on hotel paper. It was easy for me to find you. I think you'd better leave Nice."

The significance of this advice was so unusual, so far from the little orbit of my life that it was very hard to accept. But there was one thing I was suddenly sure of. "You believe me," I said.

2

Richard Amberly looked at me, surprised. I said, "You don't think I knew about his letter or his diary. You believe me —"

"I'd like to believe you. Actually, I don't think you could be quite such a good actress as to put on the show of surprise, shock, all that, that you've put on. I don't mean put on, it seems real to me. The point is, whether you're telling me the truth or not I think you are inviting something very unpleasant and possibly dangerous. As I say, I think you'd better leave Nice."

"But I don't know — I mean, you'd better read this."

This time I handed him a letter, Mr. Hatever's letter, which had fallen to the floor. I scooped it up and watched Richard Amberly as he held it under the lamp to read it. He did look older, more mature than he ought to have looked; there were tiny lines around his mouth, which was held a little too firmly; it was in fact a controlled, yet a rather sad face. Not the face of a murderer.

The words flashing into my mind seemed

to illuminate a whole course of intricate yet subterranean thinking on my part, so it became shockingly clear. My father had believed he knew something which was so dangerous to Richard Amberly that Richard would pay blackmail — call it by its name, I said to myself — rather than let the police know it. Richard had said that he'd made a mistake and that whatever this fact was, if given to the police, it would expose him to a murder charge. Murder is an unusual thing; the murder with which I knew Richard had been dreadfully concerned was that of his wife.

A murderer can look like anybody; Richard Amberly *didn't* have the face of a murderer, I thought stubbornly. He looked down at me. "This explains something of your father's course of action. But I still think he was out of his head."

"He was very sick. Desperate, I suppose. Trying to do something for me."

Richard considered that while he folded up Mr. Hatever's letter. He said, "Well — it's true that nobody can account for the vagaries of a dying man — a man who knows he's dying, who knows he's saved nothing for his daughter. A man like your father. In any event" — he handed me Mr. Hatever's letter — "it's done. I can only suggest that you —" He frowned and considered again. "Well, of course you must try to remember the names of the people to whom you sent those letters. Can you remember them? Even one or two of them? You remember mine, don't you? Try —"

I thought back to that afternoon, taking up my handbag, counting, then going out to mail the letters. "No. You don't really look at letters, other people's letters. I mean, you don't look at the names or the addresses to be sure you've got them right. I only counted them quickly. There were five. I mailed them."

Richard Amberly sighed. "They may have been — all but mine — merely friendly letters. I think though we'd better assume that they were not. I wish you had noticed the names. You see, then you could write to these people, make it very definite that this threat was made without your knowledge. Make it very clear that you're going to get rid of the diary. After you've let me read it, as I hope you will."

"I'd never have sent the letters. I'd never have let him do it —"

"I don't think anybody could have stopped your father in anything he set out to do. Not as I remember him. Well, try to think of the names. You really can't go in for a career of blackmail, you know."

"I *can't* think of any names, any addresses."

"You must have seen some of them. How did you count them? I mean, did you say, deal them, like cards?" He illustrated with a quick motion of his hands. "Or did you only thumb through them? Counting the edges. Did you notice the stamps?"

I had stood at the writing table across the room. I'd had my handbag. "I counted them on the table, down. As you would deal cards. I think I remember glancing at the stamps but only to make sure there were stamps."

"For New York? For — oh, anywhere? Airmail? What kind of stamps?"

"Stamps. That's all."

"Can't you remember my name? Surely you'd have recognized a name you know?"

I shook my head. The more I tried to remember a word, a name, a number on any of those envelopes, the more completely the black lines of my father's handwriting blurred together.

"Perhaps some of the names will come back to me," I said feebly. "I don't think so."

"Then you'd better get home as fast as you can, get hold of that diary which, if it isn't here, must be in New York, go through it and — well, see if any of the names rings a bell. Failing that" — he paused for a moment, thinking — "failing that, you'll have to go through the diary, dig out anything you can in the way of information that might damage anybody at all, write letters saying that you have destroyed the diary, very careful letters of course — oh, I don't know that I'm right. But I'm sure that you must try to disassociate yourself entirely from the diary or any knowledge of your father's having written those letters."

"You're so sure they were all blackmailing letters."

"Considering mine, I think they were," he said slowly. "You haven't asked me what your father held over me as a blackmailing threat."

I swallowed hard. "You said something about a — well, a murder charge. You said that you'd made a mistake."

"Oh, it was a mistake all right. But at the time it seemed the thing to do." A tired note came into his voice. It suggested that he had argued endlessly with himself. "At the time, to be perfectly honest, I was only too thankful for an escape hatch. That's what it seemed. It wasn't too hard for your father and Wilbur to persuade me. I can't blame them. And as a matter of truth, I didn't, at that time, blame myself. I was only thankful. So don't think my conscience has been lacerating me all this time. In fact —" He paused to consider and then said, "there's very little conscience about it. Oh, there's self-respect, pride, whatever it is. I lied to the police and it not only falls into the realm of obstructing law and justice but it — it gives me no peace!"

"If that's not conscience, I don't know what conscience is."

"Never mind that. I told the police an outright lie. The thing for me to do is go to them now and tell them the truth. I should have done it at the time she was murdered. I didn't foresee what has actually happened."

I thought only, so it *was* Cecile's murder, his wife's murder. I felt suddenly red-faced, embarrassed, sorry for him, sure that if I spoke I would say the wrong thing. Also there was a kind of echo of horror somewhere in the room as if his memories had summoned it up.

"You really don't know anything about your father's letter to me or his diary," Richard Amberly said unexpectedly. "You couldn't look like that, if you did. All right, I apologize. I am very sorry I accused you of trying to blackmail me."

I wondered vaguely what there was in my look which had finally convinced him.

He said, "You knew about Cecile's death."

"I — remember the newspapers."

"Yes. The newspapers. Well — you see, the police investigated the whole family, of course, but me first. They do. I was the husband. Cecile was killed at night, they thought about eleven o'clock. It was in the spring, April. The eighteenth. I was walking in the Park. I really was walking in the Park and consequently I had no real alibi. They didn't accuse me or charge me or arrest me but they were bearing down hard when your father stepped into the picture. Came bustling up in a cab early the next morning; he'd already talked over the phone to Wilbur who told him all about it. So your father said I was in the Park and he had seen me. He said I was sitting on a bench at Ninety-second Street under a street light. He swore up and down that he had seen me, but that I hadn't seen him, at least I hadn't spoken to him. He said he'd gone to see a friend and missed him; he gave the friend's name, the friend backed him up — said he'd misunderstood the date of their appointment and gone out. In any event your father strolled around, waiting for the friend's return, saw me. Said he started to speak to me but then decided to wait inside the foyer of his friend's apartment house where there were chairs. So he did, but he could see me. He said that he sat there for close to forty-five minutes and he said I didn't move. He then gave up and went to the ball. A charity ball. Cecile — had intended to go. Wilbur fixed the doorman, who was near-sighted and ancient anyway; he agreed that a gentleman waited in the foyer. Oh, it was all done up brown — and altogether a fake."

He leaned back, thought for a moment and went on. "But there it was, my alibi. The police had to accept it. Wilbur and your father said I had to stick to it; they said it was the only thing to do. Save me, save the family, save — I wasn't hard to persuade, not hard at all. So I said, yes, I'd been sitting on the bench at Ninety-second Street. It wasn't true."

"Oh —"

"I had not walked north at all. I hadn't even seen a bench on Ninety-second Street. I sat on a bench only a few streets away from home. I'm still not sure exactly where I was. I had some things on my mind. Your father just picked a street twenty blocks from home to make it sound more convincing and to make a longer margin of time for me.

Time for my absence from home, you see. Time for — Cecile's murder to take place."

There seemed nothing for me to say.

"The fact was I had walked south for only five or ten minutes. I did sit on a bench for a long time, smoking, thinking. As it happened, I didn't see anybody I knew. Nobody came forward and said he saw me. I had told the police during the first hurried inquiry that night that I had been in the Park but I was so stunned that I didn't say where; in fact, I'm not sure I could have said exactly where, not that night. Now understand, I was not arrested. I was not arraigned and charged with murder. I was a suspect whom the police had to investigate. Your father's statement gave me so firm an alibi that it eliminated me as a suspect. The police could not dismiss that alibi, which was totally fake but which I agreed to and claimed as true. They never found out who killed Cecile. So I must have that diary." He looked at me as if expecting me to say something and shook his head a little. "You don't understand, do you? But then nobody could understand who hasn't gone through it."

"What —"

"An unsolved murder, a murder case that has never been closed — what it does to people. The people who are concerned. The people who might have been suspects. The people" — he said somberly — "whom other people still — just a little — suspect. Oh, they don't say it, they don't even whisper it, but it's there just the same: 'That poor girl Cecile's murder was never explained. Her murderer was never brought to justice. I wonder —' I know what they're thinking. Everyone who was close to Cecile feels it. Everyone who could have got into the house. We live under a very ugly shadow. We can't go on like this."

I remembered enough of the newspaper accounts to remember the conclusion of the case; at least I had thought it was the conclusion. "But they decided it was a burglar, didn't they?"

"It was never proved. The police never found the burglar, never found some jewelry that was missing."

"But surely — I mean it's the only thing that could have happened." I stopped and then said, flatly, "Don't you believe that?"

"I want to believe it. It seems the only logical explanation. I cannot think of anybody who would hurt Cecile. The police checked —" A shadow went over his face. "They checked on every possible suspect. A burglar is the logical answer. But since I had your father's letter I've been thinking of another possibility, something that really never occurred to me until I had his letter and knew that he kept a diary and that there was something in it relating to Cecile's murder. When he came to me with that false alibi I took it as a friendly gesture, and only that — a rather dramatic kind of gesture, like your father, but merely friendly. And I accepted it. Perhaps a drowning man is not very scrupulous about the rope he snatches, but that's no excuse for me really. Now I can't help thinking that he may have had some reason to know that I had not murdered Cecile and that's why he came forward so quickly, urging me and Wilbur to take up his offer of an alibi for me."

"But if he knew that you didn't murder Cecile — what you're saying is that he knew who did murder her!"

"I don't know —"

"And that would mean that he was protecting a murderer! He wouldn't have done that."

Richard Amberly looked at me steadily. "I've got to know. I've got to have that diary. Whatever — whoever it was, I want it proved. Finished forever. Closed. No more doubts, no more questions. This diary may point the way. Your father just may have had some reason other than mere friendliness in giving me that false alibi. I don't mean that I think he was deliberately protecting a murderer."

I started to speak; he said, "Wait, listen. He knew all of us, of course. As far as I now know, he was not a close friend to anybody who might have known Cecile, or who might have killed her. But he was a friend and a lawyer of long experience. Perhaps I was inclined to accept that experience as a kind of authority for what I did. Yet I did it, I can't blame him or Wilbur. Of course, it is possible that even then your father was intending to blackmail me and he set up the false alibi with only that in mind."

"My father was not a blackmailer!" But he was; the truth struck me too forcibly. I added, "Not then. You said yourself, 'the vagaries of a dying man' —" I was to repeat that to myself many times; I was to hold fast to it.

Richard said, "I don't think that he saw that far ahead. It was only a possibility that occurred to me. I don't really think that he determined upon a course which would later give him a handle for blackmailing me. Nor can I be sure he knew or was sufficiently sure of the identity of the murderer to protect him on the theory that, later, that murderer could be blackmailed by that knowledge."

I sat very still, as you do on an airplane when the weather is bumpy.

Richard said, "But his letter to me is sheer blackmail, nothing else. He talks of this diary as if there's evidence of some kind in it. It may be only the record of my false alibi. But there may be some other evidence in it. It may be the first chink in the wall. The first glimpse of the truth. The first piece of solid evidence. The police will want that evidence. I've got to have it."

"He didn't know who murdered her! He couldn't have known or even guessed and not told the police!"

Richard gave me an odd look. "How well did you know your father?"

"Why — why, he was my father!"

"No, I mean it. How well did you know him? How often did you see him? How much did you know of his life?"

"I've been away — in schools — he was always busy. But he was very kind, very generous."

Richard's eyes and voice warmed. "I'm sure he was. He was like that. He never told you about this alibi he gave me?"

"He never mentioned the case at all. I was in Paris when I saw the newspapers."

There was a little silence. I had plenty to think about. My father, a lawyer, presumably a man of honor, a man who had a regard for the ethics of his profession, writing — call it by its name, I thought again — blackmail letters!

Richard was thinking along the same lines. He said, "No, I cannot believe that twenty months, nearly two years ago, he would have thought of anything like these letters. You couldn't have realized it but he must have gone downhill, failed in ways that you, nobody could have seen. Perhaps he did know something, some bit of evidence, which at least suggested to him that I had not murdered Cecile. Perhaps he did nothing about it at the time except provide that false alibi for me. But, perhaps dying — I've got to have the diary. If it isn't here it's got to be in New York, his office, his home, somewhere."

"You *want* to reopen the case."

"You don't understand what it means to me and the family and all the people who were close to Cecile. I can't go through life like this. I've got to end it one way or another. There may be something in the diary that will give the police something to work on. I need it. It's a simple business of self-preservation. As soon as I tell them the truth I become the number one suspect again."

"I'll find the diary if I can. I'll give it to you."

"Thank you," he said quite formally. "It's a hope, small perhaps but a hope."

"Did he know Cecile?" I asked.

Richard said, a little evasively, "Cecile wasn't — she didn't go out much. But New York is a small town really. Circles are constantly overlapping. Your father knew all of us — my mother, Stella, her husband, Wilbur. He knew Henry, of course, and Miffy, his wife. You remember Henry?"

"No, not really." All I had known of the Amberlys in the past few years had been what I had read in the newspapers. I knew that Henry, Richard's older brother, had been in Vietnam; sent out by some government department as a civilian observer who had expert knowledge of freight and shipping; in any event, his helicopter had been shot down. That was some five years ago. I had had an invitation and had read of Stella's marriage to Wilbur three years ago. I had read of the murder of Richard's wife. Somehow I had missed the account of his marriage. I said, "I read about Henry. I was sorry. I don't remember his wife."

"Oh — well, she has lived with us only since Henry was killed. I suppose you never happened to meet. . . . I've just had a thought, did your father have an address book with him?"

"Yes. I have it."

"Take a look at it. See if any of the names in it rings a bell."

"You mean those letters. I don't think I'll remember any name because I don't remember even looking at the names. But I'll get the book."

It was in a drawer of the writing table. I had already looked through it, intending to write notes to any close friends of my father's, telling them of his death. I hadn't found any names that I remembered as being close friends.

But I took the little brown book; it was a fancy little book, good leather with gold corners and initials. There was, however, a scarcity of names, and a mishmash of scrawled telephone numbers or addresses. Richard stood beside me and we both searched the book.

"Tailor —" Richard said. "A bank. Here's my name and address." There was nothing which rang a bell.

Richard worked through the little book again. "There's not a name here — except mine — that I can possibly associate with Cecile. Of course, it has perhaps struck you that one of those letters could have gone to

Cecile's murderer."

"*No* —" I said, but it came out in a whisper.

Something cold seemed to crawl up my spine. I left him with the address book still in his hands and went to stand at the fireplace where a thrifty little stack of logs was laid. I didn't light it; somehow one thinks twice before lighting a fire in any French hotel — for one reason, it is so seldom lighted it may smoke you out. But the gesture made me feel a little warmer.

I felt warmer but Richard's suggestion seemed more and more valid.

He said, "Look at it this way. Say that your father knew something that made him go out of his way to give me an alibi. That something logically would be some knowledge of Cecile's murderer. Do you think that when he's writing blackmail letters to five people whom he expects to respond promptly with money to you — do you really think he would omit such a fertile field of blackmail as a murderer?"

He waited and I said, "No —"

"I don't think so either. Oh, it's no proof. But if he knew something that proved to him that I didn't murder Cecile — and if that something was evidence leading to the person who did murder her — then I don't see how we can avoid the likelihood that one of those five letters went to the person he suspected — or knew — had murdered Cecile. It's — reasonable."

It was too reasonable. "Yes."

"If that's so, you don't think the murderer is going to like it very much."

"No —"

"I'm being very brutal. I have to make you see. A man who has murdered once doesn't have the fear and the loathing of murder that most men have. He's only afraid of being caught. You've got to find that diary. You've got to disclaim any knowledge that makes you dangerous to a murderer — or to anyone, for that matter. And also there may be something in the diary that will give the police some evidence that could save my life."

"Wait," I said. "Simply an alibi, I mean the lack of an alibi, wouldn't give the police reason to charge you with murder. They'd have to have something else — I mean some kind of evidence or — well, wouldn't they?"

He stared at me. Then unexpectedly he laughed. It changed his whole face; it changed everything about him. It was as if I had a glimpse of a different man. "Lawyer's daughter." He chuckled.

But then he sobered, rose, went to the

window again, shoved his hands in his pockets and said, over his shoulder, "There was a certain amount of evidence."

That was all. He didn't explain it. For some reason I could not possibly ask, what is that evidence? I stood there, fumbling in my thoughts, strongly aware of the still figure across the room; also of scraps of the room which I could see — the frivolous little armchairs, the pink-garlanded carpet, the rectangle of white which was Mr. Hatever's letter on the table. There was even a glimpse of myself, rather white-faced with very dark eyebrows and dark hair brushed up in loose curls. I suddenly remembered the day when my father, after eyeing my hair restively, had said with irritation that it looked like a haystack puffed out like that. I had said mildly that that was the style. "Style!" he said and took me to a hairdresser. The hairdresser had combed my hair this way and that; he had squinted and tipped his head one way and the other; his scissors had flashed. He had then taught me how to arrange my new haircut, how to brush it, what to do. "That's better," my father had said. It wasn't possible that had happened only a few weeks ago.

And now — murder, I thought; blackmail. Murder. The doorbell gave its raspy tinkle.

I said rapidly as if I'd thought it all out, "If there's really something that is evidence — real evidence, helpful evidence — in the diary, of course you should take it to the police. I can see that. But if there isn't anything, I can't see that you'll accomplish anything by telling the police, now, about your false alibi. The thing is over and settled —"

"Murder is never settled until the case is closed. You'd better answer the doorbell."

It tinkled again and I crossed the room and opened the door. "Flowers for you, Miss Hilliard," the bellboy said. He handed me a small, gaily-wrapped package which had, surprisingly, a white orchid tied to the top of it.

I had no change for a tip and no pocket in my beautiful Chanel suit. Richard Amberly must have seen my hesitation, for he came to the door and put a coin in the hand of the bellboy. I closed the door and stared at the small package with its huge white orchid on top.

"There's nobody in Nice who would send me flowers!"

"It's Christmas Day."

"There's nobody who would send me a Christmas present. There must be a mistake."

Richard leaned over to look at the tag.

"It's your name. Printed by hand. Very clear. Miss Frances Hilliard. Want me to open it?"

I gave him the box. He took out a little silver knife, sawed through white ribbons, and tore off green paper. He detached the white orchid, put it on the table and extended the white box to me.

It was not a florist's box, though. It was simply a plain white one about the size of a candy box. "Must be a present," he said. "Aren't you going to look?"

So I opened it.

I don't think I screamed; I didn't have the voice to scream. There wasn't a snake in the box but there might as well have been. There was in fact a sheaf of bills.

I whispered, "It's money. It's United States bills. Tens and twenties and —"

Richard said in a queer voice, "How many?"

It was a thick sheaf. "I don't know."

It was naïve; it was downright stupid, I suppose, but the fact is that my thoughts shot to the hotel bills — my passage home — why, perhaps in that sheaf of delicious, delectable greenbacks there would be enough to support me until I could get some kind of job. I hurled myself down at the writing table and began to count the money as fast as I could. I knew that Richard was watching over my shoulder but all I could think of just then was that magic money. I finished the last bill; they were rather dirty bills as if they had gone through many and rather dirty hands, but it was money; I sighed in sheer thankful delight.

Richard Amberly said, "Five thousand dollars."

"Yes. Oh, yes. It's wonderful —"

"Who sent it?"

I had the sensation of coming back to earth with a jolt.

"I don't know — that is — well, no, I don't know who sent it."

"It was somebody here in Nice. Somebody who knew your name and address."

All the breath went out of me; everything was gone. Finally I put out my hands and shoved the money away from me.

"Yes," he said. "It rather looks as if you had received your first installment of blood money."

Repondez s'il vous plait, I thought again, with money, blood money, or evidence of murder.

3

There was no sense in calling the bellboy and telling him to take the money back to the person who sent it. "It probably came by messenger," Richard said. "Simply left at the desk. Something like that."

The white orchid lay on the table, beautiful and mysterious. "Why was there an orchid?" I said.

He shrugged. "Perhaps to — oh, disguise the package. So it looked like a gift. Or to propitiate, disarm you, put you off your guard by seeming friendly. A very odd sort of mind would come up with that," he said thoughtfully.

But orchids have no sweet, pervading scent, and such a scent, rather heavy, somehow disagreeable, was certainly creeping from somewhere. Then I knew. I bent and sniffed at the bills, at the box.

I looked up at Richard Amberly. "It's the man, the man today! Benni, he said he was — only that's not his whole name. I didn't hear his whole name. He said the account would be settled —" I almost choked but got it out. "He talked about terms and my father. And he wanted a receipt."

After a moment Richard sat down. I could almost see him switch from his problem to mine. Yet the two problems were closely linked; they were indeed — and in a dreadful way — inseparable. "All right. Tell me the whole thing."

So I did, word for word, from the instant I had found Mr. Benni beside me, as if he'd sprung from ambush, taking advantage of my momentary inattention. There was not much to tell.

"Describe him again," Richard said. "Small, dark — perfume. What else?"

I described him again. Richard said, "No. No, there wasn't anybody questioned about Cecile who looked anything like that. I rather think Mr. Benni is an entirely different string your father has pulled. Nothing at all to do with me. So you told him to go to your father's office. He took that I suppose as putting him off until he had — oh, shown he was going to pay up. Five thousand dollars. I wonder," Richard said grimly, "just what your father had on him. Must be serious. This is a first installment. Well — what are you going to do with the money?"

I had wanted so desperately to use it; I looked at it with longing but also with loathing and pushed the stack of bills further away from me. I felt that I had to do it that minute, or I might weaken, take it, use it and forget where it came from.

He said, "You're short of cash, aren't you?" in such a kind and gentle voice that suddenly I could feel tears in my eyes.

I looked away so he wouldn't see them. "I'll be all right."

He cleared his throat. "I note that your father's partner, Mr. Hatever, didn't offer to loan you money."

"He wasn't my father's partner. They only shared offices — for many years. I don't think they knew much of each other's business."

There was a little silence. Then he put a firm hand over mine. It was warm and strong and well-shaped. He said again in that kind and gentle voice, "I'll see to the hotel bill and your passage home. That's what is worrying you, isn't it?"

I swallowed hard. "There was enough for the doctor's bills and the nurses. And the — funeral expenses."

"I take it the funeral was here in Nice."

"Yes. It was his wish. He said there was no sense in carting him off home — his words." I tried to smile.

"Was anyone with you?" he asked in an odd voice.

"Oh, yes. That is, one of the nurses. She was very kind. And the American Consul and his wife. They couldn't have been more helpful. I can borrow from the American Consul, can't I? People do when they need their fare home."

I looked up at him then and surmised something in his eyes which I could not, or at least did not, analyze except that it was different and I felt as if some kind of friendliness leaped between us. "Yes, they do. I doubt though if the American Consul can advance enough to cover hotel bills, too."

"But — if I talk to the manager of the hotel — if I tell him that I've got to go home to settle my father's estate —" My voice dwindled away, for there wasn't any estate to settle. "I ought not to have kept this suite. I was only waiting until I heard from Mr. Hatever. Of course I've got the house to sell. The mortgage doesn't cover the whole value of the house; it couldn't."

"I've been in that house once or twice. It may not be easy to sell."

I didn't suppose it would be. He lifted his hand and said in a pleasant but very impersonal tone, "I'll see to things. You can't just be stranded here —"

I broke in. "I have a little string of pearls. They belonged to my mother."

"I don't think we'll need that. But understand, I am not paying an installment of blood money."

I must have given him a startled and appalled look for he smiled. The smile lit up his whole face, banished the look of whiteness and strain — banished years, too, so all at once he looked young and strong as if nothing in the world could daunt him. "Poor joke. This is a loan. I'll expect you to pay it back as soon as you sell the house. You can give me a note. Everything businesslike."

"But — I don't know. It seems —"

"Seems, nothing, it's the way things are. You're in rather a box, you've got to get out of it. This is the first step. Besides, I've known you since you were a child, remember."

"No, not really."

He looked at me with thoughtfully narrowed eyes. "I'm not so sure. I seem to remember a long-legged child with thick black hair at some of Stella's parties. A lovely child, blue-eyed, very flirtatious, had all the boys around her."

"You're making that up."

"Well, then, you forget, I want that diary. Only you can get it for me. You'll have to go to New York to get it. As I say, you can pay me as soon as you get some money."

"All right. I mean, it's very good of you," I said stiffly. "I'll take it. I don't know what else to do. But I do insist upon a note — or —" I pulled a piece of hotel paper toward me. "What do I say?"

He laughed and again looked young and different. I had thought that his eyes were dark brown or black; now I saw that they were a lively gray. "Don't give anybody a note until he gives you the cash. First principle. I'll see about it in the morning." He went to the telephone and asked for the desk clerk.

"I'm Richard Amberly, a friend of the late Mr. Hilliard. We wish to settle up his affairs here."

There was a bubble of talk from the desk clerk who apparently — and with considerable alacrity — called the manager, for Richard went over his preamble again. "— and Miss Hilliard will be leaving tomorrow — that is, if we can get plane reservations. So will you let me know the amount of her account?"

Again there was a bubble of talk, relieved talk, I was sure. For the past few days the manager had been giving me rather troubled and worried looks; I had almost begun to avoid him. Richard motioned for a piece of paper and a pencil; I gave them to him. He listened, wrote figures down on the paper, said thank you, Miss Hilliard's account would be settled before her departure, and hung up. He then looked at the figures and raised his eyebrows. "In new francs," he said. "Let me see, that comes to — well, never mind." He stuffed the paper in his pocket. "Now I'll see about reservations. You'd better begin to pack. I'll let you know —"

"Take this money," I said, shoving the heap of greenbacks at him.

"Why — oh, all right." He didn't question my motive; I'm not sure I had one; I had only revulsion. He gathered the bills together and shoved them too, carefully, in an inside pocket. "I'll see to it until — well, I'll see to it." He came to me; I thought he was going to take my hand again but he didn't. "There's one thing that you must understand. Your father may have defended some people who didn't deserve defense —"

"He wouldn't have taken a client he knew was guilty!"

Richard's face showed no expression at all. "Perhaps not. Still, let's assume that he knew or guessed certain things about some of his clients. Lawyers do know. Or guess, sometimes very accurately. So let's say that your father may have had or preserved certain evidence about these clients."

I couldn't say that he wouldn't have done that but I had to choke it back.

Richard went on. "I'm only trying to tell you that if what we suspect is true, it's a dangerous business. Cecile's murderer — we can't be sure that one of those letters went to him, but it's possible. This Mr. Benni doesn't sound like the kind of man to yield very gracefully to threats. In any event, you have accounted for two of those letters. One went to me. It looks as if one went to Mr. Benni. That leaves only three to identify. Can't you possibly —"

"I might as well try to identify the craters on Mars."

"Yes — well, try. And in the meantime you'd better have some dinner. Then pack." He went to the telephone and called for room service.

It was rather nice to be taken care of; I listened to his order of American whiskey, rare steak, potatoes, a salad, a bombe and coffee. He didn't consult me. He put down the telephone. "I hope that's what you wanted. It's what you need. Now I'll see what I can do about reservations. I'll have to go out to the airport, I expect. Offices are closed." He took up his black homburg. I followed him to the door.

He looked down at me and put out his

hand and I said, childishly, blunderingly, but I had to be sure, "You do believe me! Don't you? Now?"

A shadow dropped over his face; he became again remote, older, too self-controlled. Later I realized that he had for a moment lost himself in my problem; my question brought him back to his own. He said lightly, though, "Oh, yes." He put his hand under my chin for a second, like the gesture of rallying or teasing or comfort you give a child. "Now if I were you, I'd stay right here. Don't go out. This unpleasantly perfumed Mr. Benni is certainly in Nice. I'll telephone to you about reservations so answer the telephone but otherwise —"

"No, no, I'll not let him even talk to me!"

He nodded. "I'll let you know."

He went out and I closed the door. After a while I heard the elevator and then I bolted the door.

I wondered what might have happened if I'd yielded to Mr. Benni, if I'd strolled and let him talk — or even, as he'd so mildly suggested, gone for a ride with him. There were not very nice connotations in the words "taken for a ride." I felt suddenly rather chilly.

Dangerous, Richard Amberly had said. Surely my father had not intentionally exposed me to danger! Yet there were those dirty bills, dirty in more senses than one.

Three letters still to identify! Suppose — just suppose — Richard's reasoning was accurate and one of those three letters had gone to Cecile's murderer.

The Riviera winter twilight is chilly. Something old and cold seems to creep from the Mediterranean over the beach, the red rocks, the twisted pines, the elegant hotels and villas. I turned on more lights.

I had to open the door, of course, for the waiter with my jingling dinner table. But then I told him not to come back for the table; the morning waiter could take it away. He left happily, intent I imagined upon some Christmas festivity.

I sat down and took a look at things. I was still appalled and half-incredulous, mainly because I didn't see how my father could have conceived and carried out a plan which was so subtle and, worst of all, blackmail. Yet in another way I could see it. I had always thought of him as exemplifying the fine and demanding ethics of his profession, but what really did I know about it? Rather, as Richard had suggested, how well did I know my father?

I didn't feel desolate as I might have done at the loss of illusions, for my father and I hadn't had that kind of idealistic relationship. And I had been in a way the child of his old age for he had married late; there was not the usual gap of only one generation between us; there were two generations. Perhaps if my mother had lived, my father and I would have drawn closer. I decided it was better not to analyze my feelings, not even to try to analyze my father. What he had done had been done, and I had to accept it.

I downed the whiskey, good Kentucky bourbon, and I downed the steak and by the time I had cleaned up the bombe and was drinking coffee I felt better, as one does. The white orchid on the table, though, bothered me; it was real — so had the dirty bills been real — and it also suggested something out of kilter, as Mr. Benni's sickening perfume had been. I got up presently and dropped the orchid in the wastebasket where it was at least out of sight.

There was nothing to be gained by sitting there over my coffee thinking. Besides, while I tried to think along a straight line — that is, that this thing had happened and that I must do something about it and that the first thing to do was find that diary — odd things kept pulling at my attention, such as the orchid. Such as some things that Richard had said and some things he hadn't said, such as an explanation of what he had called "a certain amount of evidence" against him. What was that evidence?

Why hadn't I looked at the five letters I had posted? It seemed to me then that something should have seeped through the envelopes, some intangible kind of warning, something that sent a message along my fingers and said, don't mail them, don't.

The thing to do was pack. So I went into the bedroom; I dragged down my father's beautiful but ancient pigskin bags, and almost the first thing I found was a rolled-up mass of newspaper clippings which were accounts of the murder of Richard Amberly's wife, Cecile.

They were stuffed into a small briefcase of the under-arm zipper type which itself was stuffed into a bag which held clothing. If I had seen the briefcase when I moved my father's effects from the room he no longer needed, I did not remember it. Now when I opened the big bag to reassort its contents and to add to them, I saw the briefcase and thought at once, the diary! I opened the briefcase and dumped the newspaper clippings and an assortment of other objects upon the bed. There was no diary.

The newspaper clippings were crumpled and opened to a picture of Richard's wife. She had been beautiful. I sat there, huddled down on the floor by the bed, and looked at her. Then I saw a headline and pushed the clippings away from me, yet I knew that I was going to read them.

I'd read of the murder when it happened; I vaguely remembered some of it, too much. The only detail that I clearly remembered was the most horrible one of all, and that was the fact that she had struggled and fought for her life.

I didn't want to look at those newspaper clippings. I looked at the little assortment of objects that had fallen out of the case with the clippings. There was no diary there, certainly, but there was everything else — some paper clips; some crumpled packages of cigarettes, bent and dry; a brown button, with some frayed threads hanging to it as if it had been jerked off some coat; a nail file, some old letters and bills. I took up one of the bills. It was from Paris and listed some of my new and beautiful clothes and I wondered if it had ever been paid. I would doubtless find out and soon. I shoved everything back into the briefcase, including an ink-smeared blotter but no diary.

Then I took up the clippings and smoothed them out. I wondered for an instant just why my father had brought them along with him on this trip; I wondered why he had saved them at all. The likely explanation — at least the one that occurred to me — was that at some time he had put them in the briefcase and, like the button and the cigarettes, he had simply forgotten them.

But I did begin fully then to accept the fact that my father must have undergone a kind of deterioration which had been imperceptible to me. He had been as always almost a dandy about his clothes and his personal appearance. Yet this curious untidiness seemed to suggest a hidden personality change.

I read the clippings. They were dated April nineteenth and were clearly clippings from the newspaper on the day after Cecile's murder — one newspaper. There was first a heartbreakingly beautiful picture of Richard's wife. She wore her coming-out gown, white with long white gloves. Her face was delicate, finely featured; she was turned a little so she gave the camera a sidelong, rather enigmatic look and half-smile. Her hair was very dark and smooth. There was a wide neat part up the middle and exaggerated wings at each side of her low forehead. Her eyebrows were exaggeratedly thick and arched. She was young in the picture and very beautiful. I hadn't known Cecile; she must have been older than I but in the crisscrossing lanes of New York life we would probably have encountered each other at some time if I had not been away from home so much.

The night was turning colder as it always did. The breeze straight across the Mediterranean stirred the curtains at the long window, which, like the windows in the living room, gave upon a little iron-railed balcony. I put down the clippings, got a sweater to put around my shoulders and half closed the windows. Then I read.

It was a dreadful murder. Murder must always be dreadful; this was peculiarly horrible. The lovely girl in the picture had struggled; she had been struck on the temple, half strangled and then, crawling on the floor, apparently trying to take pitiful shelter behind a tiny chair, she had been shot twice, in the head, so her beauty as well as her life was gone forever. There was a picture of her room, with everything tossed around, a chair knocked over, curtains pulled off their rods as she had struggled for her life.

I felt cold again and sick but I read on. Then at last, half shivering, I sat back and looked at the empty bags which I must pack. Richard was perfectly right; the disclosure of the falsity of his alibi would bring about further investigation and place him again in the ugly position of prime suspect. Everything, except that alibi which he and I and Stella's husband knew to be false, was against him. In brief, he and Cecile had quarreled; they had had serious differences of opinion; everyone seemed to know it — the servants, their friends, even his sister-in-law, Miffy, had admitted it under what I suspected to be pressure; Stella alone had stuck to it that Cecile and Richard never quarreled and probably nobody believed her.

Nobody seemed to know the cause of their disagreements; there was indeed, as I thought of it, a rather curious lack of information on this point, which suggested a deliberate and very determined conspiracy of silence. But at one time, after only a few months of marriage, Cecile had gone to see a lawyer about a divorce; there had been discussion of money settlements, yet nothing had been done. Sometime after their talk of divorce they were still living in the Amberly house on Seventy-second Street. With them lived Richard's mother and Miffy, who was Millicent Bell Amberly, Henry's widow.

I picked up the newspapers again and tried to weed out the exact events of that balmy night in April when somebody contrived to enter the house, enter Cecile Amberly's big and luxurious bedroom, murder her with such brutal determination, and then leave the house without being seen.

For one thing it was Thursday and servants' night out; Richard's mother was in North Carolina; she flew home the next morning. There was, that night, a guest in the house, Miffy's young brother Slade; he and Miffy had attended a benefit ball; there was a picture someone had taken at the ball showing them together, Mrs. Henry Amberly and her brother Mr. Slade Bell. Miffy looked very much younger in the picture than I would have expected Henry's widow to be; she was fair and petite; her delicate profile, a heavy bouffant sweep of fair hair above bare shoulders and a necklace showed in the photograph. Her young brother, Slade, was facing the camera; he was fair too, his eyes a little widened as if by the flash of the camera; he wore a white tie and boutonniere and was smiling.

Richard and Cecile were supposed to have gone to the ball, too; the fact that Cecile was dressed in pink silk brocade, torn and bloodied when they found her, added to the horror of the murder.

For some reason, Richard and Cecile had

not gone to the ball; I searched through the print again until I found Richard's reply to the question of the police as to why they had not gone; apparently he said merely that his wife had changed her mind.

He had then — oh, dangerous hour — gone out of the house and taken a walk along the Park. When he returned he found his wife's body. Nobody was in the house. The front door was standing open. He called the police and he couldn't go back to that hideous bedroom so he had sat on the step of the house, waiting for the police.

There were no alien fingerprints found in the bedroom. Stella and her husband, Wilbur, lived across the garden from the Amberly house; the two houses and their adjoining gardens made a little compound. Stella's house was smaller than the Amberly house. Stella and Wilbur had gone to the ball but had come home early since it was a week night and Wilbur liked to get to his office early in the morning; they roused when they heard the voices of police, searching, too late, the Amberly house and basement and the two gardens, and came at once.

The officers from the homicide department had come and done their work; Cecile's body had been taken away; police were still in the house when Miffy arrived alone. Apparently nobody had tried to reach her at the ball; she had no warning of the horror that had taken place. By that time reporters and photographers had arrived and there was another picture of her in the startling black and white flashlights; a limousine was behind her; her evening dress and white shoulders were sharp against it; she carried a fur stole over one arm and must have danced to her heart's content and her feet's anguish for she had taken off her slippers. She clutched up her long skirt and showed a small stockinged foot. Her face was lifted up and looked shocked and full of question. There was no second picture of her young brother Slade but it developed he had joined some friends at a bar; he arrived later.

Everybody but Richard had an alibi. Only Richard had quarreled with Cecile.

And then, early that morning, my father produced the alibi which was accepted by the police, that Stella's husband and my father advised Richard to adopt — and that, clearly, he had regretted ever since.

Another fact which may have influenced the police in Richard's favor was the disappearance of the jewelry. Even I could see that if Richard had murdered his wife, he could have taken and hidden or somehow disposed of the jewelry in order to give the impression of a burglar. All the same, the jewelry *had* disappeared and though, I was sure, the police had gone over the house — and possibly Stella's house, too — with a fine tooth comb, had certainly investigated safes or safe deposit boxes, and had certainly left no stone unturned to recover the jewelry and by that recovery get some kind of evidence against the murderer — though they had done all this, the jewelry had not turned up. I read the list, which was not long but was to me stunning: a sapphire bracelet, a diamond bracelet, a triple string of pearls with a diamond clasp. The estimate of its value was over thirty thousand dollars.

The substantial sum of its value was a point in Richard's favor. I had an impression that there was a certain amount of money in the Amberly family; they derived their income from the Amberly shipping line. It was an old but a comparatively modest business. Thirty thousand dollars was no trifle.

It wasn't a trifle, either; it might have been well spent if it had helped save Richard's life.

I wouldn't argue that to myself. The disappearance of the jewelry should have been a point in Richard's favor simply because it did represent a large enough sum of money to tempt a burglar.

But it was only a point.

Another point which operated in Richard's favor, although obliquely, was the disappearance of the gun which had at last killed Cecile. It had been — they knew even then — a gun of small caliber, a twenty-two; Richard had never, to anyone's knowledge, had such a gun. There had been an immediate search for the murder gun; it had not been found. There was no indication that anyone closely associated with Cecile or Richard had ever had such a gun.

That was the first day following the murder. I put down the clippings. I knew that the investigation must have gone on doggedly for weeks, for months, and had then relegated itself to that status of alertness which I thought, soberly, must be a part of the make-up of police officers so they were always attuned to any slight movement, any small indication, any underground tremor which might suggest the presence of their quarry. No, the case was not closed.

And then I thought of those other letters from my father — three more letters, if Richard was right — to be identified. One of them might have gone to Cecile's murderer.

There was an inexorable logic about Richard's reasoning. I could not prove that a letter had gone to Cecile's murderer but I could not disprove it either.

I then thought of Andre Bersche. If anybody knew anything of that diary it would be Andre.

4

Andre Bersche was my father's confidential secretary and had been so for all the years I could remember. He never seemed to change. He was a tall, lanky man, with a lantern face, bluish jaws, pale eyes and lines down his sunken cheeks which always made me think of a bloodhound. I could not remember ever having seen him smile. He had long ears, too, and long, bony hands and thin, pale hair which had gradually washed out to gray. He had always thoughtfully provided me with spending money and when I first went to boarding schools at home, had brought me packages of hard candies. He wrote letters to me in his clumsy, three-fingered typing. The other secretaries, the trained ones, did the letters and transcriptions and briefs in my father's office. Andre was the confidential secretary and so were his duties. He sent me checks; he corresponded with the heads of the various schools; for all I knew he chose the schools. He made travel reservations and got the tickets. He took me to the boat or the train or the plane. He was part of my life, yet he didn't particularly like me; as a child does, I sensed that; I was only a part of his job. But he was always there. I had a sort of accustomed affection for him. He would know about the diary if anybody knew.

Even the thought of Andre was welcome just then; he had seemed to me all but omnipotent in his curious, cross-grained way. As soon as I got back to New York I would see Andre. I had cabled to him twice since I reached Nice, once to tell him of my father's illness, once to tell him of my father's death. He had not replied; I hadn't expected a reply.

I folded up the newspaper clippings; I didn't like touching them. I put them back in the briefcase. Because it seemed to belong there, I put the small and elegant address book in the briefcase, too.

Then I packed. I packed everything; I thought only of that. At least I thought that I thought only of that, but of course it wasn't true. I kept stopping, a nightgown or a sweater in my hands, and thinking, and then telling myself to pack, not to think in circles that only turned on themselves.

When I finished at last and all the baggage was closed and locked and my father's keyring and my passport and medical certificates were in the big red handbag he had bought for me, the room had already taken on that impersonal, almost inimical look of hotel rooms, as if it wanted to say, hurry up and get out, somebody else is coming. The wastebasket was full and there was discarded tissue paper here and there. I had left out travel clothes — my polo coat, for it would be cold in New York; my beret, my scuffy loafers. But since I was still wearing the beautiful Chanel suit I decided to wear it on the plane and look fashionable and imposing insofar as I could. When I crawled into bed I left the lamp at the other side of the room turned on. But I went to sleep at once; I was almost drugged with a queer kind of fatigue as if I'd been running races or climbing mountains. I didn't wake until morning when the telephone woke me.

I could see the clear blues of the Mediterranean and the golden sun streaking across it. Richard said, "Sorry I woke you —"

"No, that's all right. It must be late —"

"I've got reservations. A plane to Paris and then a jet to New York. Can you meet me at the airport? I've got to make sure about the tickets."

I said yes.

Everything that had happened the previous day — and night — came rushing into my consciousness as if it had sat, a live thing, beside me all night just waiting for my eyes to open. At any rate, I thought wryly, it had waited.

Only it hadn't quite waited. There was something disagreeable, something faintly ugly — some perfume in the air! I shot out of bed. Mr. Benni was not in the room. Mr. Benni was not in the living room. The door there was still bolted. The door from my bedroom into the corridor was still bolted. It was my imagination. It was not my imagination. There was, I was sure there was, a trace of sickening, heavy perfume somewhere.

The French window was still open. I wondered if I had left it just like that, half open, with the cool breeze blowing the long curtains. I knew without looking that the tiny balcony outside was divided from the neighboring balcony only by a railing. I knew that that balcony in turn was divided only by a railing from the next balcony. Something about Mr. Benni had suggested that he was a man of infinite resources and perhaps experience in ways that most people would consider unusual if not unlawful.

But when I looked hard at the room and at the baggage and all about me, I could only think that just possibly my handbag had been opened, for it seemed to me that its contents were a little disarranged. Yet I couldn't be at all sure of that.

In any event, Mr. Benni was not there then.

I finally put it down to imagination, called room service for a croissant and coffee, got myself dressed, had the baggage taken down and ordered a taxi. At the desk the manager came to meet me, all smiles when he said that my man of business had taken care of the bills, and patting my hand sympathetically when he said that he hoped I'd return in pleasanter circumstances. I looked around the lobby but did not see Mr. Benni and did not smell him. Lord and Lady Tweed were not there either, for which I was sorry.

There was the usual morning bustle in the narrow streets; the shutters of all the little shops had clanged up for the day's business; delivery boys were darting along on their bicycles, squawking their horns; we passed a bakery where the fresh bread was already out of the ovens and the fragrance drifted out to me. Windows were open and maids were shaking rugs over balconies. The bougainvillaea dripped in purple and red clusters over every wall. When we reached the airport Richard was waiting for me. He was bareheaded, so his dark hair looked crisp in the sun; he carried an overcoat over one arm; he wore a gray, tweedish suit and a beige pullover under his jacket. He had two porters who saw to our luggage. The tips at the hotel had used up an alarming amount of the money I had and I was glad he paid the taxidriver. The next morning, late, we arrived in New York.

The storm which had been threatening had arrived, too; we had to circle around and around before we could land, and I rather wished that Richard was sitting beside me, as he was not, for he'd had to take what reservations he could get, and his own place was three rows behind me. He had slept most of the night — or appeared to sleep when I twisted around now and then to peer back at him. In his sleep, if it was sleep, the weary frown came back between his eyebrows; his face looked strained.

We landed in the middle of a driving snowstorm; everybody seemed rather thankful that we got down at all and were not diverted to Washington or Boston or some other landing field, and I heard one of the customs men tell another that they'd get off early for ours was to be the last plane in that day. It was the customs officer who looked over my baggage and my father's, accepted the explanation that my father had died during our trip and didn't examine my new clothes too closely but merely said that he could see that they were worn; it occurred to me that his coming holiday might have perked up his spirits and inclined him to an indulgent view.

The taxidriver told us, too, that ours was to be the last plane in that day; the rest of the flights were to be sent to Washington. "Maybe to Atlanta if this keeps up," he said cheerfully. "It's been like this all night. No let-up in sight. Radio says we can expect a real blizzard. You were lucky to get a taxi, most of the boys are pulling in. No good driving in weather like this."

I huddled my coat around me and tried to see through the driving flurries of snow. Richard gave the taxidriver the address of my father's house.

We had talked very little. Perhaps there had not been much that we could say, and certainly there had been little opportunity to say it. The plane from Nice to Paris had had such noisy engines that we'd have had to shout, thereby taking our neighboring passengers into our confidence. The jet from Paris to New York had been so quiet that, again, nobody around us could have helped hearing our conversation even if

Richard had been sitting beside me. He had come once or twice to talk for a moment about nothing, to make sure I had a rug and pillow, to drink a little champagne with me at dinner which, when I thought of it during the night, seemed a rather bravado gesture on our parts, and took me back to school-days and the history of the French aristocrats airily facing the guillotine. The thought was so absurd but also so uncomfortable that I roused fully and stayed awake for quite a long time while the man at the window beside me snored like a trumpet.

And Richard and I didn't talk in the taxi; we watched the snow and the road and lurched from one side to the other and held our breaths — at least I did — while we edged past a snowplow which suddenly loomed out of the flurries of white ahead. I didn't recognize Gramercy Park until we were upon it and I could see the locked gates through the snow and the trees sharply black and white. Richard leaned forward to direct the taxidriver. He had managed to get not one taxi but two, for we had a mountain of baggage; the other taxi was following us, its lights gleaming faintly through lanes of snow. It was cold. We turned into the short and unexpected strip that was Pennyroyal Street.

"I think this is it — yes," Richard said, and the taxi slithered to a stop.

The narrow house, typical of New York houses of its period, was veiled with gusts of snow. Steps leading up to the door were covered with snow and had obviously not been swept since the storm began. There were a few lights shining rather dimly from windows, though. So someone was there. I hadn't been at all sure of that.

Richard said, "Somebody's in the house. I'll see —" and got out of the taxi. Snow and cold swept in through the open door. Richard plunged up the steps through the drifted snow and rang the bell. The lights still shone in the house but nobody opened the door. He finally came back down to the taxi. "Have you got a key?"

"Oh — yes —" My own key, rarely used, I had placed in the zippered pocket of my handbag. My father's keyring met my hand first so I dug it out.

I was not quite prepared for the biting force of the wind when I clambered out of the taxi and Richard took my arm. We slipped and climbed up snowy steps. I unlocked the big door and swung it open.

We both went into the hall and the marble Venus in the corner seemed to adjust her marble scarf even more coyly as she gazed at us. Richard gave her a rather startled glance. There was not a sound in the house and it was cold.

It was not completely cold, merely dank as if the furnace were still going but had been turned very low. There were lights, yes, but not many of them, and every lamp had a small power bulb in it. Nobody answered when I went to the kitchen stairs and called. Nobody answered when I went up the stairs, and past the bronze boy who stood smirking on the newel post and holding up a bunch of purple grapes which at one time, I remembered, had also held lights.

I came back down. Richard said, "Nobody's been here. See —"

There was dust, a quiet layer on the table. There was — which was more convincing — a kind of utter silence about the house, as if it had not been disturbed for some time and had sunk back into its own being. It didn't exactly resent me but it didn't want to be disturbed again. I shivered a little, I think from the cold.

"It's warm enough to keep the pipes from freezing," Richard said. "Somebody has left the lights on to discourage any burglar. All right, let's leave your father's baggage. You'd better stay with us until you can get yourself organized."

"But are you sure — I mean, I can stay here, you know — I can get —" I started to say servants and remembered I didn't have the money to pay anybody. I said instead, "Andre will know what to do."

"Andre? Who's that?"

There wasn't time then, with the door open and the snow sweeping in and the taxi-drivers both waiting, to explain. I said, "My father's secretary. I'll phone to him —"

"All right," Richard said, "but come with me now. You can't stay here alone."

I didn't want to stay alone in that silent house; it didn't seem like home to me in spite of its memories. At the same time, I was already very much in Richard Amberly's debt. He must have seen the conflict in my face for he said, shortly, "If that diary is in this house somewhere, somebody might come looking for it. I'm not going to leave you here alone to meet anybody who has the diary on his mind. But I've got a notion your father would have put the diary in some — some safer place. His office — somewhere . . . We're keeping the taxis waiting."

Somehow in the wind and snow flurries I sorted out my father's baggage, and Richard and one of the taxidrivers carried it into the house. I crawled back into the first taxi and saw Richard close the house door and try it to make sure it had locked. I remember wishing, embarrassed, that I'd had a small bag with sufficient clothing for only a day or two; I had instead three, not much perhaps for the European trip my father and I had planned but too much to lug into anybody's house without notice. There wasn't anything I could do about that. Richard shouted his address to the second taxi, got into the taxi beside me and, as he directed our driver and settled back, said, "You're perfectly sure that the diary is not in your father's baggage."

"Oh yes. I looked again last night just to make sure." I thought of the things I had found, the newspaper clippings which I had read.

We lurched around a corner. I wondered queerly if the house to which we were going, the Amberly house where the murder had taken place, bore some sign, some mark of the horror its walls had known. I put that quickly out of my mind. At least I thought I did.

It seemed a long way uptown. We went up Fifth Avenue, which was a perfectly strange street, a street from another planet, covered with snow. The lights in the store windows were blurred by the wind and snow. In the middle of the Avenue at about Fifty-sixth Street a bus was slewed around in the road, abandoned except for a police car and the blue figure of a policeman, who was swinging his arms together as if to thaw them. There were almost no pedestrians and those I could see through the snow were scrabbling along close to the store windows, heads bent against the wind, their coats swirling or clutched tight. I had been right in my vague notion of the street corner Santa Clauses vanishing on Christmas Day; there was not a bulging red figure with white wig and beard to be seen. The traffic lights, though, kept on going, red and green, red and green, in this strange world.

The Park looked like a part of the same, strange planet; it was deserted, full of wild and snowy shapes and wind. Lights shone now from the great apartment buildings along the Avenue but were obscured and queer-looking. We negotiated another corner at last and drew up before a door.

The steps here had been swept at some time during the day but were coated again with snow. Richard had all the baggage brought to the door and rang the bell but then got his keys and opened the door. We and one of the taxidrivers got the baggage heaped up in a hall with a marble floor of black and white squares, and a strange and ugly speculation caught me; I wondered if the murderer had fled across those black and white squares, leaving perhaps smudges of blood. Richard closed the door with a hard bang. We stood in the quiet of the hall rather as if we had escaped the clutches of a hurricane. I caught my breath and Richard laughed. "Well, we got here; I wasn't too sure we ever would." He raised his voice. "Anybody home?" Then he laughed again. "Not that I think anybody would be out a day like this."

He went to a push button set into the wall beside a huge fireplace which was filled with white birch logs. He pushed the button but nobody came. Then there were sounds from the stairway which went up, curving, at one side of the hall. Someone said in a soft, almost childish voice, "Richard! You're home!"

It was Miffy. I recognized her full blond hair, her lovely face, her wide eyes, from the newspaper pictures I had seen; Millicent Bell Amberly, the widow of Henry Amberly.

Richard said, "Come on down, Miffy." He introduced us over the banister, as Miffy obediently came on down. "This is Henry's wife, Miffy," he said to me. And to Miffy,

"I've brought Fran Hilliard to stay with us for a while. Her father was Orle Hilliard. She's just come home; we came on the same plane. She hasn't got her house organized yet. . . . Let me have your coat," he said to me and removed it.

Miffy smiled but looked puzzled. "Hilliard?"

"You remember him," Richard said. "Orle Hilliard. The lawyer —"

"Oh," Miffy said, "yes." She had reached the bottom of the stairs and came to me, her slim hand out, smiling. She was beautiful; even more beautiful, I thought swiftly, than Richard's wife could have been. Her hand was warm and limp. She said, "How do you do?" in a very soft voice. Her wide blue eyes looked perfectly blank as if she didn't remember my father at all.

Richard said, "I think we could do with a hot drink. And some lunch."

"Oh yes," Miffy said. "I'll see to it."

She smiled at me again; it was such a lovely smile that it practically melted my bones and I had the strangest feeling that she barely saw me. She went back along the hall toward, I surmised, the kitchen regions. Richard said, "Shall we go upstairs? There's an elevator but sometimes it gets stuck."

We went up the stairway which swept in a wide curve and at the top turned into a hall which was so wide that it was like a room. Here there was another stairway, smaller, going on up; rooms opened on either side of the hall.

A man came out and said, "Well, Richard, you're home. How do you like our storm?" He gave me an inquisitive look.

He was tall and rather weedy, around sixty, with thin gray hair and a kind of dandyish air. A woman came out of the room behind him. "Richard! How did you ever manage to get home? I shouldn't have thought a plane could land in this snow."

"Ours was the last one in," Richard said. "Mother, this is Fran Hilliard. My mother," he said to me, "and my uncle, Mr. Sisley Todd."

Mrs. Amberly smiled, then seemed to recognize my name and remember the association with it, for her smile remained but her face stiffened a little. However, she took my hands warmly in her own. "My dear! I knew you were in France. I'm sorry about your father. Stella will be glad to see you again. Come in, my dear, come in —"

I followed her into a kind of library and lounge, comfortable, with worn old chairs. I sat down as she indicated a chair near a cheerful, cannel-coal fire. There was a resemblance between her and Richard in their firm features, rather willful eyebrows and chin, and direct gray eyes. Her hair was still brown, scarcely touched with gray, and done in a thick French roll. She wore a very simple, red wool dress and no jewelry except the broad band of an old-fashioned wedding ring.

Richard reached for cigarettes and went to stand at the fireplace. "Miffy's getting us something hot to drink." He then explained me, in a way, to his mother. "I met Fran in Nice and she came home on the same plane with me. Her father had had their house closed — they were on a trip together when he died. Here was Fran, stuck in a blizzard in a house with no servants. So I brought her here."

"That was right," Mrs. Amberly said, as if it were the most obviously clear and sensible course in the world. She added in an offhand way, "As a matter of fact, we're making do ourselves with no servants at the moment. Oh, it's all right," she said to me reassuringly. "You'll be no trouble at all. Two cleaning women who call themselves a maintenance crew come in and clean twice a week. There's a service that sends a cook and waitress to see to dinner. That's the way things are these days. Did you have a good trip, Richard?"

He said something about his trip, and a little clatter of glass and silver came up the stairs. Miffy came in, carrying a small silver tray. "I didn't know what you'd like," she said. She moved over to a table as carefully as a little girl, trying to be grown up, and put down the tray. "I thought perhaps a hot toddy. There's hot water. And sugar and lemon juice."

Richard went over to the tray. "Good," he said in exactly the encouraging way one would speak to a child. "Fine. Good girl."

"We might need — the fact is — well, I'll get whiskey," his mother said, and she too spoke very gently as if she really hated to remind Miffy that whiskey was a customary ingredient of a hot toddy.

She needn't have spoken so gently for Miffy either didn't hear her or didn't take it in. Miffy looked up at Richard, her great blue eyes wide open; they were a curious blue, rather light with dark pupils, but a very definite blue and shiny as the surface of the sea. She said, "I'm so glad you got home. It must be a dreadful storm. The plane might have crashed —"

"No, no!" Richard laughed, but again very gently. "It was perfectly safe. Not even a bumpy trip. The taxi was far more dangerous."

Mrs. Amberly had quietly disappeared.

I then knew that someone was staring hard at me, the way one does know. I turned and Sisley Todd was still standing at one side of the doorway, looking at me as if I were a snake.

His eyes were bright with fear. I couldn't have failed to see it. His face seemed to have shriveled up, so instead of being an elderly dandy's face, set in the lines of smiling politeness, it was the face of an old — and terrified — man.

In the same instant, exactly like a picture falling into one's lap, before one's eyes, I could see an envelope. It was a white envelope with the return address of the hotel in Nice upon it. Also upon it, in my father's handwriting, was a name: Mr. Sisley Todd.

5

I couldn't see the address; the picture blurred there. I thought it was the address of some club but I couldn't be sure. I was sure of that name though, Mr. Sisley Todd. So I knew why he looked at me like that.

Mrs. Amberly came back into the room; she quietly put a decanter on the tray.

The envelope addressed to Sisley Todd must have been on the top of the sheaf of five letters; I must have looked at it, so my mind made a picture of it, without my awareness of that picture. But I was sure of it.

What had my father known about him? My speculation leaped forward before I could stop it; he had received one of those letters, so could he have murdered Cecile? Could my father have known or accurately guessed it? Sisley Todd was a relative; he could have had a key to the house or known ways in and out of it; he would have known Cecile, he might have struggled with her, at last in terror have taken the horrible and extreme measure of killing her because — say

— she had discovered him looting her jewels. He could have come and gone unseen and unsuspected. I was horrified at the direction of my plunging thoughts and their logic, and Sisley Todd's fright.

There was a kind of rustle at the doorway; I wouldn't look, I couldn't look, yet I knew that that elderly, dandyish figure with the fear and hatred in its suddenly withered face had vanished.

I was wasting time, I thought, with a driving sense of urgency; I must find the diary. Storm or no storm, it seemed to me that Richard and I should have searched the Gramercy Park house at once, then and there, all through the accumulation of many years. It would have taken weeks. There must be an easier, quicker way of finding the diary, I decided, and that would be by way of Andre Bersche.

Mrs. Amberly came to me with a steaming glass and then discovered my wet loafers and stockings. "You'll catch your death. Come on with me at once. Richard, bring up her bags. I'll carry your drink. This way —"

Richard said something and went down to the front hall as I followed Mrs. Amberly's red-clad figure on up the stairs. She led me to a small bedroom, obviously a guest room, told me to drink the toddy while it was hot, and started the tub in what proved to be a small adjoining bathroom. I sipped obediently; Richard came with my bags, stacked them up and left as I said something apologetic about the quantity of them, and Mrs. Amberly from the bathroom said, "Now into this with you as fast as you can." She came out and smiled at me. "And then into dry clothing. We'll bring you up some lunch. If you were on the plane all night you'll want to sleep this afternoon. Now mind, drink that and get into the hot tub —"

She went away. I drank the steaming toddy; I got out of my clothes and into the tub and dressed again, in dry clothing; somehow I knew even then that one did obey Mrs. Amberly; she had that air of authority. Miffy brought up a lunch tray.

"Mother Amberly made the sandwich. I made the coffee," she said.

"Thank you. It's splendid." There was I, already, treating Miffy like a little girl who must be encouraged. I could hear it in my voice. She nodded and went away.

I wondered where Sisley Todd had gone. I didn't quite like the idea of his lingering around in the house. Yet there was only my leaping suspicion to suggest that he might conceivably be a murderer. Surely the police had investigated him as they had investigated everyone close to Cecile. All the same, I knew that one of those letters had gone to him.

And then, munching a sandwich, a little arithmetic presented itself to me. There had been five letters. One had gone to Richard, one had gone presumably to Mr. Benni. One I was sure had gone to Sisley Todd. So now there were only two to identify. Only two to account for and, so to speak, disarm. They were two too many. The first thing to do was to talk to Andre. I finished my lunch.

It is a remarkably hard thing to have a private telephone conversation in a strange house in which you are a guest. One cannot very happily, or indeed easily, prowl through a house where one has been given hospitality. Once I decided to venture down to the drawing room and library floor and got halfway down the stairs, only to hear Mrs. Amberly's voice floating out directly below me. There was a telephone there, all right, and she was using it, talking about some committee meeting. If I used that telephone my voice would float out like that, too, for anybody in the house to hear. That included Sisley Todd. I crept back to my room.

I was not looking forward to telling

Richard that Sisley Todd had had one of the letters. That had to wait; I must talk to Andre. It was very late in the afternoon before I got up my courage to take the course which should have been clear to me from the first, and that was to slip out the front door and walk over to Madison Avenue and a drugstore which had a telephone booth.

The snow was very heavy; the early twilight was darkening the street, which I could see from the windows. But it was a short block over to Madison, and drugstores abounded. I took up my polo coat and beret and remembered to take my handbag, for I'd need coins for the telephone.

I felt very uncomfortable, trying to move noiselessly down the stairs. I felt worse when apparently somebody turned on a radio in the library, for a blast of sound came out and somebody else, Mrs. Amberly, said quickly, "Sh— turn it down. Richard needs his sleep. So does that nice child, Fran."

So Richard was asleep somewhere. This seemed at first quite natural, and then quite unnatural, for I would have expected him to start at once to find the diary. I didn't exactly know where he would go or what he would do but there should have been something.

A man replied to Mrs. Amberly but it was not Sisley Todd; it was a young voice. "Miffy didn't say where he picked up this girl."

"Don't say 'picked up'!" Mrs. Amberly said sharply. "She's an old friend. So was her father. He proved to be a very — valuable friend. You can't forget that, Slade."

Slade; so this was Miffy's brother, the young brother whose picture, too, I had seen, smiling above his white tie and boutonniere. The radio was turned lower but I could hear words from it: "— bus service is almost at a standstill — alternate sides of the street parking — no school tomorrow —"

There was the sputter of a match and a waft of cigarette smoke. I crept down again and decided that nobody could see me from the library or from what seemed to be a more formal drawing room on the other side of the hall. At least nobody did see and speak to me, for I went swiftly and as silently as I could down the stairs to the front hall with its black and white marble floor.

When I opened the door the snow stung my face; I tugged the door shut behind me and turned toward Madison through white gusts of snow and wind which almost took my breath.

Sometime that day most of the sidewalks

must have been cleared but the snow had soon drifted over again. There were occasional and treacherous icy patches which were almost bare but then plunged into drifts again. It was such hard going that even in that short block I was breathless and all but exhausted by the time I reached Madison and turned. The street lights were turned on already and the snow was driving around them, glittering coldly in the halos it made. Store windows were lighted, too, and sure enough, halfway down the block there was a drugstore. I didn't fling myself inside it but the effect was the same, the wind and snow were strong. There was a clerk in a white coat at the back of the store. He glanced at me over ranks of bottles and I said something breathless about the telephone and he nodded toward two telephone booths, both of them empty, at one side. My hands were cold, I hadn't thought of gloves; my feet were cold and doubtless wet; I slid into a booth, groped into my handbag, dropped a dime in the slot and dialed. I knew that number as well as I knew my name.

I believe that as I dialed I was conscious of the door to the street opening and somebody coming into the store, for I felt a little cold gust of wind, even there in the booth. I did not give it a thought, for the bell was ringing at Andre's end. I waited and presently I had again the impression of the door to the street opening. This time a figure crossed before the glass in the door of the booth — a man, rubbing his hands together, his cheeks red, his hatbrim snowy. He said something in a loud and jovial voice to the clerk, who responded. Andre answered the telephone.

"Andre!"

To anybody else this might have been inadequate. Not to Andre, who said sourly, "So you got back. I had your cables."

"You didn't reply."

"What was there to say? When did you get back?"

"Today. Andre, I've got to see you right away!"

"It's snowing. It's a blizzard. The radio says so."

"Yes, I know. Andre —"

"Did you hear from old Hatever?"

Mr. Hatever was younger than Andre. I said, yes, but I hadn't seen him yet.

Andre sniffed. I could almost see his long nose. "Then you know there's no money."

"Yes, I know. That's one of the things I want to talk to you about."

"No use talking. That's the way it is."

"I know. I've got to sell the house —"

"You can't sell that house in a hurry. Besides, there's a mortgage —"

"Yes, I know that! But I've got to try. I want you to advise me —"

"Well —" He softened as always to an appeal for help. "I've been thinking about it. Knew you'd have to sell. We'll talk it over when the snow lets up and the buses start running —"

There was finality in his voice.

"Andre, wait! Don't hang up! There's something else. My father's diary."

There was a pause. Then Andre said, "His what?"

"Diary. Diary. You must have his diary."

"I never heard of a diary."

I couldn't let him fail me. "You *must* have it!"

"Wait a minute. Well, now — there's some cartons of papers and files I took from his office. I did it right away, after you cabled me he was dead. I knew you couldn't pay any more rent, and besides, he was already in debt for office rent. Don't know how many months he hadn't paid. Anyway I cleared out his office desk and files. I've got everything right here."

"Oh, Andre! You *do* have it. It's there!"

"I don't know about a diary. I'll have to look for it. Why do you want it?"

"It's important. I've got to have the diary as soon as you can get it to me."

"I'll have to search. It'll take some time. You and your father! Always turn to me when you want help."

That was true enough. I said suddenly, "Andre, was he different? My father, I mean? Had he — well, changed?"

"Different," Andre said, "sure he was different. He knew it. I knew it. I covered for him — much as I could. But he'd been losing cases — hadn't been getting many cases for quite a while and then he had a couple of heart attacks —"

I interrupted. "He knew that was what it was?"

"Sure he knew. Still too smart to be fooled that way. Knew it was only a matter of time. Began to think about you — not," Andre said in a sharper tone, "not that he hadn't thought of you all your life. Nobody could have been more generous —"

"I know that, Andre. I know that."

"Yes, well — said he wanted to take you on a trip. Said he'd always intended to — well, to do a lot of things, I guess, but there hadn't been time. Now he was going to take you on a trip and get so he knew you and — yes, well, it wasn't long. I could have told him that. Where are you?"

"At the Amberly house. Nobody was in the Pennyroyal Street house."

"I closed it up — got rid of that woman that used to come and clean for him. He had his meals out, mostly. I left some lights on for fear of burglars but I had the telephone turned off. I'll phone right away and have them resume service. Oh, yes, I've got some mail here. One letter's addressed to you."

Letters! "I want it, Andre. I want it right away —"

"You'll have to want then," Andre said sourly. "Think I'm going out in a storm like this?"

I thought for a second. "Is there a return on the letter addressed to me?"

Andre knew, as he always knew everything; he didn't even make a pretense of looking at the letter. "No address. Woman's handwriting. Sent from London."

"Andre, open it, will you? Read it to me."

His voice quickened. Andre was nothing if not inquisitive. "Wait —"

A voice came into my ear telling me to signal when I was through, and I got out a little stack of coins.

It was strange really how much and yet how little I knew of Andre; I knew all his twists and turns of character, I knew I could depend upon him utterly. I had only a vague notion that he had no relatives; I knew that he lived alone in a small apartment, which I had never seen, over near the river; I knew that he was a baseball fan. I knew that he liked to know all about everything that concerned my father or me.

The letter addressed to me could be a Christmas card. Probably it was, addressed to the house and either forwarded or picked up by Andre. The letter could be anything. All the same my heart was pumping and I was so hot in the little booth that, as I waited, I struggled out of my heavy coat but kept the receiver glued to my ear every second. Beyond the door I could hear the muffled sound of voices talking about the relative merits of cough medicines.

Then Andre came back. From the sound of his voice I knew what the letter was, for his words were positively gluttonous with curiosity. "Funny thing. Funny letter — It's from a Delia Clabbering. Who's she?"

"I don't know. Read it!"

"Well, all right. Give me time." There was a crackle of paper. He cleared his throat. " 'My dear Miss Hilliard.' H'm. Very funny indeed."

I didn't grit my teeth. I made myself wait and Andre went on slowly, as if examining, and trying to find some explanation for, every word. " 'My dear Miss Hilliard. I have a letter from your father. I am writing to tell you that I cannot possibly be of any assistance to you now or in the future. If I hear from you again —' " Andre's voice sharpened, " 'If I hear from you again, I shall be obliged to turn the problem over to the proper authorities. We have in England a quiet way of enforcing certain laws. I might tell you that my husband died several years ago leaving me almost penniless.' "

Andre's voice almost crackled like the paper; it rose high and thin. "What does she mean? Look here now, what's going on here? What's she talking about? It sounds to me like —"

"That's exactly what it is," I said wearily. My very bones and heart felt tired and queer. "You are perfectly right. Only I didn't do it. It wasn't my idea —"

"It was his," Andre said with perfect conviction. "It was his. Yes. He was crafty. Even when he was at his best, he was crafty. Yes — well, now — and you want a diary. So that diary has something to do with — look here, did he write some other letters?"

Andre was crafty, too, I thought dully; crafty, and quick to get every implication. "Yes —"

"How many?"

"Four. Five, including this one."

There was a pause. Then Andre gave a low whistle. "Looks as if — yes — yes, well now. We'd better have a talk about this."

"That's what I've been telling you."

"Yes. Now then — H'm. First thing I'll do is go through these cartons. See what I can find. Evidence, that's the ticket. He had to have some kind of evidence —" He stopped, and I could almost see him examining the letter. "Letter seems to come from a lady," he said, meaning a lady in his terms. "Good writing paper. Simple. I told you it was mailed in London. Sure her name, Delia Clabbering, doesn't mean anything to you?"

"I'm sure."

"She's not scared," Andre said after a pause. "Or maybe she is, at that. She threatens you with the law. They say that the English have a very efficient way of dealing with blackmailers. I wonder what your father —"

I cut in. "I don't want to know. Andre, write her a letter. Tell her it was a mistake; tell her —"

"Oh, I know what to tell her. I'll put it in general terms. I'll tell her you know nothing of your father's affairs or that your father wrote to her — yes, yes, all a mistake. Sign your name. Shut her up. I hope," he added dourly.

Well, I hoped so too. London seemed very far away but at least I had the name of one person with whom I could communicate, to whom I could say, it was a mistake, I don't want your money, it was all a mistake.

Andre said, "Something to do with her husband. She says he's dead. I wonder what —"

"Andre, get your letter off airmail."

"Airmail won't go in this kind of weather."

"The storm won't last forever."

"All right, all right. Tell you what, I'll go through these cartons. See you tomorrow. Buses ought to be running by then. We can't talk about this in some stranger's house. You come to your father's house, say about four. I'll be there."

"Can't you make it earlier? In the morning?"

"Huh." He gave a dry laugh. "Go through all these things tonight? This is going to take time."

"But Andre, I've got to have it —"

"Four o'clock tomorrow is the best I can promise. That'll have to do."

I knew Andre when he turned stubborn.

"All right —" Andre always liked me to

repeat instructions — it was his clerkly type of mind — so I did. "Four o'clock tomorrow at home. Andre —" I knew the answer before I asked it, "Has your salary been paid?"

"No," he said promptly, "nor the loans I made to your father, either. I've got the amounts all down in my account book. Soon as you sell the house you can settle with me. I can wait till then."

"You'll have to wait till then," I said and thought with dismay, yet at the same time in a queer way understanding my father — loans.

"All right. I'll get busy looking for this diary. Or," said Andre, "anything else that could be blackmail evidence. Dear me," he said, but with a kind of relish in his voice, "well as I knew him, I wouldn't have thought he'd do this. Still though — yes, he'd changed. I told you, I covered for him. But he'd changed. Wanted to leave you some way of getting money, didn't he? Oh, yes, that'd be the way of it. Dangerous." He sighed and said with a kind of sober regret in his voice, "He wouldn't have done this when he was himself, younger. No. He had his ways — maybe not always right up to snuff, but then you wouldn't have known about that. Nobody did but — well me, maybe. Maybe some other people thought he sailed too close to the wind sometimes. Still — no, he wouldn't have done this. I told you he'd changed."

"I know. Don't keep telling me. All right then — tomorrow at Pennyroyal Street at four."

He hung up without saying good-bye; he never bothered to say good-bye. But I knew that all his bloodhound instincts had been aroused. He would find the diary if it was humanly possible, or even if it wasn't.

How quick he had been to guess, and guess accurately, the meaning of the diary and the meaning of the London letter! That was like Andre too. I clicked the receiver and dropped in the additional coins, which clanged sharply.

So that was the fourth letter. There was only one left to discover. First, Richard; next, Mr. Benni with his perfume and shiny hair; then, Uncle Sisley. Now, Delia Clabbering. Whatever her letter referred to, it seemed clear that it did not refer to Cecile's murder. Perhaps, in fact, the fifth letter had nothing to do with Cecile's murder. I wished I could be sure of that.

The red-faced man trudged past the door, a package in one hand, turning up his coat collar with the other hand. I knew that I must get back to the Amberly house. I pulled my coat on and went out of the little booth; I thanked the clerk, who gave me a pleasant nod and said it was a bad night.

It was indeed a bad night and growing worse; when I pulled open the street door the snow and the wind and, now, the darkness fell upon me. Lights shone from store windows upon streets that were swept almost bare of pedestrians. Those who were out huddled close beside buildings, ducking their heads, hurrying. I reached the corner of the cross street and turned into it, and then it was really dark with the coming of early winter night. Street lights seemed far away and all but smothered in snow.

I didn't turn around because I had the slightest, atavistic sense of pursuit. I turned around only to escape for a few seconds the biting savagery of the wind and snow sweeping across the Park and along the canyon of the street. I turned to clutch my coat more firmly around me and to walk backward for a little space and get my breath.

But I turned in time to see a man's figure, silhouetted against the street light on Madison Avenue; it ducked out of sight, swift as a lizard, down some areaway. The street was then empty. He ducked out of sight too swiftly, too instantly.

I then remembered, queerly at that time, my impression while in the telephone booth in the bright little drugstore, that the outer door had opened and closed. Yet nobody had crossed my line of vision. I had, a moment later, heard the door open again and this time the red-faced man had come in, had talked in loud and jovial tones, had made his purchase and left.

I also remembered the second telephone booth, beside the one where I had sat and dialed and talked to Andre. It was the booth nearer the door. I had assumed it to be empty; I had not so much as glanced that way when I left the drugstore.

There had been something too swift, too surreptitious about that figure sliding away from the street and the lights on the corner. I had an ugly notion that a man was crouching in the shadow of the areaway, waiting for me to decide that I had been mistaken, waiting for me to go on, waiting for me to become engrossed with my immediate struggle with the storm. I whirled around, grasping my coat, and tried to run toward the Amberly house.

6

I didn't hear anybody running behind me; I couldn't have heard and I didn't stop to look. I passed one house with lights streaming mistily out, and then another which was dark, and my breath was like knives in my lungs. I thought the Amberly house must be the next one and I stumbled and slid and ran full tilt into a man. He caught me in his arms. "Fran! Where on earth have you been?"

It was Richard and I couldn't answer. I couldn't breathe. He cried, loudly through the wind, "I've been at your father's office —"

So he hadn't taken a quiet, long nap, ignoring the diary. It was easy to leave and probably return to the Amberly house unobserved; I had proved that myself. The thought flashed across some level of my awareness and was gone.

He shouted, "Your hands are like ice."

He held my hands, he held me, and my breath began to come with less pain. *"There was a man —"*

The wind swept my gasping words away.

He put his face close to mine. "What did you say?"

"There was a man. He ducked down into an areaway."

I could feel him look over my shoulder. "There's nobody now. Nobody at all. Are you sure? I'd better look —"

He left me standing there and ran, jogging through the snow. It was so thick that only because of the street light I had glimpses of his figure as he stopped to peer down into the nearest areaway; he ran on and then disappeared completely around the corner of a house. The wind surged across the Park and along the street. Richard came back out of the snow and darkness. "Nobody there now. At least I couldn't find anybody. Why did you think he was following you?"

I had to shout in his ear. "The next booth —"

"What?"

"The telephone booth. In the drugstore —" The wind hurled everything I said out into the night.

Richard said, "We'd better get back to the house."

"No — wait — I want to tell you —"

He didn't hear me; a violent gust of snow caught us as if it had teeth. Richard put his arm around me and I leaned against it, thankful for it; we reached the steps of the Amberly house, struggled and slid over the snowy steps for a second; then the door opened into silence and warmth.

It didn't seem possible that only a door, thick and wide though it was, could transport us from such cold and wind and swirling snow, into warmth and silence and a smell of soup. Richard led me back, through a lighted dining room with white and black squares on the floor like the hall, and into a small room; this was narrow, with bookcases along the wall and an old-fashioned rolltop desk. He turned on lights as we entered; he took off my coat and then went to plug in an electric heater which stood beside the desk. "My father's hideaway," he said. "Nobody will hear us here. Nobody knows we're here, except the women in the kitchen. Warmer?"

I nodded. He pulled up a chair before the heater; he knelt down and took off my sodden shoes. I thought rather dismally that it was a good thing I had all my baggage with me, for the day had taken its toll of my shoes. He took my feet in his hands and began to chafe them vigorously. "Warmer?" he said again.

"Yes —" My teeth had been chattering; I didn't know it until they stopped and I could talk clearly. "Did you find the diary at my father's office? Would they let you look for it? Andre took his papers but he doesn't know anything about the diary —"

Richard said, "I told them I was representing you — okay? Anyway there were only a few people there. Hatever is in the country for the holidays. I didn't find the diary. I think they'd have let me look but they said your father's secretary had taken all his papers."

"Yes — yes, he did. I've just talked to Andre. That's why I went to the drugstore."

"Andre — the secretary? Oh, I see. You didn't want to use a phone here. Yes — well —"

"He doesn't know anything about a diary. He's got some cartons, things he took from my father's office. He's going to search. But, Richard, there's one name — I mean one letter — it's all right. That is, it's going to be all right as soon as she gets my letter — I mean, Andre is going to write to her and sign my name —"

He sat back on his heels, and still holding my feet in his hands, said, "You'd better begin at the beginning."

So I did. I went over it all. Richard nodded when I told him that Andre was to write a letter to Delia Clabbering at once; he nodded when I told him that I was sure that

Andre would find the diary.

And he nodded briskly when I told him that I had remembered one of the letters; the letter must have been on top of the little stack; I was sure I had remembered the name on it.

"I thought you would, given time. Well, there's another letter you can check off then —"

"Wait, it was Sisley Todd."

He stared at me. "Uncle Sisley? Are you sure?"

"Yes. And then the way he looked at me — yes, it was Sisley Todd. The address was some club —"

Richard jerked a little footstool over to the heater, put my feet on it and rose.

I said, faltering, "But the police must have investigated him when Cecile — when she was —"

"Oh yes." Richard's face was rather white and set. "Oh, yes, I told you. They investigated everybody who could possibly have got into the house or been close to Cecile. Uncle Sisley was one of them." He had, naturally, every detail of that investigation clear in his memory. "Uncle Sisley was at his club. He thought of going to the ball, decided against it, played bridge with some cronies there in the club until about ten-thirty and went up to his room and to bed early. The doorman at the club didn't see him leave until about four in the morning when I think Stella or Wilbur phoned to tell him that Cecile had been murdered. Then he took a cab here. He wasn't much use — but who could have been? He did his best to rally. I remember that he made the police let me have a drink, which I sorely needed by then. I don't think he could possibly have had anything to do with Cecile's murder. I don't think he could possibly know anything about it. Unless it's something he doesn't know that he knows. He's a bit of an old fool."

"He's scared," I said. "He looked at me, he heard my name and he was scared."

"Well, I wonder. He really is an old fool, you know. A nice old fool in a way. Rich too. He certainly would not have wanted Cecile's jewelry. All these people your father wrote to have got to have some kind of money — or at least some way to get money; otherwise he wouldn't have written the letters."

That was, of course, a sine qua non. Delia Clabbering had declared herself penniless, though. And I didn't think that Richard himself was rich or anything like it.

He said, "Uncle Sisley was my father's

stepbrother. Never married. He must have had an idea once. Possibly when he was in kindergarten. I doubt if he's had an idea since. But he's a likeable old duck just the same. I wonder what your father — I'd better ask Uncle Sisley."

"Yes —"

He looked down at me. "That checks another letter off your list. It leaves only one."

"Yes."

He said almost casually, as if he had to say it yet didn't want to alarm me, "Do you think your friend of the white orchid could have been in the next telephone booth and followed you tonight?"

"No! I'd have smelled his horrible perfume."

He grinned a little. "It *must* have been horrible! We can't be sure that the man you saw was really following you, you know. On the other hand — tell me again as much as you can remember of your talk with Andre — I mean, particularly, exactly what you said and what a man in the next booth might have overheard."

I told him again, as accurately as I could remember it.

"So he could have heard you ask about the dairy. If anybody *was* really there and it *was* somebody who is interested in the diary

—" He thought for a moment. "In a way that would be good. It would show him that you don't have the diary and that you've never read it. Yes, that would be good."

"Good —"

"Safer for you," he said shortly. "He could also have heard you repeat the time and place where you'll meet Andre tomorrow. Of course, your part of the conversation did sound as if Andre said he had the diary, didn't it?"

I thought back. "I said — yes, I said to Andre, 'You *do* have it. It's there.' Something like that. And I said that it was important and that I must have it. Then we talked about Mrs. Clabbering's letter."

He said slowly, "But probably there was nobody at all in the next booth, you know. Did you hear anything, his voice, the dial, any movement?"

"No."

"It seems unlikely that anybody could have been there, I mean anybody interested in you. I can't imagine anybody following us from Gramercy Park, hanging around in the storm all this time and following you when you went to the drugstore. Nobody could have known in advance that you were going there —"

"Your Uncle Sisley," I said suddenly.

"Oh, Lord, yes. I suppose so. Shall I get him down here now and get it over with?"

I nodded. I didn't want to face Uncle Sisley but as Richard said, I wanted to get it over with, too.

He went away and I sat there holding out my feet to the electric heater; my stockings were dry by then but my slippers were still soaked through.

Safer for you, Richard had said. It seemed extraordinary, preposterous to accept even a possibility of physical danger to me. Yet there had been a stealth, an effect of surreptitiousness in the way that shadow of a man had ducked out of sight. I wouldn't think about it.

So I brooded over the trivial problem of getting to a store and getting some overshoes — which seemed just then unsurmountable. Perhaps Stella could lend me overshoes.

Richard brought him in and closed the door firmly behind them. Uncle Sisley just gave me a darting kind of glance and then looked away.

Richard started it. "I told Uncle Sisley you had something to say to him."

"So," Uncle Sisley burst out in a high-pitched voice. "So, you're together in this! I wondered about it when you brought her home! You, Richard! I'd never have thought it of you —"

"Wait a minute," Richard said. "Wait a minute."

I broke in; I had my piece to speak. "It was all a mistake."

"What! What do you mean? Of course, it was a mistake. Your father took advantage of it. He was a liar and a cheat and now he's got a daughter who's a blackmailer —"

Richard took him by the arm. *"Listen to her!"*

Uncle Sisley wouldn't. He was red in the face, his angry eyes squinted up to shoot me murderous glances. "I shouldn't have written the letters! But I trusted that woman and, what's important, I trusted your father. He said she'd given him the letters and he said he'd destroyed them at once, that minute. To protect me. But he didn't destroy them, he kept them and he put the whole thing in this diary and *you* —"

His letter had had nothing to do with Cecile's murder. A wave of understanding was sweeping toward me and I could see its outlines.

Richard said, "It's all right. Don't fuss. It's all right." The wave of understanding had reached him.

I cried, "I knew nothing of what he wrote

in his letter to you. I have never seen the diary. I don't want any money. It was a mistake —"

"Tosh," said Uncle Sisley violently.

I had never heard anybody actually say the word *tosh;* I was for an instant diverted.

Richard was quicker on the uptake than I. He looked a little red, too, and rather swollen somehow about the face. I didn't realize that he was all but choking with suppressed laughter and perhaps some released tension until he spoke. "Uncle Sisley, I take it that these letters — that is, well, it was a breach-of-promise suit, was it?"

Uncle Sisley darted him a look that could have killed him. "Yes! That is, it could have been. Still could be! You know it. You're in this with the Hilliard girl. You — you cad."

This was another word I'd never heard spoken. It was more or less stunning.

Richard said, "You must believe me. There are no letters from you — at least if there are, Fran knows nothing of them, and if there should be any letters among her father's effects, she'll return them to you at once. Her father wrote that letter to you without Fran's knowledge. She's trying to tell you that. She does not want money. She does not want anything." He spoke very slowly and deliberately, like pounding one nail at a time into Uncle Sisley's head. "Understand?"

"Then why did you write me that letter?" Uncle Sisley said to me.

"But I tell you she didn't! Her father wrote it. He did it when he was dying. He wasn't himself. Fran has seen no diary —"

"Then why did she come here, tracking me down?" said Uncle Sisley with a triumphant air of I have you there.

Richard sighed. "She didn't. I didn't know you were here. She didn't know you were here —"

Uncle Sisley interrupted. "You could have known. The heating system at the club is being repaired. Naturally I came here to stay. Your mother or Miffy could have told you. Or Stella, for that matter. I've been here close to a week. You could have known."

"I didn't," Richard said patiently but very deliberately and emphatically. "Fran didn't know it. She didn't even remember your name on the envelope until she heard it —" He stopped. I was sure he instantly regretted even that admission, and Uncle Sisley seized it like a juicy bait.

"There, you see! She knew about that

letter. Oh, maybe you're not in it with her, Richard. I'd be sorry to think that my own nephew would stoop to such perfidious actions. But she knew it. Don't let her fool you."

By now none of Uncle Sisley's vocabulary would really have surprised me. Still *perfidious* was something to think about.

Richard had made a mistake, I think out of sheer frustration, for Uncle Sisley was indeed rather trying. *"Fran knew nothing of the letters."*

Uncle Sisley might not have been the world's shining light when it came to intelligence but he had an animal cunning just the same. His mouth pursed up; his eyes became even brighter. He mulled something over and then pointed his finger at Richard. "So there were other letters! Mine wasn't the only one! Why — why, that's how it happened that you went to see her. That's why you brought her here. She sent you a letter, too —" He then had what must be, if Richard were correct, the second idea of his life, and he turned so purple he nearly burst with it. "It's about that alibi! I always knew there was something fishy about that alibi." He puffed. His idea was nearly killing him but he brought it out. "Old Hilliard — he didn't see you at all. There wasn't any alibi.

So —" It was Uncle Sisley's day for ideas. He immediately had a third one, which was nearly the end of him, as a matter of fact, in more ways than one. "And that girl knows all about it!"

Richard looked a little alarmed, not so much at Uncle Sisley's idea, I thought, as at Uncle Sisley's purple face. "Here, you'd better sit down."

"With you!" Uncle Sisley puffed. "Never with you! Never at your table. I'll never take your bread and salt —"

"That's all right, but you can't get a taxi just now. There aren't any."

This practical note seemed to cool off Uncle Sisley a little. "Well," he said. "Well —"

"Uncle Sisley, now listen for just one minute. Fran knew nothing of what her father wrote you. She doesn't give a hang how many women you promised to marry. Understand?"

This, again to my surprise, seemed to touch Uncle Sisley's pride. He squared his shoulders, touched his tie, smoothed back a curly gray wisp of hair which had fallen over his purple forehead, and said, "One does these things. Dear, dear. Gets carried away. Marriage — no, no. Not for me."

Richard's eyebrows crooked up. I thought

he was going to laugh. He said gravely, however, "Certainly not, Uncle Sisley."

"You should have listened to me when you married," Uncle Sisley said. "I told you not to. Told you —"

"Yes," Richard said sharply. "Now we've got this all clear, haven't we, Uncle Sisley? No diary, no letters, no money, nothing."

"H'm." Uncle Sisley gave me a look which did not imply forgiveness. "Very well — certainly if you say so, Richard. But what about that alibi Orle Hilliard gave you? If this girl knows the truth — It *is* the truth, isn't it? Orle Hilliard did not see you that night."

Richard said after a moment, firmly yet with affection, "Leave this to me, will you?"

"Well — well — dear me. If you say so, my dear fellow."

"I do say so. Forget the whole thing."

Uncle Sisley gave me a look which did not imply forgetting. He said, however, in a stately way that the dead past must bury its dead, which seemed a little obscure.

Richard pressed him. "Not a word to my mother. Not a word to anybody. For your own sake, you know, Uncle Sisley. My mother —"

This got through to Uncle Sisley. He

looked frightened. It was not the fury of fear with which he had greeted me but it was an uneasy fright just the same. "My dear Richard," he said in a hurried yet still stately way. "Something like this coming to the ears of a gentlewoman! Your mother! Never!"

He couldn't or perhaps didn't try to restrain himself from shooting me a deadly glance when he said gentlewoman, clearly implying that I was not of that breed.

"And now remember," Richard said, "Fran will go through her father's papers. If she finds any letters which belong to you, she'll return them. When she finds the diary she intends to destroy it."

"Unread, I trust," said Uncle Sisley. "Unread —"

The door opened and Miffy came quietly in. She glanced at the electric heater, at Uncle Sisley and me and Richard, all in one long sweep of her beautiful eyes. She saw my wet shoes, too, and I thought that just a flicker of placid surprise touched her face. She said, "Mother says cocktails are ready. She says we must have an early dinner to permit the caterer's cook and waitress to leave early."

"Thank you, Miffy," Richard said.

Uncle Sisley didn't offer Miffy his arm;

the effect was the same as he bowed her out of the room. Richard gathered up my soaked shoes. "Well, that's done."

Uncle Sisley had had on his conscience whatever imprudent letters he had written, that was sure, but it seemed also sure that he had nothing else, certainly nothing concerning Cecile's murder. He had been very quick though to pick up the matter of Richard's alibi.

I said, soberly, "He's brighter than you think he is. He guessed about your alibi."

Richard turned off the electric heater. The red bars faded before he said, "It wouldn't surprise me if it hasn't occurred to a number of people that that was a very timely alibi. My mother knows; I told her. Wilbur knows and I'm sure Stella knows. Uncle Sisley didn't until just now. He'll not say anything, though."

The fragrant odors of soup and a roast wafted through the dining room. We avoided the elevator with its ornamented door and went up the stairs again. Mrs. Amberly met us in the hall above. "My dear child, you shouldn't have gone out in this storm! Richard, I thought you were asleep!"

"I had an errand downtown. I met Fran on the street. There's not a taxi to be had."

"But Fran — going out on a day like this!"

Mrs. Amberly looked puzzled.

Richard said to me, "You'd better get some dry shoes."

So I went rather quickly on up to the guest room and dug into my bags for more shoes. High-heeled pumps they were this time, which made me feel quite dressed up. It was dark outside; the snow was still hissing against the window panes.

When I went downstairs Uncle Sisley, forgetting everything but his manners, offered me a cocktail, met my eyes and sprang back as if I had offered him a cocktail loaded with cyanide. He retired to stare down at the fire and drink in a desperate and despairing manner which really touched my heart. Yet I didn't see what more I could do to relieve his apprehensions.

Miffy was sipping at her own martini. Richard was standing before the fireplace. Another man, young, fair, and good-looking, eyed me from a deep lounge chair. His eyes were as blue as Miffy's so I knew at once who he was. Richard said, "Slade Bell —" and Mrs. Amberly said, "Miffy's brother."

Slade got out of the deep chair, came to me and put out his hand. "I'm delighted, Miss Hilliard," he said. "I remember your father —" and spilled the whole contents of his martini on my skirt.

"Oh, I'm so terribly sorry. This is dreadful! Miffy, where's something — a towel — I'm so frightfully sorry, Miss Hilliard. I hope you'll forgive me. I'm afraid I've ruined your lovely suit. Surely from Paris."

Richard said, "I'll see to it," and applied a handkerchief to the spreading stain on my skirt. Mrs. Amberly appeared from the hall with a linen towel, apparently from some nearby washroom. "Try this, Richard."

Uncle Sisley stealthily and swiftly refilled his glass. Richard looked queerly white and angry as he scrubbed away at my skirt. Slade Bell kept up his apologies; he was so sorry, it was so frightfully awkward of him, really he was sorry. Mrs. Amberly, I thought, gave Richard a rather troubled look and then said to me firmly, "I'll send this to the cleaners. I don't think there'll be any stain. Now you'll feel more comfortable if you run upstairs and change to something else. We'll wait —"

Once in my room again, I got out of the suit, hoped Mrs. Amberly was right about the cleaners, remembered something I had heard my father say to the effect that good alcohol never hurt anything, reflected briefly that good alcohol certainly seemed to offer some solace to Uncle Sisley, and yanked out a black silk dress which happened to be another Paris purchase and was, in my proud opinion, a triumph of dressmaking. It was easy to get into. I added my mother's pearls and gave myself, even in that hurried moment, a rather pleased glance in the mirror, for I was sure that I looked quite sophisticated and Parisian. It seemed too bad when Slade clumsily burned a hole in the dress with his cigarette, as he did later in the evening.

That was after dinner, during which Mrs. Amberly kept up a flow of light conversation which sounded as if it was her habitual task, a glum-faced waitress whose name nobody seemed to know stalked around the table and a fat woman in white peered in once or twice from the pantry.

Richard telephoned for a taxi and while we were still having coffee a taxi miraculously came and the caterer's cook and the waitress, bundled up now in scarfs and coats, departed. We went up to the library and somebody turned on a radio. The weather bulletin stated that there was as yet no prospect in sight of the storm's easing up. Stella telephoned and talked to me and answered a small perplexity in my mind when she told me that her mother couldn't keep a permanent cook or any permanent domestic help not only because the house was big and times had changed but also because there had been a murder in the house.

7

She didn't say it so badly. She said it only after she had exclaimed about my arrival, said that she was sorry about my father and she'd like me to stay with her if I felt like it until I had made some kind of living arrangement.

She was warm, brisk and friendly; it was as if we had seen each other every day of the past four or five years, during which in fact even our correspondence had dwindled away. Richard had told her, she said, that my father had left only a house, which I intended to sell, and not much money; she supposed I'd be wanting to look for a job and she thought that perhaps "my husband" could help. "My husband" had easily got a job for Slade in one of the branches of the bank. She was very proud when she spoke of — "my husband." She sounded young and sturdy and sensible, and I could see her freckled face and full forehead and the determined sparkle in her hazel eyes.

"Besides," she said, "I do have a cook. I help out with the cleaning but the cook's been here ever since I was married, in spite of — oh, you know — Cecile."

I must have failed to answer her for it struck me only then that there did seem to be a rather odd arrangement for domestic chores in the Amberly house.

Stella said, "It's one of those things. They come, you know, and stay for a while, and then they just leave and won't say why. I suppose maids in the neighborhood talk to them. Or somebody tells them about — about *it.* Gets them upset. So Mother gave up getting permanent help. It's hard for her. Hard for Richard, too. Reminds him all the time of Cecile."

I still said nothing, for the photograph of Cecile's room, with the draperies torn away from the window and the chair overturned and the ugly marks of struggle everywhere, was in my mind. Stella said, "Surely you know about that!"

"Yes."

"Horrible," Stella said. "Some dreadful burglar. But it's all in the past. I wish Miffy and Richard would sell that house and get rid of it." She took a breath and said in a voice that didn't sound quite so sensible and sure of itself, "To tell you the truth, I don't like being there alone myself. Silly but — oh, well, I didn't mean to talk about all this. All I meant to say is that you are welcome here at my house and I'll do my best to make you comfortable. Have you thought much about what kind of job you want?"

I found that I had, which rather surprised me; my subconscious must have been buzzing right along. "I can teach languages or work in a travel agency."

Stella thought it over. "There might be something in the Foreign Department of the bank," she said, but dubiously. "I'll ask Wilbur." Her voice changed. "Fran, I shouldn't have told you that about the house and — and all that. It's only that we — that things — that everything has been different," Stella said in a burst, "since Cecile's —"

Murder is a hard word to say when it means what it meant to Stella. She said, "Since Cecile. All the time. In so many ways. No matter how tactful people are they can't forget and neither can we and — it's been dreadful."

Richard had told me; he had said I couldn't understand what murder did to people.

"Yes," I said.

"Well" — Stella's voice steadied itself with determination — "I hope to see you tomorrow. If this snow only lets up. Good night, Fran."

I said good night and hung up; the telephone extension was in a little alcove in the hall opposite the stairs, between the living room and the library. A teakwood screen, carved on both sides, which looked deceptively lacy — deceptively, because in fact it was very heavy, as I soon discovered — curved around the telephone, giving it an air of privacy which was also deceptive, for anybody could hear anything through the lacework of the screen.

I rose from the little bench and started back to the living room and bumped into Miffy's brother Slade. He had a highball glass in his hand and I instinctively stepped back, jarring against the screen. He caught it and had to exert himself to put it right.

"Heavy," he said, laughing a little.

It was then that the cigarette he was carrying in his other hand burned a hole straight through the sleeve of my dress and stung my arm. I jerked it away. His eyes widened. "Oh, I'm so sorry! How clumsy of me. I hope I've not burned you. Or your dress! Oh, I'm afraid I have. Really, I'm terribly sorry." His eyes were dancing, though.

I told myself that I must be mistaken; that his blue eyes were not amused and purposeful. No, he couldn't have first spilled a martini on my dress and then intentionally burned a hole in another dress.

He was so young, I thought, a boy; he must be still in school. I remembered though that he wasn't still in school, that Stella's husband had found a job for him, and I had a flashing sympathy for Stella's husband who was also about to be asked to find me a job. While all that went through my mind I had brushed off the spark of cigarette and found that, indeed, there was a tiny burned hole in my sleeve.

Just then, too, Richard came to the door of the living room and stopped. Slade looked at him. "So stupid of me. First a martini, now my cigarette. I was only trying to catch that screen, it's heavy —" He turned to me. "I hope you'll forgive me."

I could have forgiven him at once if only his eyes hadn't danced like that. But I said something, I don't know what, and Richard came across to me, lifted my hand and looked down at the tiny hole in my sleeve with its burned brown edge and a speck of my skin showing through.

"Did it burn you?" Richard said to me. He was angry; I now knew a kind of white set look in his face.

It had stung a little, not much; I hurriedly said that it hadn't burned me. Richard turned to young Slade, who was sipping from his highball glass and eyeing us over its rim.

"I rather think that's a Paris dress," Richard said. "It'll take something to pay for the damage you've done."

I felt as if I should say, no, no, it was only an accident. I didn't, for young Slade said, "Richard, what would I use for money? You know what the bank pays me. I'd starve if Miffy hadn't taken me in here to live." He laughed. But then — I think at the look in Richard's face — he said rather hurriedly that he must thank Richard, too, for giving him a home; Miffy owned only half the house, of course; and that he hadn't meant to burn my dress, it was an accident and he was terribly sorry. Miffy came out and said mildly, "What's the matter?"

Richard became gentle and kind at once. "Slade had an accident with his cigarette. It burned Fran's dress."

Miffy's wide eyes turned to me. "Oh, I'm so sorry."

"It doesn't matter," I said quickly and at that point Uncle Sisley's before-dinner cocktails caught up with him. He said good night to Mrs. Amberly, calling her his dear, dear Sally, he took Miffy's hand and kissed it, he saw me and bowed until he nearly lost his balance, but had no recognition whatever in his glassy eyes and Richard got him off up the stairs. I said good night to Mrs. Amberly and tried to thank her. I said good night to Miffy but she was standing at the window looking down at the snowy street and didn't hear me. Slade had disappeared.

I too, once I had gone into my room, went to the window and looked down three stories. The flying snow made halos around the street lights. Somewhere there was the chug, chug of a snowplow. I thought of the men who had to work all night, all over the city, trying to clear it of its crippling encumbrance of snow.

It seemed a year since Mr. Benni had approached me on the Promenade des Anglais. It seemed a year since Richard had come to me with his news of the diary. But tomorrow Andre would have the diary. I had to account now for only one remaining letter. It occurred to me that its recipient might reply — as Mr. Benni had replied and Delia Clabbering had replied.

If the fifth letter had in fact gone to Cecile's murderer it was rather chilling to consider what form that reply might take. A murderer, Richard had said, is not afraid of murder, he is only afraid of being caught.

I made myself listen to the hiss of the snow against the window and the chug of snowplows, which would come nearer and then go farther away, and at last I went to sleep.

By morning the snow had banked up against the windows and sifted into the room through the crack I had opened; I mopped it up with a towel. I got a sweater and skirt from one of my bags. The red sweater and gray herringbone skirt had seen considerable service in school but were warm and comfortable. I went downstairs, past the second floor with its living room on one side and library on the other, and down to the dining room on the first floor where I found Stella.

She greeted me with a firm and friendly handshake and said she had mushed across the garden. Indeed I could see the marks of her floundering footsteps; the long window gave upon a rather eerie space of snow-shrouded paths and shrubbery and benches, which in summer must be the garden. She said that breakfast was waiting for me, that Wilbur and Richard and Slade had gone to their offices.

I didn't think Richard had gone to his office; I was sure that he was trying to track down the diary. I wondered how and where. Stella said that Wilbur had insisted on going to the bank, although she didn't see how he was going to get home if the snow kept up as the weather reports said it would, and that, besides, nobody ever did much business in New York during the week between Christmas and New Year's, and did I like my egg soft or hard — all in the same hearty breath. She gave me the same feeling of staunch friendliness she had given me over the telephone the night before.

She was a little older than I, not much. She had scarcely changed at all; her light brown hair was straight and bushy, her eyes a bright hazel, her chin and forehead broad and rosy, freckles on her cheeks. She said that she wished I could have come to her wedding and I said I was sorry I couldn't and wondered where I had been sent that summer. To a village near Deauville, I thought, along with some other girls who were tutoring in French.

I wished that I knew where Richard had gone. I wished that he had left some sort of message for me.

"My wedding was lovely," Stella said, measuring coffee. "We went to Bermuda for our honeymoon." Her brisk, common sense manner dropped away and her pleasant face looked very bleak. "But then we had a bad time, you know. Nearly two years ago now, two years in April. That was only the spring after I was married. Richard and Cecile had been married early the same year I was married. They had a very quiet wedding. Cecile's parents wanted a small wedding. They were going to live in Jamaica, right away. Poor Cecile. It was dreadful, I can't tell you — but it's in the past."

How very wrong you are, I thought dismally. It's not in the past; it's about to come into the headlines and back into your lives again, your life and your Wilbur's life and Richard's. I thought of Mrs. Amberly and how kind she'd been to me and Stella asked me if I wanted sugar in my coffee.

A little color came into Stella's cheeks when she said in an embarrassed way that she hoped I wouldn't pay any attention to what she had said about the house. "Wilbur heard me. He says I talked as if it is — well, haunted in a way by Cecile's murder. I was explaining why this big house is a problem — the housekeeping, I mean. But any big house is a problem that way. Miffy and Richard really ought to sell it."

Somebody — Slade and Stella herself — had said something of the ownership of the house but I suppose I looked puzzled, for Stella pushed back a bushy lock of hair and explained that Miffy and Richard owned the house jointly. "My father left it to Henry and Richard together. I suppose he thought they'd sell it. It's too big and cumbersome by today's standards. But then Henry died, so his share reverted to Miffy. They ought to sell it. But Miffy says it is home."

"She's so young, much younger than I'd have expected."

Stella gave me a queer but very straight look. "Miffy? She's thirty-six."

"I can't believe it! She looks about sixteen!"

"She was married to Henry ten years ago — yes, just about ten years ago. She was twenty-six when they were married, I remember that. Henry was killed five years ago. Yes, she's thirty-six. We all feel sorry for her, as if we ought to do our very best to make up to her for Henry's loss. But Miffy isn't the only one to miss Henry; we all do. That is" — Stella's sturdy honesty came out — "Richard misses him and so does Mother, I know. Henry was so much older than I that I really didn't know him the way I know Richard. Poor old Rich. He had to give up his own profession and take over at Amberly Shipping after Henry died. Richard is a lawyer, you know."

"No." I was startled. "I didn't know that!"

"Oh, yes. He'd started a practice, a good practice, too. But somebody had to go into the company and of course there was nobody but Rich to do it. That kind of shipping has passed its heyday, everybody says. But the company is still sound, makes a living for Mother and Miffy and Uncle Sisley. I get some income, too. Richard always wanted to be a lawyer. It seemed a pity he had to give it up."

So Richard had known, as only a lawyer could know, exactly what my father had done and how far he had fallen. Yet he had said with a compassion which I now understood more fully and even more thankfully, "the vagaries of a dying man."

Richard himself, though, had experienced what must have been to him a breakdown in his own ethics, when he accepted the lie my father offered him. Richard himself had experienced a human struggle between right and wrong and wrong had won. It occurred to me that perhaps only experience in one's own failure develops understanding and compassion for failure in other people.

We had taken our coffee into the dining room and were idly watching the snow through the French doors when Stella said with a kind of desperate honesty, "Nothing really has been the same since — well, since Cecile and — and all that. Sometimes I don't want to see even — even friends.

Things happen. It may be only a word or a look but — You see," she said with a burst, "the case was never really closed! Of course it had to be a burglar, but they never found him."

"I know —"

"But it's worse for Richard. He was in love with her," Stella said firmly. "He adored her."

I looked at Stella's floundering footprints, in the snowy garden outside the windows. The snow had already smoothed them over a little; before long there would be scarcely a trace of her progress across the garden. Of course Richard had been in love with Cecile; he had married her.

Stella was trying to say something else to me and finding it hard; she was twisting her firm hands a little, her hazel eyes were bright. "Did your father tell you?"

"What? Oh. The alibi. No. Richard told me."

"Richard!"

"I knew nothing of it until then."

"I see," Stella said in a voice that proclaimed that she didn't see at all. After a moment she said, "Yes, well — Wilbur thought you knew. He was sure your father must have told you. Wilbur said — he told me to tell you — that is," Stella said desperately, "you are an old friend, you see and — Wilbur thinks — Wilbur asked me to say —"

I took pity on her. "Wilbur wanted you to advise me to keep the fake alibi a secret."

"Yes! The police believed that alibi! It doesn't matter whether it was true or not. Richard didn't — couldn't have killed Cecile! I told you. He adored her. There's no question of that! Wilbur thinks it's best to leave things as they are."

The edges of her footprints in the garden were blurred. A bench looked like the rounded back of some strange animal, bent over in the snow. I said at last, "What do you think?"

"What do —" I heard her draw a sharp breath. I didn't look at her but I could almost feel the struggle that took place between her innate honesty and her obvious devotion to Wilbur and to Richard. Then she said stoutly, "I agree with Wilbur. Wilbur is right, I'm sure."

She wrapped herself in coat and hood and scarf and kissed me on the cheek and avoided my eyes. It was hard for Stella, I thought, pulling a French door shut after her, and watching her wade determinedly through the heaped-up snow.

Dear Stella, who had a struggle with her conscience, too. It couldn't have been easy for Mrs. Amberly to accept my father's lie either. On the other hand, my father's lie might have saved her son's life.

The complexity of human relationships is never simple to follow; it is like intricate lacework, but lacework made of steel. I knew that I would have accepted that lie with nothing but thankfulness; I'd have stuck to it till I was blue in the face for a perfectly clear reason: Richard had not murdered Cecile and I knew it. Stella and Mrs. Amberly knew it.

The day went along quietly, too quietly in a way, for Richard did not return and did not telephone. I thought of everything to account for his absence and his silence except the perfectly obvious course he took.

Mrs. Amberly called me into the library and chatted for a long time about Stella and how very happy she was before it struck me that Mrs. Amberly was putting a great deal of emphasis upon Stella's happiness with her Wilbur and that Mrs. Amberly, too, believed that I must know of the alibi my father had given Richard. So in her own way she was saying, please keep it quiet; please preserve our status quo.

She didn't say it in so many words. It was not, however, very pleasant to realize that Stella and her husband and Mrs. Amberly

— and even Uncle Sisley for his own reason — considered me a source of potential danger.

Uncle Sisley was nowhere to be seen. Miffy drifted around the house, watching the snow from the windows or listening to the weather reports. It was mid-afternoon when I started out quietly, surreptitiously indeed, taking care not to be seen and questioned, for the house near Gramercy Park.

I had not forgotten my impression of a man following me perhaps the night before, certainly sliding very quickly out of sight when I turned; I was perfectly aware of an unpleasant little tingle of uneasiness, even as I opened the closet door off the black and white marble hall and borrowed, without permission, some overshoes, which I thought belonged to Mrs. Amberly. I let myself out the front door into the snow and remembered that fleeting shadow of the previous night altogether too well. But still the surmise that he was following me was a very feeble surmise indeed; it had no firm and tangible basis. My promise to meet Andre was firm, and, besides, Andre, who was always overprompt, would be at the house when I arrived.

I hadn't heard from Richard at all, but I knew that he couldn't have forgotten my appointment with Andre; I was sure that he would arrive at the house, too. I was not at all afraid.

I thought that I had allowed myself more than enough time; I hadn't. I hadn't really anticipated the sheer physical struggle of making my way through the storm. It was as if it turned itself into my enemy, fighting me at every step. I waded and slid through the snow as far as Madison Avenue and there I wasted some time trying to get a taxi. There were no buses anywhere and the snow blew in icy clouds and whirls along the bitterly cold street. I thawed out for a few moments in a drugstore and eventually made my way over to Lexington. If the sidewalks had been cleared, then snow had covered them again, but there was a sort of lane in the street, between banks of snow which had been scooped up on either side by snowplows. The cleared lane was slippery and covered with thin patches of snow and people were walking there in the middle of the street. There were not many people, only a few, muffled up, heads bent. I took to the middle of the street, too, and it was easier going, not much easier but a little. I took the Lexington Avenue subway downtown.

The car was almost empty. It was a queer kind of holiday for New Yorkers, the blizzard plus Christmas week. When I got up to the street, at my stop, I felt again rather as if I had stumbled into some strange world, altogether unfamiliar.

But the Park was the same and the grilled iron gate and the trees and shrubbery laden with snow. The pleasantly dignified entrances to the Players Club and the National Arts Club loomed up with lights through the whirls of white. Pennyroyal Street had apparently been considered too short and unimportant to have been cleared at all. I waded along a vaguely trodden-down path in the middle of the street again until I reached number ninety. Here to my surprise the steps had been shoveled, not recently but sometime during the day. The shovel stood, neatly reversed, on the step beside the door and all but proclaimed Andre's finicky presence.

The snow was in my eyes; my hands were cold and numb even in the gloves that, this time, I had remembered to wear, but managed to get out my father's keyring and open the front door. I was almost pushed into the hall by a sudden gust of snow and wind but I got the door shut behind me and caught my breath. At least it was quiet in the house. Indeed it was almost too quiet. It was also much later than I had intended it to be.

I took off my coat and gloves and called, "Andre —"

I took off my snow-covered beret and called, more loudly, *"Andre —"*

Nobody answered. There was not a sound in the house but something was different. I looked around and the marble Venus looked cold and distant in spite of her coy simper. Then I knew what was different, and that was the musty, dusty, closed-in smell of the house. There was instead a smell of Mr. Benni.

8

I was perfectly, horribly sure of it and I clutched up my coat and beret in one swoop and started for the door. The storm then played one of its many roles during those days and stopped me. It was quite literally impossible to run out into the battering snow and wind without fastening my coat and pulling my beret on tightly, and the moment of pause gave me a moment for common sense to take over.

The thing to do was clear and imperative. I must speak to Mr. Benni, tell him it was a mistake, I had never seen a diary, he'd get his money back and I didn't want it and — yes, it was imperative. I must check off Mr. Benni.

He had not offered to harm me; I could not be afraid of him. The first thing to say must be a loud and firm declaration that he could have his five thousand dollars back, and that should make him listen to me. Here was the phantom, the vanishing Mr. Benni. I might not have another such chance.

I then realized that all my father's baggage had been removed from the hall where I had left it. There was the lamp I had left turned on, the worn Oriental runner, the brown velvet curtains at the end of the hall, the long stairway with the bronze boy holding the bunch of purple glass grapes on the newel post. But the baggage was gone, so somebody had removed it.

I was sure that Mr. Benni was now going through the baggage, at his leisure, hunting for the diary which was not there, and the certainty gave me the impetus I needed. I trudged down the hall to the library, Mrs. Amberly's overshoes making squishing sounds. The house was so still that the sounds seemed very loud. There was a dim light over my father's desk in the library but nobody was there.

Somebody had been there, for the baggage was open, clothing was strewn helter-skelter over chairs and floor, and the slim briefcase which I had placed in one of the bags lay, caved in and empty, on the floor beside the desk.

I went to the desk. The clippings about Cecile Amberly's murder had fallen to the floor, too; it chanced that her face, that beautiful face above the white dress, looked up at me. I looked away. The top of the desk was littered mainly with the contents of the briefcase — paper clips, bills, the package or two of cigarettes, a nail file, some battered-looking folded letters, the worn-out blotter. There were also the usual accoutrements of my father's desk, the ornate inkstand, silver and tarnished; a huge blotter roller; a picture of my mother in a silver frame, also tarnished; a picture of me as a five-year-old staring soberly into the camera. The litter from the briefcase was mixed up with them.

But where was Mr. Benni? The scent of his perfume lay within this room, too, although it didn't strike me with such unpleasant force as it had when I came into the hall from the fresh, cold air.

I debated going upstairs. I wondered if, disappointed, Mr. Benni had gone about the long and tiresome business of searching the house and, having heard me enter, was hiding somewhere, waiting for me to leave. If so, he made no sound whatever.

I was sure that Andre would soon arrive; I listened for the rasp of Andre's key. I listened for the doorbell announcing Richard's arrival. I gathered up the clippings about Cecile Amberly's murder and put them on the desk. I pulled open a drawer of my father's desk and found that Mr. Benni, or somebody, had been searching there, too, for the contents — letters, bills, whatnot — looked as if they had been stirred up with a spoon.

If the diary had been in that drawer Mr. Benni would have found it; still I went quickly through the drawer and then through the other drawers of the desk, which were in much the same state of disorder. It was a rather disconcerting disorder really, for my father had saved things which there was no reason to save, old theater programs, advertisements, old calendars, bits of string. Andre had been right; he had changed.

I was, I know, looking for a book; since I first heard of a diary I had visualized the book, a flat little black book or perhaps not so little but rather thick, perhaps labeled diary or perhaps just a memo or even a small account book. There was no such book in the desk and I didn't really expect to find it in such an obvious and not at all secure place. I still heard no sound whatever from the house and Andre didn't come. Richard didn't come either.

For a moment common sense had suggested a frank and even rather amicable talk with Mr. Benni (who had attached a white orchid to his money, which struck me then as definitely a propitiative gesture). This moment was vanishing rather rapidly. I certainly could not have brought myself to search the house for him.

I began to think, or at least persuade myself to believe, that Mr. Benni had finished his search and, disappointed, had left the house as stealthily as he entered. Although he wouldn't have entered it stealthily. He would have gone boldly up the steps, manipulated the lock somehow — a dubious accomplishment but one which, from what I had seen of Mr. Benni, I felt was almost certainly within the range of his talents — searched, and then left.

Clearly he was in New York. It was quite beyond the range of any sort of coincidence that anybody else connected in any way with my father would use the same perfume with which Mr. Benni doused himself.

The question, of course, was where was he then? And where was Andre? I looked at my watch and it was nearly five o'clock. I looked at the windows and they were black. It was not like Andre to be so late for an appointment. Also it did not seem possible that Richard would fail to arrive.

But I had to allow for delays in getting around New York that day. I had been late myself; I tried to reckon the time it had taken me to slip and slide along the middle of the street, reach the subway, go down the stairs, wait for my train, arrive at my station, struggle through the snow again — no, I couldn't reckon the time.

There was something almost inimical in the silence of the house. I was at home there, yet actually I was not at home at all. I decided to wait a little longer, glanced down at the litter on the desk and presently picked up one of the folded pieces of writing paper which I had taken to be old letters, carried around by my father for no reason at all. It was soiled and creased. I unfolded it.

It was an old letter — no mistake about that — but I knew why my father had carried it around. I read it — I couldn't help scanning through it after the first few words. There was no address; it began, "My lovely darling soon to be wifie." It went on in terms which were so immature that they were not even funny and was signed with many crosses, Smoochie. I believed it because I saw it, in scrawly handwriting under the light from the lamp.

It was drivel; it was written by an adult, which was unbelievable. I found two more letters; they were written on the same paper, folded and creased as if they'd been carried around the same way, and were the same kind of letters. An adolescent in his senses would have been ashamed of writing them. But there was one thing that was mentioned in all three letters and that was marriage, in no uncertain terms, in terms that any judge would consider positive proof of promise of marriage, and I knew who Smoochie was.

That was the one cheering thing about the little pack of letters; they were clearly my father's hold, if I had to call it that, on Sisley Todd. Clearly they had nothing to do with Cecile's murder. My only problem was to get those absurd letters back into the wrinkled old hands which had been foolish enough to write them.

I looked at my watch again. Richard wasn't coming. I was aware of a growing uneasiness; Richard hadn't said that he would meet Andre and me but I had been sure that Richard would come. I had been sure that Andre would come, too.

It was very cold in the house; without knowing it I had become chilled through. It felt almost as if some window had been opened and left that way so an icy draft crept along the floors. The telephone stood on the desk and I dialed Andre's number. He had had it connected again, as he promised; there was a dial tone and I could hear it ring but Andre did not answer.

I debated. It seemed likely that Andre had

come, cleaned the steps, waited for me and left, which would be like him; punctual himself, he demanded punctuality of others, and was never exactly patient. He was probably returning to his apartment then. It was dark and getting later by the moment. Neither Andre nor Richard was coming. I decided to leave.

I put Uncle Sisley's letters into my handbag. I left the desk lamp burning. The house was still perfectly silent, so still that it seemed to me that I could almost hear the relentless fall of the snow. In the hall at the foot of the stairs, beside the newel post with its absurd bronze boy and purple grapes, I knew where the cold air was coming from, for there was an icy little draft upon my face. I put on my coat and beret.

I ought to find the open window, if there was one; frozen pipes would be expensive to replace. I stopped, my hand on the newel post, and heard cautious footsteps somewhere above. There was a little creak of old wood, then another. Then there was a little wait as if somebody were listening for sounds from me, listening to make sure that I had left the house; perhaps listening to make sure that I was still there. Mr. Benni. He hadn't gone after all.

My careful reasoning, my plan for a sensible approach to him, everything in fact that was sensible at all disappeared. I heard another cautious footstep somewhere above; I knew that whoever was in the house had to be coming down from the third floor, the attic floor. Before I had more than recognized that fact I was tugging the door to the street wide open; I was out in the snow. I closed the door hard after me and ran down the steps.

I bumped into somebody, who muttered an apology as if it were his fault; I slid across an intersection, I hurried because I knew the street light might disclose my presence. I was not at all sensible; I was afraid.

I made it to the subway and looked behind me and there were stragglers, bending against the storm; nobody seemed to pay any attention to me while I waited on the platform and nobody else got into the car which I entered when the train came.

A subway ride is hypnotic; the speed, the rush of sound, the glimmer of stations passed or the bleak brightness of stations where there is a stop, all of it is hypnotic. I only wanted the stations, the time, to pass quickly. I stared at a newspaper which a man in the next seat had procured, and didn't see anything beyond a headline about the blizzard.

We reached my station at last. I wrapped my coat around me and trudged up the stairs, looking behind me instinctively. Nobody at all followed me up the stairs.

There was a drugstore on Lexington, near the subway entrance. I went into it and again found a telephone booth and dialed Andre's number. Again I could hear the repeated buzz at the other end and I waited and waited but Andre didn't answer.

I lingered in the drugstore for some time; I bought some toothpaste, fumbling for my coin purse and seeing the little sheaf of Uncle Sisley's letters. When I thought ten or fifteen minutes had passed I tried Andre's number again and still there was no answer.

Perhaps it had been Andre in the Pennyroyal Street house. Perhaps he had not heard my arrival. Perhaps he had been searching while he waited for me. No, he couldn't have been searching; I'd have heard it, unless of course his search had extended to the attic. I decided that it was possible; there were some old trunks and boxes in the attic — I didn't remember just what. But it seemed to me quite likely that Andre had remembered them and begun to search them for the diary.

It seemed to me quite likely indeed that it

had been in fact Andre from whom I had fled in such unreasoning terror.

I couldn't linger much longer in the drugstore. The clerk was beginning to give me inquisitive looks. I said something about the storm and a telephone call. He said, yes it was a bad night. I thanked him for the use of the telephone and went out into the street. It looked very bare and queer, windswept and cold, with the street lights glaring and the store windows too bright, and everywhere it was too empty except for the snow and the wind.

The cross street to Madison had been in use that day; also the sidewalks, which were patchy with snow and ice but had once been cleared. There were humps of white which were automobiles, parked, covered with snow and immobilized. After I crossed Madison I took to the middle of the street again, between more white humps of parked cars. I reached the Amberly house and saw lights coming from the library above. Then, of course, I had to ring.

Slade opened the door. His eyes began to dance. "You! Richard is raising hell. Come in —" He called up the stairway. "She's here! She's back!"

He helped me off with my coat, he bent to tug at my overshoes; his cheeks were pink as if with not too well suppressed merriment. Richard came running down the stairs.

"Where have you been?" Richard sounded angry.

Slade straightened up. "Can't a girl go for a walk without your making such a fuss?"

I didn't want to talk within the hearing of Slade's alert and, it seemed to me, mischievous ears. I had to. "I went home."

Slade hung my coat up in the closet and thumped the overshoes down on the floor.

Richard said, "I left a note for you. I didn't want you to go to — out in the storm —" he said, making a quick substitution of words as if he didn't care to take Slade into our confidence. Slade was aware of it and chuckled. "Don't mind me. I'm going upstairs. I'll leave you two alone."

"Go ahead," Richard said and stepped to one side as Slade, still chuckling a little, went past him, up the stairs and out of sight. Richard then drew me away from the steps, toward the dining room; again there was the fragrance of cooking from the kitchen and the sounds of voices. He said, "I told you not to go there. I left a note for you. I pushed it under your bedroom door before I left this morning."

"I didn't see it. I didn't see any note at all."

"Was Andre there?"

"No. That is, I don't know. I was late. But — somebody — Mr. Benni had been —"

Richard caught me by the wrists. *"What?"*

"So I thought I could tell him I'd give him back his money and that it was all a mistake and I could check him off the list, you see. But he wasn't there — not then. It was later, after I'd looked through the desk and waited for Andre, and I was leaving. Then I heard somebody upstairs but I lost my nerve completely, I don't know why, and I just ran —"

He pulled me up closer to him, holding my wrists. "Fran," he said.

I was beginning to feel very warm and safe. "Yes, it was silly to panic like that."

"No, no, it wasn't silly."

There was a long pause and I only felt Richard's warm clasp on my wrists and his presence. Somebody dropped something with a clatter in the kitchen and somebody else giggled. Richard said, "Don't do it again."

"Don't —"

"That kind of thing. Going alone to the house, like that. You've got to understand that it's dangerous."

"I wasn't afraid. Not really. That is, until I heard the footsteps coming down from the third floor, the attic, I'm sure. There are some things stored there. I don't know why I lost my head like that. It must have been Andre. I didn't wait to find out."

"If it was Mr. Benni I don't imagine he'd have been in a frame of mind to listen to sweet reason."

"He'd been there. It was his perfume."

"I wonder," Richard said thoughtfully, "if Andre *could* have gone to the house after all —"

"If he saw Mr. Benni, Andre would have called the police and got rid of him! It must have been Andre I heard on the stairs. Why didn't I wait and ask him if he'd found the diary!" I said impatiently.

"He hadn't this morning."

"This morning! You talked to him?"

"I went to his apartment." His voice was low; he lowered it further. "We had a long talk. At first he was suspicious of me. After I'd told him the whole story he talked — a little grudgingly but talked. Said only that there was no diary. I suggested that we go through your father's papers just to see if we could discover anything — I mean anybody liable to blackmail. After some more talk he agreed and we started to go through your father's records; he let me help although he kept snatching things away from me and saying that was confidential. Nothing of any special interest turned up, as far as I could see, and certainly no diary. He had worked all night, he said, looking for the diary and hadn't found it. I told him you wouldn't be at the Gramercy Park house this afternoon so he said he was going to give up for a while and get some sleep. Practically threw me out."

"Oh." It sounded exactly like Andre.

"So then I went to the office. I hadn't reckoned on the difficulty of getting around in the storm. It took forever. I tried to phone to Hatever and question him; there's just a chance that he might know something. But his telephone was out, due to the storm. I got home a while ago. If that was Mr. Benni in the house, he's gone by now. Putting as much distance between him and the house as he can, as fast as he can."

"I couldn't reach Andre. I phoned and phoned, on my way back here. He didn't answer."

"From the way he acted when I left he wouldn't answer the last trump just then. He was determined to get some sleep. He's a little on the cranky side, isn't he?"

If Andre had decided not to, he wouldn't answer the telephone, he wouldn't answer the doorbell, he would scarcely budge for a fire siren. I said yes.

Richard said, "And if Mr. Benni got the diary, that's another defeat. I should have started to search that house the minute we arrived in New York. But it looked as if it would take six months. I was so sure your father had put the diary in some safer, some more secure place. As a matter of fact I still think so."

I said slowly, "If Mr. Benni found the diary — oh, in a desk drawer or somewhere else in the house — he wouldn't have searched my father's baggage, would he?"

"Maybe he searched that first. The question right now is whether it was Andre or Mr. Benni you heard in the house. We'll talk to Andre and find out if he was there and if he found the diary —"

There was a slight sound on the steps. I looked up. Miffy was coming down the stairs, her lovely eyes on Richard. She came all the way down and put her hand on his arm.

"You two are always alone together like this. What do you find to talk about so much?"

9

We went upstairs. Richard sat down at the telephone in the hall. Paying no attention to any listening ears, he asked me for Andre's number, dialed it and again it rang and rang and there was no answer.

"Still won't answer," he said. "What's the number of the Gramercy Park house?"

I gave him the number and he dialed that but there was no answer there either. Miffy's eyebrows were lifted inquisitively. There was a foot, though, in a very elegant shoe, dangling from an unseen leg and footstool in the library. I guessed it was Uncle Sisley's foot.

Richard said to me, "Not there. We'll try again."

Miffy said, "Who?"

"Nobody you know, dear," Richard replied absently and I felt suddenly reckless of listening ears or eyes too, dug into my handbag and marched into the library. Uncle Sisley, whom at that moment I could not help thinking of as Uncle Smoochie, looked up and I shoved his letters at him.

"Yours," I said, turned around and marched out of the library again.

Miffy's eyes were round and curious. Richard understood, for his lips pursed in a soundless, rather amused little whistle. He said, "That's done? Where —"

"In the briefcase. All the time. I found them this afternoon."

"Found what?" Miffy said. "You two act as if you had secrets all the time."

Richard put his arm around her. "Nothing, Miffy. Really nothing —"

She put her head against his shoulder and smiled at me. There was something a little possessive in that smile as if it said: Strangers, do not trespass.

I heard Uncle Smoochie clearing his throat in a rumbling and embarrassed way in the library. I fled upstairs. I felt ruffled and indignant. Uncle Sisley had written his own stupid letters, I hadn't. And Miffy wasn't Richard's owner, she was his sister-in-law.

After a hot shower and after I had dressed and brushed up my hair, I began to feel less indignant. It really didn't matter what Miffy did or said, or how she said it.

I hoped that Uncle Sisley wouldn't think that I had read his drooling letters but was sure that he would think I had — as indeed I had, as much as I could stand, and sufficiently to recognize them for what they were.

It had been a good plan of Richard's for Andre to hunt through any records of my father's cases. I didn't much like that idea, though. I had an uneasy feeling that there was no telling what we might find and that it might be better not to know. Still, if we couldn't find a diary, it was the obvious and sensible alternative course. Surely it wouldn't be difficult to identify any case concerning Mr. Benni — if there were a case concerning him. Andre had already written to Delia Clabbering, I was sure. Again I went through the little arithmetic of the letters. Richard, Uncle Sisley, Mrs. Clabbering, Mr. Benni. And one more — Mr. or Miss or Mrs. X. For the hundredth or, it seemed to me, perhaps the millionth time, I tried to see the letters I had so casually counted and mailed; I shut my eyes and tried and tried and finally went down to dinner.

It was much like dinner of the previous night except Slade did not spill a martini upon my dress, and Uncle Sisley, apparently in a fit of remorse following his previous night's desperate debauch — or perhaps merely feeling in consequence a little liverish — did not drink at all. I caught one or two rather wistful glances at the cocktail tray and once or twice caught him watching me covertly. He looked away immediately; I didn't know whether he was brooding about Richard's alibi or his own recovered letters.

Stella and Wilbur came to dinner. It took me a moment or two to realize that they — by they I mean Mrs. Amberly, Stella and Wilbur — were bringing up a big gun in their defense and the defense of Richard's false alibi in the way of Wilbur. Although in fact it might have been Wilbur's idea that by charm and blandishment alone he would insure my silence.

The exasperating irony was that I certainly wouldn't have told the truth to anybody, ever; it was Richard who intended to do that. Their efforts with me were wasted.

Wilbur was indeed a big gun. He was huge, broad-shouldered, tall, thick-necked and muscular. He had a big voice, too, which boomed out jovially.

He had thick dark hair, crew-cut, a thick red face, and small black eyes which were shrewder than I would have expected. He engulfed my hand in his great red fist and beamed down at me with a vast smile and cold eyes and said he was delighted to know

Stella's dear friend.

Stella looked proud but worried. Mrs. Amberly was cool and very self-possessed. Richard was a trifle grim and serious, and I guessed that he, too, had summed up the situation and knew exactly what Stella, his mother and Wilbur had in their minds.

I wished I could tell them that I was on their side and I could not interfere in what was so importantly Richard's own affair. I only hoped that he would stick to his decision to find the diary before he went to the police and told them the truth about his alibi. But if Mr. Benni had the diary, there wasn't much chance of finding it, ever.

We should have searched the Gramercy Park house at once. If Mr. Benni could find it, we could have found it.

But if Mr. Benni had found it, why had he lingered in the house? The obvious answer was that he had heard me come in and call Andre, he had waited; he had eventually become convinced by my silence that I had gone and had started downstairs himself.

But there was always that chilling and altogether too logical possibility that the fifth letter had in fact gone to Cecile's murderer — and that murderer wanted the diary, too.

It couldn't be that I had sat there in my father's library, alone and listening for what now seemed a long time, while Cecile's murderer quietly searched the attic!

Dinner was just about what I would have expected. The maid who served it was different, short and bouncy and smiling instead of long and glum, but again nobody seemed to know her name. Mrs. Amberly did not need to do so much talking, for Wilbur took over and told what he clearly thought were witty anecdotes of the storm. Stella laughed dutifully but crumpled up her napkin and worried it all through dinner. It would be quite easy to dislike Wilbur very much; indeed, as the evening wore on and we played some half-hearted bridge and he told me, after every hand, exactly what mistakes I had made, I began to think that it would be quite easy to throttle Wilbur.

I wanted to talk to Richard. I wanted to make plans to go the Gramercy Park house and find the diary — if it were still there and if Mr. Benni had not, by now, found it himself.

I wondered suddenly what had happened to the note Richard had left for me, telling me not to go to Gramercy Park that afternoon. This question struck me with peculiar force just as my partner made a no trump bid and I was counting my hand for the best suit and there happened to be not much to count. Oddly too, for no clear reason, another surmise shot like an electric current into my mind: if it was not a burglar who had murdered Cecile, if it had been somebody my father had known, then suppose it had been one of the people now in this room, quietly playing bridge while a blizzard closed us all in together.

It was a paralyzing kind of surmise. I said three hearts before I discovered that I had only four rather feeble hearts and had to sit there while my partner raised the heart bid. I didn't actually hear this raise; I was thinking only, suppose, just suppose one of the people in this room deliberately, intentionally took that note Richard left for me and didn't give it to me. Suppose that person went to the Gramercy Park house to get the diary. And suppose that person believed that I knew far more of the contents of the diary than it was safe to permit anyone to know and had consequently intended to get rid of me! A murderer, Richard had said, is only afraid of being caught.

The cards were dancing before my eyes. It seemed to me that everybody in the room must have heard the dreadful course of my speculations. My partner said, "We have it for four hearts," and I reminded myself that whoever it was in the Gramercy Park house that afternoon, he had not come near me.

My partner was Slade. We had made up exactly two tables of bridge and had drawn for partners. Richard was at the other table. Somehow I played the hand out. By the time I had finished I had returned to a more normal and practical state of mind. I really did not think that Mrs. Amberly or Uncle Sisley, Slade or Miffy, Stella or her hearty husband had stolen into the house that April night and shot Cecile. No, I didn't think that. But all the same it seemed to me that there was a kind of chill in the room, in the house, that had nothing to do with the storm.

Yet the room was quiet, isolated by the snow; there was the little slap of the cards, the voices — nothing unusual, nothing ominous at all, except in my thoughts.

Once or twice when Richard was dummy he rose and went to the telephone in the hall; it seemed to me that everyone was aware of his errand and that everyone listened, but perhaps I imagined it. Perhaps, too, I imagined a feeling of tension and strain.

Certainly, though, Wilbur overdid this great and sudden chumminess to me; he even rose and hugged me hard when I made game — from the dummy hand, as a matter of fact.

Miffy might look and speak like a child but she could add. She said, "Why, Wilbur, you've lost seventy-two cents. I shouldn't think you'd hug your opponent."

He laughed loudly. "I never lose a chance to hug a pretty girl." He added, ha, ha, ha, and I didn't see how Stella could stand him, but at the other table she smiled happily. It struck me, oddly, that perhaps Wilbur was not always so agreeable.

At eleven Stella said they'd better go home before they were entirely snowed in, and Wilbur agreed.

He kissed me good night, a hearty smack which would have hit my mouth if I hadn't seen it coming and ducked so it hit my forehead.

I caught a glimpse of Richard's face with rather satirically lifted eyebrows. Stella kissed me, too, quickly and in an embarrassed way as if Wilbur had gone a little too far in his efforts to gain my admiring friendship — and secrecy. But Wilbur was quite content with himself and his idea of lady-killing. He said good night heartily to everybody and swooped down the stairs, with Stella under his great arm. Presently we heard the bang of the French door in the dining room; I think we all listened for the glass to shatter but it didn't.

Uncle Sisley shuddered. "Wilbur nearly knocks the house down when he shuts a door. What a perfect ass he is!"

I felt that at any moment I might begin to like Uncle Sisley, even knowing the worst about him as I thought I did.

Richard went to the telephone again and still Andre did not answer. He then tried my house number again. I was standing beside him and could hear the buzz, over and over again in the empty house. It seemed imperative, as if somebody must rouse to answer it. Nobody did.

Richard put down the telephone at last. "He wouldn't have stayed in the house, would he?"

I considered it. "He might have, because of the storm. There's a telephone extension in what was my father's room. Andre might not hear it."

Again the storm entered the stage and played its not unimportant role. Richard went to a window in the library and pulled back the crimson curtain. I followed him. The snow drove blindingly against the window. Looking down to the street was like looking at a wild scene on another icy and deserted planet.

I said low, “There’s no use in trying to go back to the house.”

Richard thought it over; the wind slashed snow against the windows. He shrugged at last. “I doubt if we could get there now,” he said and let the crimson curtain drop into place again.

The storm had changed the whole city; it was no longer a civilized and orderly place. It even controlled and put its mark upon people. Ordinarily we would have called a taxi and searched till we found Andre — discovered whether or not it was Andre I had heard on the stairs — and found out whether or not the diary had actually been in the house and Andre had found it. There might easily be some hiding place in the big, old house of which I knew nothing.

We turned away from the window. Mrs. Amberly and Uncle Sisley were talking about some bridge hands; Mrs. Amberly, as always, was adept at keeping some kind of light conversation going. It struck me that she had had to learn that art, protectively, during the past year and a half. Miffy and Slade were standing at another window, holding the red curtains back too, looking down at the street. We were all drawn by the storm as if by a magnet; we all had to look down whenever there was a lull or whenever we heard a snowplow. Miffy and Slade looked queerly alike standing there. They didn't speak, but when they turned from the window they looked as if they had just had a long conversation.

I made my manners to Mrs. Amberly and went to bed. I wished that I could ask Richard what he thought had happened to that note and why. I very much wished the question had not thrust itself up out of that part of the mind — instinct, reasoning, whatever it is — which simply cannot be controlled and whirls off in its independent course, casting up the strangest and most unwelcome froth. I wished I could be sure that the ugly suspicion it had cast up was merely froth.

Perhaps half an hour later Richard knocked softly at my door. I was still awake, sat up, turned on the light and said, "Come in."

Richard came in and closed the door behind him. He was wearing a dark gray dressing gown and soft-soled bedroom slippers. "I found out what happened to the note I left for you."

He spoke in a whisper. So did I. "Who took it?"

"Miffy." He sat down on the foot of the bed.

I stared at him. "But why?"

"Well — it's like Miffy. Do you mind a cigarette?"

"No. Here —" I pushed a package toward him but he had his own in his pocket. He reached for a packet of matches on the bed-side table.

"You see, I pushed it under your door when I left. You weren't up yet. I didn't want to wake you. I remember that my note didn't go all the way under the door, a corner stuck out. I thought tonight that it might have been the day for the cleaning women to come and that one of them might have picked it up. So I asked Miffy and she said no, they hadn't been here today. I said you had lost a note I'd written to you and she said she had taken it." His voice was perfectly casual.

"Why would she do that? She didn't give it to me!"

"No, she forgot. She went to her room and got the note. Here it is."

He pulled an envelope out of his pocket and gave it to me.

It had been torn open. He said, "Yes, she opened it. She said so."

I stared at the envelope and then I stared at him. "But — but you don't —"

"No, well, you don't understand Miffy."

I thought that over. "No, I don't understand her at all."

"It's hard to explain. I suppose she opened it for a perfectly simple reason, she wanted to see what it was. I didn't address it to you, look here —" He turned the envelope over and of course it was blank, no name, nothing to indicate that it was intended for me. Except the certain fact that it had been pushed under my door.

This did not seem to occur to Richard. "She was going along the hall, saw the corner of the envelope sticking out from under the door and pulled it out and looked at it. Then she read it."

There was no Dear Fran, no salutation of any kind. It read merely, "Don't go out today. I'll talk to Andre." He had signed it R, with a vigorous sweep of the initial.

I looked at it, I looked at him. He said, "Miffy said she thought Andre was probably a hairdresser and then she forgot the note altogether."

The note was short, still it didn't sound at all as if Andre were a hairdresser. Miffy's curiosity, Miffy's forgetfulness, if it was indeed that, might have cost me my life. Suppose Mr. Benni, or whoever was in the house, had decided that what I knew of the diary was too dangerous to be permitted to exist and that consequently I was too dangerous to be permitted to exist!

But the ugly hypothesis had wedged its way into Richard's mind, too, for he said, "When I came home this afternoon late, and found you'd gone out in spite of my note, I thought everything. I was sure you would understand why I was going to see Andre and why you shouldn't go to meet him. If there was really anybody, say Mr. Benni, in that second telephone booth in the drugstore last night, and if he really overheard you make an appointment with Andre at four o'clock, then — well, when I got home and you were not here I thought of everything. I tried to phone to you at the house. I could hear the phone buzz but you didn't answer."

"I must have gone by then."

"I questioned Mother, I questioned Miffy. I phoned to Stella, I thought you might have gone there. I was on the phone to Stella when you arrived. But that note — I had to know what had happened to it because —" He stopped and looked at nothing and finally said, "Because."

"I know why. If it was somebody here — somebody in the house, somebody who knows about the diary and thinks I know and —"

"No!" he said. "No!"

But he had thought of it. He'd thought of

it for many months. He had never been perfectly sure that a burglar had killed Cecile. There had been times when he must have thought, was it somebody close to Cecile, close to him, somebody in the house?

I said flatly, "We must find the diary."

"I'd hoped we'd have it by now. None of us can go on like this."

"Your mother wants to. Stella and Wilbur want to. They're afraid I'll tell about the alibi."

"Yes, I know. Wilbur doesn't want to rake the thing up again."

There was another silence. I tried to say, if it wasn't a burglar, then who do you think killed Cecile? I couldn't say it, bluntly like that.

He put out his cigarette and pulled a paper from the pocket of his dressing gown. "Do you trust me?" he asked, half smiling. "I want you to give me a power of attorney. Same kind you gave Hatever and for the same reason."

I took the paper and it was a simple form. "There's a pen in my handbag."

He rose, found the red handbag and gave it to me, watching, still half smiling while I rummaged and then signed the power of attorney.

"You didn't even question," he said with

a little laugh. "Far too trusting. I should tell you that I'm a lawyer —"

"I know."

"Oh. You know what a power of attorney is?"

"Of course."

"I'll not sell your house. But I do want to have your authority to see what I can find out, if anything, about your father's affairs. His banks, the safe deposit records, everything. There just might be something that Hatever has overlooked."

"All right."

"I'll go first to see Andre. Then I'll let you know just as soon as I know anything at all. Don't go chasing out in the blizzard and a closed-up house again —"

"I had to go this afternoon. I was sure Andre would meet me."

He sighed a little. "You mustn't blame Miffy for forgetting the note or for reading it either. She's as curious as a child and as — as — well, that's the way it is." He looked down at me for a moment and then, unexpectedly, he leaned over, smoothed out my pillow, put his hand on my cheek and kissed me. It was the lightest of kisses, quick and comforting and like a feather, yet it lingered warmly on my lips as Miffy opened the door.

Again, I thought. Again! She knows. She *is* fey. She knows whenever Richard and I are by any chance alone. She knows he kissed me.

I felt as if his kiss must be visible, still on my lips. Miffy said, “I thought I heard talking.”

Richard said, but gently, “You might knock, Miffy.”

Her lovely eyes widened. She said, unbelievably, “Why?”

Richard took her arm. She was wrapped in a pink silk dressing gown, simple and sleek; her blond hair hung disheveled and yet lovely around her shoulders. “Never mind,” he said, almost as unbelievably, “come along.”

“I saw you kiss Fran,” Miffy said. “You mustn’t kiss Fran.”

I wanted to ask why.

I wanted to say that so much that for a second I thought I had said it. Richard laughed; it was a light, perfectly mirthless laugh. “Good night, Fran,” he said, drew Miffy out into the hall and closed the door.

10

That night the snow stopped. It stopped suddenly, yet stealthily; it stopped with utter silence, yet all at once through that silence sounds began and became louder and clearer, for the whole great city had started digging itself out. There was the sound of snowplows everywhere when I awoke. Sidewalks were being scraped, there were the sounds of voices, men shouting at each other as they worked and as if they were released from frozen paralysis. When I looked down at the street there were pedestrians wading along energetically through banks of snow; a maid wrapped in a coat was walking a dog around the drifts the snowplow had sent up against the sidewalks. A delivery truck came along the path in the middle of the street. The sky was still gray and a little threatening as if it said, all right, I'll let you off today but look out, I may send down a smothering pall of snow again at any moment. But still there was no more snow.

Uncle Sisley went out for a walk; I saw him leave, swinging his walking stick jauntily and wearing ear mufflers below a French beret, which looked rather peculiar but sensible. Mrs. Amberly set out briskly, after making a long market list. Richard had already gone by the time I went downstairs. From the dining-room windows I could see something of Stella's house, neat and trim, and I thought I saw her open an upstairs window and whisk snow from the ledge.

That morning Miffy told me why Cecile and Richard had disagreed.

We were in the library. Miffy had some knitting in her lap. "Richard scolded me last night," Miffy said.

"Oh." I stopped thinking of Andre and Richard and listening for the telephone, and looked at her. She bent over her knitting.

"He said I shouldn't have come into your room like that. But I did hear your voices. I thought it was odd. So of course I came in."

I think I opened my mouth, decided it was hopeless and shut it again. She continued. "Of course I didn't knock, why should I! But there Richard was, bending over you and kissing you." She glanced up then; there was only the shine of her very blue eyes. "Wasn't he?"

"He — I — yes." And it's none of your business, I wanted to say.

She put in several stitches and then said, "Dear Richard. He didn't mean anything by that, you know. We are so close. Naturally, I understand him."

Do you indeed, I thought, and still couldn't say it. Not to Miffy.

There was a cannel-coal fire in the grate again that morning; I watched it and wondered who had carried the coal and who had lighted it.

Miffy said, "I just thought I'd tell you."

I couldn't have checked my quick and surprised look at Miffy and she met my eyes and smiled.

The implication was clear — and why not? Richard was attractive. Miffy was beautiful. Miffy had been a kind of inheritance from his brother, in a queer way; a charge and a care and — a wife?

She said, "Richard was terribly unhappy, you know, in his first marriage. It was dreadful. Everybody knew it."

"Stella — Stella says he was very much in love with her."

"Of course she would say that! She told the police, everybody, that Richard adored Cecile. She still sticks to it. That's only to protect Richard. To keep people from thinking *he* might have killed Cecile. No, he didn't really love Cecile."

"He married her," I said, on a queer wave of anger.

"Oh, perhaps he thought he loved her. In the beginning. When he married her. But he didn't know. Her parents knew. They should have told him. But they didn't. They were only too glad to get her married off." She put in one stitch, carefully. "They went off to live in Jamaica just as soon as they got Cecile off their hands. They didn't even come back when she was murdered. They should have told Richard about her. How was he to know!"

I wouldn't say, what was there to know. "But he — he must have known Cecile well."

"Why, of course he thought so. In a way he had. She was younger than Richard but — oh, you know New York. You think you've known people forever and know them very well, but really you don't, you just see each other now and again." She whirled the knitting around. "But he hadn't known *that.* They kept it a secret. But we knew it as soon as they were married. Everybody in the house knew it. I don't see how it was kept out of the newspapers later at the time of the murder, but it was. That was why Richard and Cecile quarreled and why they didn't go to the ball that night." She put down her knitting. "I'll show you her room. It's beautiful."

"No!"

"Yes — do come — it's on the top floor. They had the whole floor remodeled when they were married. Come —"

I didn't exactly want to go with her, yet somehow I did. We took the elevator. We stood in the hall and Miffy pressed a little button; there was a rumble which came closer and stopped. We went into the small cage and it went up and the door opened on the fourth floor.

There was a hall there, too, and a few closed doors. Miffy went to the door of the room which would overlook the garden. There was suddenly a key in her hand. So she had planned to show me this room! She opened the door.

I couldn't help looking at the room which I had seen in those newspaper pictures. It was not quite dark, although blinds and curtains were closed. Miffy flitted across it as if she knew her way very well, neatly avoiding chairs and a bench; she pulled the ropes of some heavy blue curtains — the curtains which had been dragged off their rods in that horrible struggle a year and a half ago.

She opened blinds; the cold gray light showed the room. There was an enormous bed — that, too, I had had a glimpse of in the newspaper clippings. There was the chair which had been knocked over. I could see now that it was upholstered in pale blue with little gold figures in it. Suddenly I felt almost as if I had seen the room in the shambles of that dreadful night, almost as if Cecile still lingered somewhere, looking out of the mirror perhaps and watching us, her dark hair neatly parted in the middle and her glance a little sidelong and knowing.

Miffy said, "It is a good room to hide bottles in. Plenty of hiding places. We could never find them all."

Miffy didn't even look at me. She went to another window and drew open more pale blue draperies with a swish that sounded loud. She opened the blinds. Her slim figure was silhouetted against the gray light. There was a balcony outside. I could see heaped-up snow and a balustrade, heaped and rounded with snow, too. Probably in the summer there were flowers.

So that was the reason for the quarrels, for the disagreements, for the suggestion of divorce which had come to nothing. Poor Richard. Poor young Cecile.

Miffy said over her shoulder, "She'd been at it that night. She'd dressed and we all thought that she might be in a condition to go to the ball. But then Richard found her

— she could hardly stagger. There wasn't anything to be done. So Slade and I went to the ball."

Miffy rubbed her slender wrists. "It's cold in here. I suppose the heat's turned off. We never use this room now, of course. I keep it locked; the maids might be curious."

Richard, I thought, must have gone through hell. And Cecile, that young, lovely Cecile with her slanting smile. I said, "Couldn't anyone stop it? Or anything —"

"Oh, Richard tried. One doctor after another. Twice he induced her to enter a sanatorium but she always managed to slip away. He tried everything."

"Cecile must have tried —"

"Cecile! It was all Cecile's fault. She wouldn't try to stop. It was all her doing."

"But — but perhaps, she couldn't. I mean, she needed help —"

"Needed nothing! She was just a wicked, wicked girl. Ruining her own life, trying to ruin Richard's life."

"It's tragic —"

Miffy said, "Oh, I don't know. She brought it on herself."

"You don't mean the — *the murder!*"

Miffy said positively, "Of course, it was a burglar but Cecile certainly was drunk when he killed her. Who knows what really happened? What provocation she gave him? It was dreadful for Richard but he wasn't in love with her. He couldn't have been. Really I think it was a kind of marriage of convenience, in a way. I mean, it just sort of happened because it seemed so suitable. I never thought it was a real love affair. It was one of those things — propinquity, something like that. Aided by her parents." She shifted away from the subject. "Stella wants us to sell the house. Richard and I own the house together."

Stella had told me that. I didn't like the big cold room with its pale blue draperies and pale blue carpet. I turned to the door and Miffy said, "But I don't want to sell it. Neither does Richard. It is our home."

The implication was there again; this time there was a clear suggestion that it would be their home after their marriage. It was very still in the room and in the house; from there we could not even hear the sounds of the snowplows and the delivery trucks and taxis and cars.

I said, "I think I hear the telephone," and went out.

"No," Miffy said, "you can't hear anything from here! Don't hurry. Where are you going?"

I saw the stairs, winding down. I wondered if a murderer had run down those stairs, or if he had slid stealthily into the elevator which still stood, its door open, its little buttons glimmering.

"I'm sure it's the phone," I said and hurried down the stairs, my hands sliding along the banister. I didn't hear a telephone at all.

The library seemed warm and protective. Presently I heard the small rumble of the elevator. Miffy came through the hall and into the library. "You didn't hear a phone," she said gently. "You ran. You didn't like that room. There's nothing there now."

There was a certain amount of evidence, Richard had said. I didn't want to talk to Miffy about it; I had already heard too much. Yet I had to ask her. "Did the police know that — that Cecile drank?" I said.

"Oh, of course. How could they help knowing? There was the autopsy, you know. I've forgotten what percent alcohol but —"

"Never mind," I said, my voice sounding harsh.

She went on, "And besides there were bottles in the room. Half empty some of them, some of them full; they were hidden in the queerest places. A man from the police department seemed to know exactly where he'd find them and he did. There was one wedged in at the top of the windows, behind the cornice for the draperies. No, there were two there, I remember. Full ones, unopened. There was one —"

"I don't want to know —"

"And of course we had to tell the truth. She did drink. Every one of us knew it. Only Stella insisted that she didn't and that she and Richard never quarreled. But somehow the drinking part was kept out of the papers."

I didn't think Richard would have quarreled with Cecile. I said, "Richard must have felt very sorry for Cecile."

"Yes, he did! I just couldn't understand it. She would scream at him and — of course the servants heard it and the police knew. Besides, once Cecile went to a lawyer and talked about a divorce and money settlement but she changed her mind . . . Stella," Miffy said thoughtfully, "is a very stubborn girl. Stella interferes."

Something about it sent a kind of tingle over me; I wanted to say, what does Stella interfere about? And then the telephone rang.

Miffy made a swift move but I was nearer the hall and I reached the telephone first. It was Richard. I was conscious of Miffy standing very close to me. Richard said,

"Andre's not at home. I phoned, no answer. I went to the two banks Hatever had mentioned in his letter. Hatever was right. They couldn't dig up a thing anybody had overlooked."

"No safe deposit box?"

"No. I'd rather hoped for that. All this and traffic conditions took time. I phoned to Andre again; still no answer. Tried your house and no answer. So I went to Andre's apartment. He didn't answer the bell so I got hold of the superintendent. I told him Andre might be ill, something might have happened. So he finally told me he'd look inside his apartment and he did. I stood in the hall. Andre wasn't there. Has he called you?"

"No."

"We'd better go to the Gramercy Park house. Can you meet me there and bring the key?"

"Yes. Right away."

"You can get a taxi if you're lucky. Try Madison or Fifth."

"Yes, I will."

"I'll be waiting for you."

I put down the telephone and Miffy said, "Are you going to your house?"

"Yes."

"I thought Richard said it wasn't open.

That's why he brought you here."

"There's nobody there. It's been closed."

I ran to my room for my handbag. Miffy followed me. "You must be in a hurry. Why are you in such a hurry?"

"Richard is going to meet me."

"Well, don't run. Here —" The elevator cage was now at that floor, its door open. Miffy went into it and smiled at me. "I'll take you down."

"All right —"

But as I stepped into the cage I remembered Richard saying, sometimes the elevator gets stuck. I didn't want to get stuck in the elevator just then. I drew back so quickly that Miffy whirled around from the little panel of buttons and stared at me.

"It's all right — thanks — I'll run downstairs —"

I didn't wait for her to speak; I ran down the stairs and got my coat and beret out of the closet. Luckily Mrs. Amberly or somebody had a supply of overshoes. I snatched up a pair that didn't fit; they were too small, Miffy's probably. I burrowed about until I found another pair and by the time I had pulled them on, there was the quiet rumble of the elevator again. Its door opened and Miffy just stood there framed by the door, in the dim light, her slim hand on the panel of buttons. She looked like a portrait standing there.

I said, "Tell Mrs. Amberly where I've gone, will you?"

"She's lunching out," Miffy said. "We had such a late breakfast and talked so long, I really didn't think about your lunch. I'm so sorry."

I said, of course, and that was all right or something like that, and the shadows in the elevator made it look as if Miffy were smiling a little. I opened the big front door and went out into a snow-covered, cold, but once again an active world.

I waited a while on Madison, near the drugstore from which I'd telephoned to Andre. Already there was slush on the street crossings and the snow there was gray and grimy. I waded through a heaped-up drift of snow when a taxi came along and stopped for me. It took a long time though to plow through traffic, for the streets were narrowed by the heaped-up snow.

When we turned into little Pennyroyal Street, Richard was at the door of number ninety and came to help me over the heap of snow at the curb.

The steps had not been cleaned since the previous day. The shovel was still standing decorously turned in. I unlocked the door.

Richard thrust it open and then turned to me with a fleeting kind of grin. "Mr. Benni here?"

I went into the hall. The air was musty and stale but there was no trace of perfume. "No — not now. Andre," I called. "Andre — *Andre* —"

There was no reply. There was no sound at all. Richard was apparently transfixed again by the blank gaze of the Venus in the corner; he stared for a second and shied his hat at her white curls. It fell into position a little on one side and gave her a hideously raffish look. "Ouch," Richard said, snatched his hat off the marble curls, and put it down on his coat, on a bench. I started for the library and Richard followed me.

"Things are just the same as I left them," I said, and wished I had hidden the newspaper clippings. Richard glanced at the clutter on the desk.

I was sure he saw the clippings but his face didn't show it. He said, "What's all this?"

"Things that were in a briefcase." I took off my coat while I explained it. "I found them like that yesterday, dumped out on the desk."

Richard stood for a long moment looking down, almost as if counting. "Funny things to be carrying around."

"Well, yes. Nothing important; I suppose they just happened to — to collect —"

He lifted a used blotter, held it under the lamp and said, "Have you got a mirror in your handbag?"

I got out my powder compact. He opened it and held the blotter in front of the tiny mirror. He said, "I can make out Del — Del — something — it may be Clabbering — I think it is. I need a larger mirror."

"Delia Clabbering! That's the woman —"

"Yes, of course." He raked over the odds and ends of bills, paper clips, old cigarettes. "Is anything missing?"

"Why, I — no. No, I don't think so."

"Look again. Mr. Benni was here. I want to know what he took."

I looked. "There's nothing gone really — that is — yes. I think there was a button. Just a brown button, nothing important, I don't see that."

We both hunted over the desk though as if it might be important. Richard said, puzzled, "What kind of button?"

"It was a button from a man's coat, I think. Brown. Some threads hanging to it. Nothing but a button."

"It may have rolled off somewhere."

Because it was gone it began to seem important. We both got down on our knees.

Richard pulled the lamp around to give us more light. We searched the figured Oriental rug, we groped beneath the desk, we looked all around it; we pushed the leather desk chair back. There was no button.

"Buttons," Richard said, "don't walk away." He rose and stood by the desk. "Your father was very definite about a diary. But suppose Mr. Benni took that button. Suppose that was what he wanted. It doesn't seem likely, yet suppose the button was in fact some sort of — oh, evidence. Suppose this blotter is evidence."

An ordinary brown button. A handsome address book that meant nothing. A blotter. "That's where I found your Uncle Sisley's letters. They were in the briefcase."

Richard picked up the blotter again and held it close to the tiny mirror.

"Look here."

I went to him and bent to see close under the lamp. "Why, there are words. Or parts of words."

"Yes. It looks like 'believed divorce' and something I can't make out. Oh, 'marri—' no, 'remarri', that's clear, and 'bag you' — no, 'beg you' — some more I can't make out, but there's a signature. I believe it *is* Clabbering." He looked at the blotter and I looked at it. Finally he said, "I think it could be read, 'believed our divorce was legal,' something like that. There's a blur. Then something to the effect that she had remarried and she begs somebody to — oh, perhaps forget the whole thing. Forget he was in fact still married to her, do you think?"

"My father advised her to write this letter?"

"Yes, I think so. He may have advised her to throw herself on the mercy of the husband she believed she was divorced from, tell him she had remarried and beg him to let it go at that. Now, you see, since her second husband — at least the man she thought she married, and obviously it became a marriage which nobody ever questioned — now that he's dead, she doesn't propose to be blackmailed. She can't be blackmailed. It fits in with her letter to you."

"Then that — that blotter was —"

"Evidence. Your father saved it."

"He did that," I whispered. "You're a lawyer, too. You understand, you realize the codes of ethics he —"

"He was dying!" Richard said. "Stop thinking about it. Now listen, you're sure that only that button has disappeared?"

"Yes. Yes, I think so."

"Well, then I don't think Mr. Benni is

going to bother you again."

"But he was here?"

"Of course he was here and found the button, and that button was worth five thousand dollars and a trip to New York, to him. Worth perhaps much more. At least that's what I think. And I think Mr. Benni is gone and I doubt if he'll return. The urgent thing right now is Andre. A man can't just drop out of sight. I think I'll take a look around the house."

"But if he's here, he'd have heard us —" I began and then as Richard went out into the hall and glanced up and down it and then up the stairs, I followed him; again I felt that curious, icy little draft on my face. I was bolder in Richard's presence than I had been alone, the night before. "There's a window open," I said. "I'd better close it."

Richard came after me up the stairs. The icy little draft became colder, I stopped in the upper hall, for I saw Andre's overcoat.

11

It was Andre's long black overcoat; he'd worn it for years. It was Andre's plaid muffler, green and blue, which he'd worn for years. It was Andre's black felt hat, curled and worn and shabby. All of them lay in a heap on the bench.

Richard understood; he began to search but I found Andre. He was in my father's room. A window was open for about ten inches, icy air blowing through the room. I saw the long figure on the bed, covered entirely with a queerly splotched sheet.

I don't know what I said — perhaps I screamed — and Richard pushed me aside. I couldn't see past his bent figure; I could only see the ridged bunch which distorted feet made under the sheet.

Richard took me into the hall; he shut the door carefully behind him. I didn't even say, is it Andre. He took me with him back down to the library and the telephone. I don't remember moving. I did hear him speak into the telephone. He gave his name and gave the address and repeated it, Ninety Pennyroyal Street. He said he had found a murdered man; his name was Andre Bersche. He spelled it. There were some questions and a wait and then apparently someone else came on the telephone and Richard repeated his name, my father's address and the fact of murder. He then said that if they could find a Lieutenant Garrity he'd like to talk to him. I believe there was a little more talk. Then Richard put down the telephone. He looked at me. "I'm so sorry —"

"I hope it was quick."

"It was. It must have been. There's a bruise on his temple."

"How —"

"I think first a bruise that knocked him out. Then a revolver shot."

There was only one thing that I clearly remember in that strangely short interval before the police arrived. That was when Richard said, after a long silence, "If that fifth letter did go to Cecile's murderer, then it must have been Cecile's murderer who killed Andre."

I was thinking of Andre; I was thinking of his worn and familiar overcoat and hat, seeing him in them as I had seen him so many times. "Why?"

"Because of the diary. Andre must have found the diary. That, or whoever murdered him believed he had found the diary. And he — the murderer — is in terror." He stood at the desk; it chanced that his hand on the desk touched the clippings about Cecile's murder. He said then, "But there's no proof."

"If Andre had the diary —"

"Oh yes. If Andre found it and had it with him, the murderer took it. Andre's pockets are empty — not even a billfold there."

"When —" I whispered presently.

"Yesterday afternoon, I should say. Before you came. Andre must have arrived —"

I said huskily, "Somebody had swept the steps. It must have been Andre."

"Yes — well then, he must have gone upstairs for some reason. Searching perhaps —"

"He was — it's my father's room."

"Searching then, almost certainly. He was killed. Then, you came. The murderer heard you. You thought he came down from the attic. Probably he hid there. Waited — listened —"

I remembered it too well, the silent house, the sense of a live quality in that silence as if it listened to me.

"Then he must have believed that you were gone and finally started down the stairs." He looked at me. "Another minute —" he said and stopped.

"It didn't happen," I said but I was afraid again, afraid as I had been the day before. More than anything, I was thinking that I had been the cause of Andre's death. Perhaps he hadn't been fond of me but I had known only kindness from him.

Only then another and urgent danger shot into my mind. I jumped up out of my chair. "Richard! You *can't* tell them about that alibi! Not now. They'll say you did it. You knew about the diary. They'll say you knew Andre had it. They'll say you killed him —"

"I think they're here," Richard said, listening, and went to the door.

I heard them, the doorbell ringing and stopping as Richard opened the door, the businesslike voices, the brisk footsteps on the stairs, every sound and movement that follows violent death.

They did not take us to the station for some time, not until more cars and more men had arrived; not until I had waited for a long, long time there in the library. There seemed to be a great deal for them to do before they asked me for a statement. I thought that Richard had made some sort of statement but I didn't then know. There was, however, no further opportunity to talk to him alone and persuade him against telling them, then and there, of that false and now doubly dangerous alibi.

In fact, the first time I had any chance at all to talk to Richard it became instantly too late. He came into the library and a man came with him, a youngish man with a nearly bald head and very old and cold green eyes. Richard introduced him. His name was Lieutenant Garrity. He wore a neat brown suit and highly polished brown oxfords and his tie was as green as his eyes. He seemed to know my name. Richard said to me in a perfectly flat voice, "Lieutenant Garrity worked on the case when Cecile was murdered. I thought we'd better talk to him." And then he came out with it, facing Lieutenant Garrity, whose green eyes were very narrow. "That alibi of mine was false. I had no alibi at all."

I couldn't have stopped him.

There was a queer kind of flash in Lieutenant Garrity's green eyes. Then he laughed a little but it wasn't like a laugh. "I see. Old Hilliard — I mean your father, Miss Hilliard — invented it."

Richard nodded.

"I see," Garrity said again. "Yes. I wondered — still we couldn't prove it. Well — what's the connection between that murdered man upstairs and your fake alibi —"

Richard turned to me. "Can you tell it, Fran?"

It was of course my father's act, my account to give. But I said sharply, "There's no use in not telling it now!" I heard my own voice cracking upward with tension.

Garrity put down a natty cashmere overcoat he was carrying over one arm. "I'd like to hear, Miss Hilliard."

So I told him; I began with the letters I had mailed for my father; I didn't stop until I told him how we found Andre. I heard my voice going on and on like a record that's been set in motion, and I really cannot remember that I had any particular feeling. It simply seemed to me that Richard had given up; they would charge him with both murders. Garrity listened to the whole recital; he only moved once and that was when Richard made me sit down and Garrity put one foot on a straight chair and leaned his chin on his hand.

But he looked at the objects on the desk. He took the small address book with its handsome gold corners and looked through it and asked if any of the names or addresses meant anything to me. He got down on his hands and knees and looked for the missing button as Richard and I had done. He seemed very much interested in the button; he questioned me about it at some length, yet he seemed a little puzzled, too. Abruptly though he dismissed the button and questioned Richard about his interview with Andre the previous morning. Richard told everything he had told me of it. He questioned both of us about our efforts to talk to Andre over the telephone and the times when we had telephoned. He questioned Richard about his visit to Andre's apartment house that morning. He went to the door and snapped out a low order to somebody outside; I heard part of it, enough to know that he was sending police at once to Andre's apartment.

Before they took us to the precinct station they asked me to identify Andre and I did; someone had closed his eyes. I saw them, then, carry him away. His black hat and shabby overcoat still lay over the bench and a policeman in uniform gathered them up carefully and took them away. Another policeman, a thin young fellow in his blue uniform, was apparently taking up a sentinel's post at the door to the library when we left.

They took us to the precinct station in a police car; the heater had been turned on and it was suffocatingly hot. The little room at the precinct station was hot, too, and there was a hissing radiator near me. They took our fingerprints and our formal statements.

And then they really questioned us. Garrity did most of the questioning, although another man, also in plain clothes, elderly and very tired-looking, seemed to exert some sort of tacit and strong authority.

Sometime long after dark Richard asked permission to use the telephone; someone said he had every right to get a lawyer if he wanted one; I had the impression that we had both been told that; Richard said, no, not at that time. He didn't use the telephone himself, however; a young man with a stenographer's tablet did it for him and told Mrs. Amberly, when she answered, merely that Mr. Amberly and Miss Hilliard would be delayed in getting home.

It was late, too, when somebody brought in hamburgers and cartons of coffee and cream and sugar and paper cups. Richard and Lieutenant Garrity entered into a friendly-appearing contest over paying for them; Richard let Garrity pay and to my amazement there was a kind of twinkle in Richard's gray eyes when Garrity grinned frankly and said, "You win," satirically and gave some money to the young policeman who had brought in the food. We ate. It was like a grotesque picnic. The lights on the desk and in the ceiling glared down.

I don't remember the exact sequence of the questions, I do remember that there was nothing I was not asked to repeat, to elaborate upon, to describe, it seemed to me, a dozen times. Gradually though, the questions to me seemed to narrow themselves down to a few salient repetitions. Was I sure that someone had been on the stairs, in the house, the previous afternoon? Was I sure I did not know who it was? What had the footsteps sounded like — a man's or a woman's? I didn't know.

How long had I known Richard? I didn't know exactly that answer either. I only knew that I had known him slightly in a rather remote way since I was a child. How long then since I had seen him — that is, before he had come to Nice to see me on Christmas Day?

Christmas Day and Nice and the bougainvillaea and the blue sea seemed to me then in another world, another way of life, nothing to do with a room in a precinct station and a hissing radiator and the light shining down upon my face and the faces of men who were questioning me and had every right to question. I told them I couldn't remember, not for some years. They asked me again in a few moments and got the same reply.

They questioned me most about the diary and I could tell them only what I knew. I did gather that they had found no diary in Andre's overcoat; Richard had found nothing at all in his pockets. They questioned me over and over again about the letters and again I could tell them only what I knew. I was growing very tired and the room very hot; I felt a little dizzy and someone gave me more coffee.

At some time they — or Richard and I — discovered that Mr. Benni might have taken my own key to my father's house and that he could have done so if in fact — as had been my impression, or rather the impression his perfume had left in my room in Nice — he had crept in at night. Richard, I think, brought it up and asked me if I had had two keys to the house. When I said I had had my own key and my father's key, too, Garrity asked me to look in my handbag. I did and my key was gone. So perhaps I had overestimated Mr. Benni's ability to enter houses or rooms at his will. But Andre, I told them when they asked, had had a key. That key was gone, too, along with the contents of Andre's pockets.

There was some talk then about why Andre had been murdered in my father's room upstairs and I said that he might have been searching for the diary. They questioned me in detail about my conversation with Andre over the telephone; they asked exactly what I had said and what he had said, and the location of the drugstore.

It seemed to me that they all assumed that Andre had been murdered on the afternoon of my appointment with him and it seemed likely to me. Yet nobody said so, in so many words. There was still an autopsy report to be secured and to mull over; there would be a great mass of details, proved facts to discover and to investigate.

They asked me for Delia Clabbering's address and I didn't know it; if Andre had had her letter to me in his pocket, that was gone, too. But their questions about the letters seemed to indicate that, at least for the present, they believed what Richard and I had told them. I hadn't wanted to tell them about Uncle Sisley's romantic carrying-on; it had to come out and did.

They questioned me over and over, putting their questions in very expert and different ways, about the fifth letter, and of course there was nothing I could tell them except that there was a fifth letter. Whether or not they accepted or even entertained the surmise that it had gone to Cecile's murderer, I couldn't tell.

They went back, too, from time to time to the diary. Nobody seemed to comment upon my father's astounding attempt at blackmail; I felt that nothing really in the way of the changes and shifts and variations of human conduct could surprise them. Once though, during a slight pause, Garrity said in an oddly reflective voice, "I knew Orle Hilliard." It sounded as if that explained a great deal; I looked at him but he seemed to be examining the polish of his brown oxfords with narrowed green eyes. It seemed to me, however, that there was a kind of mute agreement in the room, hovering in the air; certainly, in a way, my father had been well known and that was in criminal law. Richard stirred and said suddenly, breaking into that silence, "Remember he didn't do this for himself. He had all this — material. He needed money. He didn't blackmail anybody for himself. It was only when he was dying and leaving his daughter without any money at all —"

Garrity cleared his throat and said, "Yes, of course."

That had not occurred to me before; it didn't exonerate my father perhaps but it seemed important to me.

The snow drove against the window, more insistently than the hissing of the radiator. Garrity asked if I had ever known Cecile Amberly. He had asked that before; I replied again; no, I hadn't known her. The repetition of the question was the only indication I had that they might be trying to establish a link between Andre's murder and Cecile's.

They finally took me into another room, a small room with a table and some straight chairs and a calendar hanging on the wall beside a window. A young policeman sat in a corner of the room while they questioned Richard.

The door to the corridor was open. I could hear a sound of telephones and the mumble of voices in the distance as the station went about its business. Sometimes a draft swept along the floor as if some door had opened upon the winter night and slowly closed again. Occasionally a policeman thudded leisurely along the corridor. Someone had carved a heart on the leg of the table near me; I studied it for a long time before I made out the irregular hacked design of a heart. I wondered who had done it and why.

Time went on and I began to think that

perhaps they were not going to arrest Richard then and there and charge him with murder; surely if they had intended to do that, it would have been done at once, not after a wait of what seemed to me many hours.

But time went on, just the same. Once the young policeman asked me if I wanted a drink of water. I said no thank you. He went to a fountain which was in the corridor, barely out of sight; I could hear the gurgle of water.

There was at last the opening of a door, voices near at hand, the tramp of footsteps, and Richard and Garrity came along the corridor. They came into the room and if I hadn't known the truth I'd have said there was a friendliness between them. Garrity said that he was sending us home in a police car. So at least Richard had not been arrested that night.

Lieutenant Garrity had a few words to say about newspapers. "I'm going to give you both some advice," he said, rubbing his bald head again. "You don't have to follow it. It's a free country. But it's a request as well as advice. Keep this business of the diary and those letters to yourselves. Don't even talk to your family or your friends about it."

Richard seemed to understand more than

Garrity said; I didn't; Garrity sensed this and spoke directly to me. "You see, Miss Hilliard, newspaper reporters are very acute and they have long memories. They're going to jump to some sort of connection between your father and the murder of Andre Bersche and the alibi your father gave Amberly. Now, it won't do much good for any of us to deny that that alibi was false. We can try to keep that quiet for a while but there's no point in it. Sooner or later everybody's going to know that the investigation into Cecile Amberly's murder has reopened — that is, it was never closed but that we're now looking at some different — call it views. This false alibi — well, the only thing I want to say is, you can't avoid somebody's making some very close guesses about that fake alibi, so we may as well admit it was false, openly. But that diary and the letters — that gives us something to work on, I hope. Anyway I want you to keep quiet about both the diary and the letters."

I nodded. I only wanted to leave.

Garrity turned to Richard. "I wish you had kept the letter from Orle Hilliard."

Richard shrugged. "I told you, I tore it up, threw it away. Before I left Nice."

Lieutenant Garrity said nothing. I, too, wished Richard had kept the letter. It would have proved at least one point. But Garrity was polite and easy when he told us that we could go.

I was not prepared for what happened the instant we emerged, following the broad, blue-overcoated back of a policeman from the door of the precinct station, and that was a succession of blinding flares of light and voices and faces coming out of the dizzying lights.

Richard grasped my arm. The policemen made a kind of lane for us down to the police car. But the photographers and reporters followed just the same, the flash bulbs popping and questions hurtling from everywhere. The policeman swung open the door and Richard pushed me into the police car. He then stopped for a second and looked out at the faces of the reporters surrounding him. More flash bulbs glared. He said something about being sorry, no statement, nothing to say, sorry —

He swung into the car beside me and shut the door and the policeman who was driving shot away from the curb.

"It's their job," he said. "It doesn't take long for them to get any news. You okay?"

"I was afraid they'd arrest you."

"No," he said slowly. "They need some firm evidence. They questioned me a long time about my visit to Andre's apartment yesterday morning. But we did meet at his apartment, not at your place. They would have to show some kind of proof that in fact I had gone with him, or met him at the house where he was murdered — at least that's what I think. And of course they aren't sure until after the autopsy just when he was killed. They think that whoever killed him opened that window and let in freezing air in order to confuse the time of death — I mean the condition of the body, all that — and give the murderer a chance to establish an alibi of some kind."

"I understand." Andre, whom I had known all my life and who had been my one source of authority. I suddenly remembered his speaking once of my mother; he'd said she was a dear and good lady and she'd have wanted to be proud of me.

Richard said, "Try not to think about him."

A disembodied voice came from nowhere, speaking to the policemen riding in the front seat. It was, of course, from a radio. Both men listened intently. After they had delivered us they were to go to some address in the east eighties; somebody reported an attempted entry. New York was never quiet, never asleep.

They let us out in front of the Amberly house and said good night in a polite and oddly friendly way.

Richard glanced up at the windows above the door where lights showed dimly behind the drawn curtains. "They're still up," he said. "They've heard the news. Well, here we go. I think Garrity is right about keeping quiet the diary and the letters. He put it as advice and a request but it's an order." He unlocked the door.

He took my coat. I pulled off my beret and felt as if it had been years since I had put it on, there before that mirror. I jerked at my overshoes and Richard bent to help me. I started up the stairs and somebody above cried, "Here they are —"

Slade came to the top of the stairs and Mrs. Amberly and Uncle Sisley crowded after him. They stood like a receiving line but not exactly a welcoming line as I came up into the hall. Stella was there, too, and Miffy, of course, and Wilbur. Stella cried, "We heard! We heard! Reporters have already been here."

Her eyes were bright and troubled. I looked at Mrs. Amberly and there was the same troubled look. Richard was still in the hall below; I wished he would hurry. Then Wilbur came thrusting his way around

Miffy, his elbows squared, his chin squared, his little eyes furious. "You little fool, you! I thought we could trust you! We took you in like a friend. You little cheat and liar —"

He stopped there, for Uncle Sisley hit him on the chin. He crashed down to the floor with the effect of a huge tree going down. He knocked over a little table and sent small objects, ashtrays, a lamp and a little china shepherdess, crashing down, too.

Richard sprang up the steps. Uncle Sisley stared at Wilbur, smiled, and lifted his own chin in a jaunty, didn't-know-I-could-do-it, kind of way.

Miffy said, "You'd better get up, Wilbur."

12

Wilbur scrambled up, rubbing his chin and looking at Uncle Sisley in a dazed way. "I didn't see you coming! You couldn't have done that if I'd seen you coming! I didn't see you coming!" I imagined that that was the first time Wilbur had ever had such a thing happen to him and I hoped it would do him good.

Uncle Sisley straightened his coat airily. Wilbur advanced upon him. "I'm going to twist your silly head right off your neck —"

"Try it," Uncle Sisley cried, carried away. "Try it!" He danced back, squared off with his fists and pranced like an elderly little rooster. "Fran's a nice girl. You can't talk to her like that. I won't let you!"

I was briefly thankful that Uncle Sisley, since the return of his letters, now considered me a friend rather than a dangerous enemy. Wilbur lowered his head, doubled up his fists and started for Uncle Sisley just as Richard brushed past me and stepped between them. "All right," he said. "All right, let it go. Mother, will you take Fran upstairs. See to her —"

Stella, her childish freckles standing out in her white face, seized Richard by his coat lapels. "Your alibi when Cecile was murdered — do they really know it wasn't true?"

Richard said, "What have you heard? Who told you?"

Everybody talked at once. The newspapers had begun to telephone and inquire about me, about Richard, about our return from Nice, about my father's death. Then one reporter had arrived at the house. He had pushed past Uncle Sisley, who had opened the door.

"I tripped him," Uncle Sisley said, "on the stairs. But he kept right on going."

Mrs. Amberly took over. "He had remembered about the alibi, Richard. He seemed to be a very bright young man," she said sadly. "He asked if I was sure that the alibi Mr. Hilliard had given you was correct. I said certainly —"

Richard put his arm around her. "Sorry, Mother," he said. "Well — but — but the police accepted it and —"

"The police know now that it was a false alibi —"

Wilbur interrupted; he shouted; he turned alarmingly scarlet. "I knew it! I told you so! That girl Frances Hilliard knew all about it! She told the police! I knew it!"

"I told them myself," Richard said sharply.

Wilbur gave a kind of incredulous bellow, and Richard turned to his mother. "What happened to the reporter?"

"Oh, he left. After telling us about" — she turned to me — "about — *that.* He said the man — Andre Bersche, the murdered man — had been your father's secretary and he'd been found — you and Richard had found him, in your house. And — oh, Richard —"

"It's going to start everything over again, isn't it, Richard?" Miffy said gently. "All that about Cecile and everything. Isn't it?"

"Yes," Richard said.

And of course he was right, but it didn't start until the early morning editions of the newspapers. Just then, aside from another outraged bellow on Wilbur's part, Richard's announcement seemed to take the starch out of everybody. Uncle Sisley's fighting spirit flickered out and he sat down on a footstool and just stared rather vacantly at Richard. Stella blinked as if she wanted to cry but wouldn't let herself and told Wilbur they'd better go home. Wilbur rallied sufficiently to snarl at Slade, who happened to stand in his way, and tell him that he'd better get on the job and keep regular hours or he'd be fired in spite of being a relative.

Wilbur then gave me a look which could have killed, caught Stella's arm and jerked her down the stairs. In a moment, again, the French door in the dining room slammed; the glass didn't shatter this time, either, but it must have been a near thing. Mrs. Amberly said firmly, though looking drained and white and older, that we had talked enough, it was very late. She said it must have been dreadful for me and sent me to bed and I was only too thankful to go.

I was in bed when she came with a glass of hot milk. "Here. I've put a little brandy in this. Try to sleep."

She said good night and no more, and left. The house seemed very quiet. The hot milk was liberally laced with brandy; there must have been really a walloping slug of it, for I knew I couldn't sleep, yet I barely touched the pillow when I did sleep. I awoke late, to another gray and overcast day. The sky seemed to press down upon the whole city. Yet it did not snow.

I found Richard and Miffy in the dining room. Richard was reading the newspapers.

"Is it bad?" I asked.

"Not as bad as it might be. Nothing yet about the alibi."

He got coffee for me and I looked at the papers. There were headlines, of course.

There were the salient facts. Murder. Andre Bersche, for many years confidential secretary to Orle Hilliard. Orle Hilliard, the well-known criminal lawyer, died recently in France. Body found by his daughter, Frances Hilliard, and her friend, Richard Amberly. Miss Hilliard a guest at the Amberly residence.

There was as yet no outright statement from the police about the false alibi. Perhaps there hadn't been time. But I could see then that Garrity was right; it could not have been kept a secret for long. Someone would have nosed it out and already they were on the scent.

There was a picture showing a girl huddled in a polo coat, her beret on the back of her head, her eyes wide and startled in the glare of the flash bulbs. She seemed to be somebody quite apart from me. Richard's face was more familiar to me but it, too, was sharply black and white and strange. There was a picture of the Amberly house. Obviously it had been dug out of the files and been taken at the time of Cecile's murder; spring foliage showed on the shrubbery at the door, and a dotted line led to the fourth floor where Cecile had been murdered.

Merely the printing of the picture suggested a link between Andre's murder and

Cecile's. The reporter who had called at the house the previous night was not the only reporter to have a swift and accurate gift for putting facts together which might be related.

The murder of Cecile Amberly was brought back into focus in much of its detail. "The Amberly house was the scene of a shocking murder" — "A year and a half ago the young wife of Richard Amberly, Cecile, was found —"

Orle Hilliard had come forward and said that he had seen Richard Amberly at Ninety-second Street and Fifth Avenue at the time when, according to medical evidence, Cecile had been murdered.

There was nothing stated outright. Still any reader would begin to think, there's something fishy here. And indeed there was something fishy. I wondered how soon the fishiness of the alibi would come out in the headlines.

Miffy said, "It's not a very flattering picture of you, is it?" It wasn't. Richard, returning with coffee, heard the remark and said rather sharply that I hadn't been posing for a beauty contest. But then he seemed to repent the sharpness of his tone and patted Miffy on the head in a conciliatory way.

"Probably Garrity gave this to the

papers," Richard said. "Sounds like him. Merely facts. They say that you had made the appointment with Andre in order to talk to him about selling your house."

Miffy's blue eyes widened. "You sound as if that wasn't the real reason she went to meet him. What was it then?"

It would be very easy for either Richard or me to make a slip about the diary and the letters. Richard retrieved himself that time. "But it was the reason," he said mildly. "That's why I went with her."

This instantly diverted Miffy who said, "What do you mean?" By the time Richard had talked about real estate agents and markets and the state of the stock market, as if that had something to do with selling the house, I thought that Miffy had forgotten her original question. I couldn't be sure though; not with Miffy.

There were two callers that morning. Lieutenant Garrity arrived first and took me to the drugstore where I had used the telephone booth and talked to Andre. Richard came with us, in a police car.

The drugstore clerk proved to be the pharmacist; he had been the only one on duty the night the storm was at its worst; he remembered me.

"Sure. She came in — went to the telephone. Was there a long time."

"And you recognize her?" Garrity asked.

"Sure. She wasn't wearing any kind of overshoes. I thought she'd catch her death of cold. Sure, she had on that same beret and coat. I remember her."

"Do you remember anybody else who was in the store at the same time?" Did he, Garrity meant, remember anybody who came in and entered the booth beside the one I was using and overheard my end of the talk with Andre? He didn't.

There was a man who got some cough medicine, not a regular customer, he didn't know his name. Somebody might have come in and gone into the first telephone booth but if that had happened he didn't remember it. "I was preparing some prescriptions. Counter there is high. Might have had my back turned." His eyes were very curious. Garrity asked him to report it if the man who bought the cough medicine happened to come in again, and thanked him.

"It's not very likely that the cough-medicine guy will come in again and even if he does he may not have seen anybody in the next booth," Garrity said on the way back.

"So that line is blocked," Richard said.

"A description of somebody in that booth

at the same time as Miss Hilliard was in the other one would have" — Garrity adjusted his green tie and said — "helped —" He didn't add if somebody really was in that first booth but might as well have said it.

Once in the house we went back again to the little room off the dining room. Richard plugged in the electric heater; Garrity took off his overcoat and said that so far the diary had not turned up but they had not yet been able to make a really thorough search of the Pennyroyal Street house. "Most of the stuff in your father's briefcase just doesn't seem to mean a thing, Miss Hilliard. The paper clips — far as I can see, they're just paper clips. Same with the cigarette packages. Nothing in them but a few dried-up cigarettes. That's really all." He shot me a disconcertingly knowing look. "Laboratory's been at them. Nothing there at all. But the blotter was used by Mrs. Clabbering all right. She remembered using it after she'd written a letter in your father's office, at his dictation. I talked to her this morning, early."

"You —" I swallowed. "How did you get her address?"

"Talked to a guy I know at Scotland Yard. Didn't take him long to find her. She was perfectly willing to talk — didn't enjoy it, I suppose, but talked. She'd been married once, thought her husband had divorced her. Remarried. Husband number one turned up. She went to your father. He advised her to ask husband number one just to keep quiet about the whole thing. So she did, and he did, and husband number two never knew a thing about it." He glanced at Richard as if forestalling a question. "Husband number one has nothing to do with any of this. Can't have. He died, too, only a year or so ago, but Mrs. Clabbering didn't know that. We checked after we talked to her. So he's out of the picture. So is she. That leaves the button."

Richard said, "And Mr. Benni?"

"Oh yes. Only his name is Benntovici. But that button was worth five thousand dollars to him all right. Worth his life — and he's got away with it."

"What did he do?" Richard said.

"Well, I knew when I heard about that button that somewhere, sometime, there'd been a case that had something to do with a button torn off a man's coat. It rang a bell. But I couldn't, last night, recall the exact case. So I checked it out and sure enough this Mr. Benni of yours, Miss Hilliard, was a racketeer, a gangster, had his dirty finger in a lot of dirty pies, but nobody could ever get him for anything. You could hardly think of any racket that you didn't suspect Benntovici — Benni — had something to do with. We've got some shots of him — looks young, very dapper, always used perfume — oh, it's your Mr. Benni all right. He wasn't one of the big fellows, one of the bosses; he was their henchman though and did whatever he was told to do, as far as we could make out. Well, anyway this button —" He sighed and rubbed his bald head again.

"It was like this. Simple. A man was murdered, he was hooked up with the numbers racket. He had a man's coat button clenched up in his fist when we found him — rolled over in a ditch, out of some car out on Long Island, a deserted stretch of road. Benni was suspected, nothing proved. The button disappeared."

"Disappeared!" Richard said.

Lieutenant Garrity looked a little grim. "Well, yes. Nobody knew what happened to it — or would admit what happened to it. But the fact is —" He squared himself around to face me directly. I thought that perhaps he didn't want to say what he was going to have to say. "The fact is, Miss Hilliard, your father's secretary, Andre Bersche, had been around the station house. One oldtimer remembers that. He was friendly with some of our men — maybe too friendly, I don't know. They missed the button that day. Nobody knows or ever admitted how or where or what happened. Doesn't look as if anybody would let a piece of evidence simply walk out like that." He frowned. "I realize that this sounds like bribery of one of our men. I really don't think that any of the men then in charge of the case were bribable. I've had their records looked up. The only thing I know for a fact is that Bersche was there the day the button disappeared. Actually it wasn't known at that time how important that button was going to be — except perhaps by Benni's attorney, who was Orle Hilliard. Later it developed that the police case might have rested on that button."

"My father wouldn't have sent Andre —" I began and stopped because obviously he would and had.

Lieutenant Garrity looked as if he would feel sorry for me if he could permit himself to do so. "Your father," he said, "was not a scoundrel. He wasn't even what I'd call a shyster. There were times when he was brilliant — especially when he was younger. But — well, he was ruthless. When he took a case he defended his client and there were no holds barred. Sure, he sent Bersche to get hold of that button. I don't know how Bersche contrived to do it. I don't think we'll ever know just how he did it. But I'm sure he did. And because of that button and Mrs. Clabbering's statement I'll say that I believe your story about your father's diary and his blackmail letters. I don't say Orle Hilliard would have attempted this kind of thing, blackmail, when he was in his prime. He was too smart. I'm sure he wouldn't have done it for himself. As Amberly here" — he nodded at Richard — "pointed out, clearly he didn't do it for himself. But when he knew he was dying penniless, maybe nothing in the way of ethics seemed to matter to him. Maybe the only thing that mattered to him was some way of getting hold of some money to support you."

After a moment I said, "Thank you —"

Garrity went on briskly, "You can see for yourselves. Last night all that you told me about the diary and the blackmail letters seemed a little — well, I wanted some more — some proof. Some backing. Now I've got it. Mrs. Clabbering. The button. You see?"

I saw. Richard said, "What about Benni?"

"Well, now," Garrity said, "at the time the button disappeared the police had managed to get a look at Benni's clothes, couldn't find a button missing. But later on, a week or two later, somebody got hold of a coat of Benni's, hanging in a garage somewhere — garage belonged to one of his chums, as a matter of fact — and a button was missing. So the button we had had was very important. But here we were. We didn't have the button. Nothing could be proved. We couldn't even charge Benni. Benni left the country. But of course he could have been brought back. That button could have hanged him."

"Even now," Richard said.

"Even any time," said Lieutenant Garrity sharply. "Obviously he followed you here. Arrived by air yesterday. Landed in Washington. Had to come here by train. He's still in New York. No," he corrected himself, "he may not be in New York but he's not gone back to France or Italy yet. We've checked with all the airlines and steamship lines." He shrugged. "He could be anywhere."

"Do you think he murdered Andre?" Richard said.

"No," Lieutenant Garrity replied promptly. "And I'll tell you why. I think all he wanted was that button and the diary. He got the button, at least I'm convinced of that. The diary —" He sighed. "I don't know. That I think doesn't matter though.

It's what we can prove that's important. But — no, I don't think he murdered Bersche. And besides" — this time Lieutenant Garrity looked sorry for Richard — "he couldn't have killed your wife. Whoever killed Bersche used the gun we couldn't find —"

Richard said, "The gun —"

"Sure. The one somebody used to kill your wife."

In a strange way it was not news; it was only a confirmation of something that had already, stubbornly suggested itself, over and over. All the same, it was a shock, too.

Richard said at last, "You're sure —"

"Same markings on the slugs. Same gun. No doubt of it. Benni was in Italy or France, anywhere. He was not in this country when your wife was murdered."

"Yes," Richard said. "Yes, I see." He turned his back toward us; he absently rolled up the top of the old-fashioned desk, disclosing a pigeonholed interior, rolled it back down again and finally said, "Who?"

Garrity eyed Richard rather narrowly now, no longer looking sorry for him. "We're back at the same questions, aren't we? Yes, who? Do you think Orle Hilliard knew who killed your wife?"

"I don't know. It looks like it."

"Maybe he only had an idea," Garrity said. "But maybe Orle wrote one of these blackmail letters to your wife's murderer."

"Of course. That's logical."

"No proof of it," Garrity said. "Still, if that's so, maybe that fifth letter scared the daylights out of somebody. Maybe that somebody really was in the drugstore when Miss Hilliard talked to Bersche, heard that conversation she had with Bersche, heard her ask about the diary, heard her speak as if Bersche had said that he had the diary, went to the house, met Bersche. If all that's so, you see, it explains why there's been no attempt to shut your mouth," he said to me, "permanently. He thinks you do not have the diary. Excuse me. But murder is not polite. All right. I think it possible that somebody did hear Miss Hilliard inquire about that diary and promise to meet Andre Bersche. I think he must have heard the time she was to meet him. Somebody had turned out the desk in the library. Maybe it was Benni, but once he got his hands on that button I think he'd leave. Maybe Andre Bersche searched the desk —"

"No," I said. "He'd have tidied it up. He'd swept the steps. I'm sure. He was like that."

Garrity looked at me; Richard looked at me.

Finally Garrity said, "Assuming all this, that Orle Hilliard knew something, threatened somebody, and that somebody is either your wife's murderer, Amberly, or certainly has the murder gun, assuming all that —" He stopped; he looked at nothing for a long time, his eyes very pale green, then he rose. "We can't assume anything," he said. "All we know is, it's the same gun. I'd like to know where that gun's been for nearly two years. Any ideas about that, Amberly?"

"No," Richard said in a tired voice. "I told you, two years ago. I don't know anything about the gun."

"You told me you had an alibi, too," Garrity said as flatly.

"I lied about that. I'm not lying about the gun."

Garrity eyed his freckled, blunt hands. "You can figure this case several ways," he said soberly. "Guess you can figure any case several ways. You believe that Orle Hilliard knew something of your wife's murderer which induced him to come forward and offer you that fake alibi."

"I think that's how it happened."

Garrity's green eyes lifted to Richard in a flashing glance and then went back to his hands. "You believe that whoever killed your wife killed Andre Bersche because

Bersche had that diary and the murderer had to have it. Well —" Garrity rose and took up his coat. "We'll have to take a look through those records that Bersche took from your father's office, Miss Hilliard. That's a first step. If we find nothing there we'll have to go through every inch of the Pennyroyal Street house."

I said, "He came down from the attic stairs."

Garrity glanced at me. "I think it likely that if Bersche's murderer was still in the house when you arrived, he went to the attic merely to hide from you and wait until you left. But we'll search all those old trunks and boxes, if we need to, as soon as we can. Meantime I want you to be there, Miss Hilliard, when we go through your father's records. I'll send a police car for you sometime this afternoon." He looked at Richard. "You can come, too."

Richard went with him to the door; there was a curious kind of tie between the two men. It was as if they would have liked each other had circumstances permitted it, though in cold fact one was the hunted and the other the hunter. Once in a while, in some unguarded instant, something almost like understanding shot between them.

The police car was leaving when the

second caller arrived in a taxi; it was Mr. Hatever. He squeezed himself out of the taxi, clambered over the soot-stained heaps of snow, saw me and took off his hat.

He hadn't changed at all since I was ten; he was just as round, just as florid, just as shiningly neat, and his enormous spectacles were just as owlish. So were his bright brown eyes. His fat cheeks, purple from the cold, were the color of the frosty bloom on plums. He shoved his hat back on his head, took both my hands, kissed me, exuding a rich odor of face lotion, and said in mellow tones that he was terribly, terribly sorry about Andre; he had heard the news on the radio and knew I was at the Amberly house. The roads had been partially cleared only that morning and he had taken the first train.

Richard took his overcoat, which was a little too long and designed, I suspected, to flatter his bulging figure; it had an astrakhan collar and he had astrakhan earmuffs which fell out of one pocket when he shoved his gloves in with them.

"Very cold," he said smiling. He had dimples, one on each side of his rosy lips. He didn't look at all like the man who could have written me the kind but very reserved letter. But I think I had somehow always known that Mr. Hatever's rosy, smiling appearance was rather at odds with Mr. Hatever's shrewd common sense. However, he had called on me and that was a friendly act and I thanked him.

"No, no, not at all." He adjusted his enormous, horn-rimmed spectacles. "Is there somewhere we can talk in privacy? Not meaning you, of course, my dear fellow." His spectacles flashed at Richard. "Anything we have to say — I feel sure that Fran has taken you into her confidence. The papers said that you came back from Nice together. It was very kind of you and your mother to offer her your hospitality. If I'd known dear Fran was coming, I'd have insisted on her coming to us."

Dear Fran felt as if already she'd had too much of Mr. Hatever, and Richard led the way again back to his father's hide-away. It seemed to be the only room in the house where anybody could be sure of no interruption and I wasn't too sure of that, ever, not with Miffy anywhere in the vicinity. Perhaps that was why I took a chair beside the rolltop desk, facing the door. Richard closed the door.

Mr. Hatever rubbed his hands over the electric heater and said that I needn't be troubled about the office rent my father had owed him. “All that can wait, dear Fran, all that can wait. Friendship, you know. It amounts to something over thirty-five hundred,” he said rather thoughtfully. I didn’t blame him for the thoughtfulness.

“I am sorry I can’t pay you now. As soon as I sell the house —”

“Yes, yes, of course. Not that I myself would want — or indeed permit you to pay this debt. Old friendship, yes. That means more to me than anything else. Unfortunately” — he shook his head until his rosy jowls quivered — “unfortunately, expenses being what they are — advancing every day — yes, expenses. I wish I could tell you to forget this debt.”

“I am terribly sorry.”

“Oh yes, yes, my dear, certainly. Don’t give it a second thought. I’ll help you sell the house. Too bad though that Andre was killed there. Diminishes the value, I’m afraid. People don’t like murder —”

Richard said, “When did you last see Bersche?”

“Why, I haven’t seen him since shortly after Orle Hilliard died. He came in to the office to help me as soon as I had a power of attorney from Fran. We went through Orle’s desk — checkbook, all that. Then Andre brought some cartons, gathered up everything and had it taken away. I have not seen Andre since. I have not talked to him since. His death — his murder — was a very great shock to me. A personal grief. Too bad . . . Of course, the newspapers don't come right out and say there's some link between Andre's murder and your — your poor unfortunate wife's murder, Amberly, but they do suggest — yes, well, perhaps to a lawyer's mind, like mine. Yes, yes. Was that alibi Orle gave you the truth?"

I could have choked Mr. Hatever if I could have got my hands around his starchy collar and the rolls of fat on his neck. Yet very soon now everybody would know.

Richard said, "No."

"Ah yes. Ah yes. At the time I wondered. Very pat, you see. Very pat. Very like old Orle, as a matter of fact. Do forgive me, dear Fran. Forgive me."

Richard said, "We've been wanting to talk to you. I tried to phone you several times."

Mr. Hatever's spectacles glittered; he interrupted. "About Orle's estate?" He spread his fat hands with their shining and manicured fingernails. "There wasn't any estate. I told Fran. I wrote to her —"

"Yes, she knows that. But is there the least possibility that anything was overlooked? A safe deposit box anywhere, for instance?" Richard said.

Mr. Hatever's eyes were very sharp. "No." He seemed to consider it judicially. "No, I can't say there is any such possibility. I don't think I missed anything. Went over every single thing that could be found. It was rather a job — Orle had changed. He got so he saved everything, things that should have been thrown out. Still I would have found the check stub for box rent, something. No, I covered everything, I'm sure."

"You don't think that he could have put anything in a savings account or a safe deposit box under — say — another name?"

Mr. Hatever managed to look indignant. "My dear Amberly! Really!" He thought it over and said, "That is, he might have if he'd wanted to. But if he did, there was no record of any such thing."

"You must have known something of his cases —"

"No, no! We went over his financial records, nothing else, nothing. I knew very little of Orle's professional affairs. Nothing, indeed. Oh, we took offices together many years ago. Always remained on cordial terms. When he was short of money — well, I paid our rent. But years ago our — shall I say our professional paths diverged. No, Mr. Amberly, I can't tell you anything at all about his law practice. Nothing!"

"I hoped that you could," Richard said. "There's a diary we want —"

"Diary!" cried Mr. Hatever. "I forgot! It's in my pocket." He tugged at his coat pocket and my heart leaped up into my throat. Mr. Hatever pulled out a book. It was a small black volume. The word *Diary* was stamped on it in gold letters.

I clutched at it; Mr. Hatever looked slightly surprised at my eagerness but relinquished it. My whole attention was focused upon the book in my hands; it was only at the very fringe of my consciousness that I felt that something, somewhere in the room had moved. I hoped that within those pages there was evidence, real evidence, which would clear Richard, and I was afraid to hope it. I didn't know what the diary might reveal. It might be a deadlier Pandora's box, for all I knew. Something in the room *had* moved. This time the impression was strong enough to pluck at my awareness and tore my gaze from the diary. The door, across the room, stopped moving.

It was then perfectly still. The rosy reflection of the red electric heater on the polished panels of the door had barely stopped moving, too. I went quickly across the room, ignoring Richard's and Mr. Hatever's questioning looks, and flung open the door. Nobody was there. Nobody was in the dining room. If anybody was in the kitchen, I could hear nothing. I couldn't see much of the hall but there was no hurrying shadow, no hurrying footsteps, nothing.

Richard, close to me now, said, "What is it?"

"I thought Miffy — I mean someone was at the door. It doesn't matter."

"Oh," Richard said. He, too, looked toward the hall, listened and then drew back into the little room and closed the door but this time stood with his back against it. Mr. Hatever quite naturally was looking rather surprised. But he cleared his throat, blinked and said, "The diary was overlooked. Andre must have missed it. One of the office girls found it. Actually it was on a bookshelf, in with some books. The girl properly turned it over to me. I thought you'd like to have it — sentimental reasons."

If he only knew what that diary meant! I said, "Thank you."

"Oh yes, and here is the power of attorney you gave me. I've done all I can. You'd better have it back."

I took the paper and said thank you

again. Mr. Hatever said he'd better be getting down to the office. "Wouldn't surprise me if I didn't have some people from the newspapers to talk to. Dear, dear — poor Andre."

Perhaps he was aware of the eager way I had clutched the diary to me for he shook his head. "There's nothing in the diary, really. I looked, of course. Thought perhaps some of poor Orle's cases — debts — loans — something like that, might be noted. But there's really nothing in it. It was your father's property so I brought it to you. Only my duty. Yes, I'll be getting along. Call on me for anything you want. That is" — a prudent impulse pursed up his rosy lips — "that is, of course, if you really don't have any cash, I can lend you — not much perhaps — expenses, all that — terrific. But still, until you've sold your house — I'd be delighted —" He didn't sound delighted.

Richard said, "She's all right for the moment. I'll try to get you a taxi."

I suppose I thanked Mr. Hatever still another time. In any event Richard ushered him out.

I stood looking down at the diary. I was almost literally afraid to open it and read. But I opened it. I read. By the time I heard Richard's quick footsteps returning through the dining room, by the time he appeared in the doorway, I knew what was in the diary. Mr. Hatever had been quite accurate; there was nothing at all.

13

"But there must be," Richard said. "There's got to be. Give it to me."

He looked through the book. It was not very thick; it was undated, except in a few places where my father had made a note of the date and apparently initials, sometimes a name and a word, lunch or dinner, the place and the time, and that was all. Even these were desultory entries, as if he had not had the heart or the interest to keep the diary up regularly. "It's only an engagement diary," Richard said. "I wonder if these names could mean anything." They didn't, as far as I could see. They weren't in fact names for the most part but merely initials. The diary was in fact a jumble of nothing.

But the contents of the briefcase had proved to be not entirely a jumble of nothing. There could conceivably be some kind of significance, some kind of code in the diary; I suggested that, although rather feebly, and we went over every page of the little book again. There wasn't anything at all or if there was it was far too ambiguous even to hint at a significance.

"Looks as if he'd use it for a week or two, then forget about it, then use it again for a while. And only for dates," Richard said finally.

He closed the book and gave it to me. "Perhaps if you read it over and over, something will strike you, but I doubt it."

He was disappointed. He had hoped for much from that diary. So had I. And so had the police! I said, "I suppose we'll have to turn this over to the police."

"Oh yes. But it's the wrong diary."

"Yes, I see."

"So where is the right one? Will you let me see the power of attorney you gave Hatever?"

I gave it to him; he read it carefully and gave it back to me. "That's all right. Same kind you gave me. A power of attorney can be a pretty inclusive instrument. You can do anything, with a power of attorney — buy, sell, dispose of property, anything. But this document is limited to exactly what Hatever did for you, merely an inquiry about your father's estate."

"Mr. Hatever wouldn't take money from my father's estate!"

Richard laughed shortly. "No, on the face of it, I don't think he would. He couldn't appropriate anything with that limited power of attorney, even if he wanted to. But he did know your father. Your father knew him. It's possible that he found the diary, the real one, and for reasons of his own, and very important reasons, doesn't intend to give it to you."

I said, "The gun — Cecile —"

Richard nodded. "Yes. Your father could have had something on Hatever — but Hatever had nothing at all to do with Cecile or me or — no, Hatever didn't kill Cecile and he didn't kill Andre. I think that Andre may have found the real diary."

I said slowly, "If whoever killed Andre has that diary, the real diary, what will he do with it?"

"If it incriminates him he'll destroy it at once. Or destroy the part that affects him, tear out the pages and burn them or something. But if he has a certain kind of mind, I suppose he could use the rest of the diary as your father used it."

"For blackmail."

"Of course he'd have to know the names, know some specific threats to use for blackmail. He'd have to get them from the real diary. There's nothing in this one."

Several times I felt that someone was in the dining room and was sure that it was

Miffy but if so she didn't open the door.

"Maybe the police can make something of it," I said at last.

Richard seemed as doubtful as I but put it in his pocket. It was a queer kind of anticlimax, that hit-or-miss engagement book.

We had lunch. Mrs. Amberly said that Uncle Sisley had gone to his club to get some clothes and Miffy said that Slade was at the office and it was a pity he'd insisted on going because transportation was still very difficult. Mrs. Amberly said that if he didn't leave for the office before noon, as had happened that day, Wilbur would talk to him very seriously, and for a second I wondered if it could have been Slade who had seen or overheard the transfer of the diary from Mr. Hatever to me. He would have told Miffy perhaps.

But Miffy was curious and Miffy was never far from Richard. Stella did not come near and I was sure that Wilbur had outlawed me. The telephone did not ring because somebody had taken it off the hook. Mrs. Amberly spent the afternoon apparently answering notes on a heap of Christmas cards on her desk, and Miffy worked away at her knitting, but, I thought, knew it whenever Richard lighted a cigarette or I took a long breath. Uncle Sisley arrived home and I found out who kept up the cannel-coal fire, for he staggered in carrying a bucket of coal and knelt at the blaze. He was very jauntily dressed in a brightly checked tweed jacket, very dashing black slacks and a yellow tie with small black figures in it, which I first thought were bumblebees but then discovered were boxing gloves. Richard went to take the coal bucket, stared and said, "Where's the fight?"

Uncle Sisley glanced down complacently at his tie. "Of course I took a few lessons in my youth, in the manly art." Only Uncle Sisley would have said the manly art.

Miffy said softly, "But Wilbur really *didn't* see you coming, Uncle Sisley, I was watching. Besides, Wilbur was so mad he wouldn't have seen anything —"

Uncle Sisley's face fell, but only for an instant, and he said. "Tosh." This seemed to restore him so he said "Tosh" again and the doorbell rang. Richard went to answer it and it was the police. They had come for Richard and me.

Uncle Sisley's jauntiness left him, he teetered back on his heels and looked rather shrunken. Mrs. Amberly's lips tightened. Miffy said, "But where are you going? What do the police want?"

"Just to talk to us," Richard said. "Don't wait dinner for us. It may be some time before we get back."

The cannel coal had blazed up and was snapping and crackling and I didn't want to go. I went downstairs and took some comfort from Richard's hand tucked under my arm. He got my coat out. He helped me into Mrs. Amberly's overshoes again. He gave me my beret. I only happened to put my hand in my coat pocket and found the money.

I knew it was money by the cold, somehow rather greasy feel of it. It was rolled up tightly with a rubber band around it; I could feel the rubber band, too. Then I caught Richard's look and I said, "There's more —" and pulled out the roll. It *was* money, greasy and dirty, rolled up tightly; there was more than money.

A tiny slip of paper was stuck in under the rubber band. Richard took it out, carefully. There were words stuck on the paper with transparent tape. The words were printed and read, "Silent more to came." Richard held it and we both looked at it and knew exactly what it meant.

" 'Silent,' " Richard said at last. "I suppose that means for you to keep quiet about the diary. 'More' means more money.

'Came' — he couldn't find the word 'come' and did find the word 'came' and used it. There we are. 'More to came.' "

"The words look as if they were cut from a newspaper."

"It's one way to get a message across without giving anybody a sample of handwriting —"

" 'More' and 'to' and 'came' look like newsprint. 'Silent' is different." We both looked at the word *silent,* which was in heavier print, almost script, and its background was a tiny rectangle of glossy white paper.

I could hear the engine of the police car outside. I thought I heard someone upstairs in the library say something to somebody else. I was sure I could hear a particularly sharp crackle of the cannel-coal fire. At last I said, *"Who?"*

"Can you remember putting your hand in that pocket — I mean, when you last did that?"

It wasn't possible. He saw the futility of that question in my face. "Well," he said, "let's see how much." He counted the bills quickly.

It seemed to me that it was very still upstairs; it almost seemed to me that somebody — not Mrs. Amberly nor Uncle Sisley nor Miffy precisely, but somebody — was listening and it was somebody who had to know what we said and what we were going to do about that money. "Two thousand," Richard said. " 'More to came.' "

14

He sniffed the bills and held them toward me and I said, "No perfume."

"Can you think back to — oh, back to Nice? I mean your coat, where it's been, who could have had the opportunity to put this in the pocket?"

Anybody could have had the opportunity. I said so after a moment. "Even on the airplanes. Anybody —"

Richard was looking very strained and white. "It *could* be somebody here, of course. Your coat's been hanging in the closet half the time."

"The coat was in the hotel in Nice. The money could have been slid into the pocket — oh, anywhere. Even while I was wearing the coat. For that matter, on the street, in the subway — in the Pennyroyal Street house — anywhere —"

The doorbell rang again. Richard shoved the money into his pocket and opened the door. He gave both money and diary to Garrity who was sitting in the back of the police car, and Garrity turned on a little top light and looked. He counted the money; he examined the slip of paper that went with it; he peered closely at the decorative script of the word *silent.* He flipped through the diary. He listened to everything we had to tell him. He questioned me about my coat, when had I last put my hand in the pocket, and I didn't know. He made me give a kind of recital of where my coat — and I — had been, when. I went over the entire past five days as minutely as I could and he said, turning off the top light, that it was a rather well-traveled coat. "You don't remember anybody pressing close to you at any time, anywhere. Airport? Street? Anywhere?" I didn't.

We went south on Fifth Avenue; the lights of the great apartment houses along the Avenue shone through the early winter dusk. Garrity questioned me and questioned me and I watched the lights of the Fifth Avenue stores flash past. The street was again almost deserted; the decorated windows with all their Christmas trim seemed like a bright pageant played to empty seats. Presently we turned on a side street. It would have taken a matter of seconds to slide that roll of bills into my pocket, I reflected.

Garrity finally veered to the diary. "Sure

there's nothing in it?"

"Nothing that seemed to have any meaning."

"I saw Hatever today." Garrity sensed my surprise. "Your father's associate! Had your power of attorney! Sure, I went to see him. That power of attorney interested me — all sorts of hanky-panky could go on if somebody who had a power of attorney had a looting turn of mind, too. But it's a fact, there was nothing to loot. We've investigated that, too."

"You've had a busy day," Richard said a little dryly.

"Yes," Garrity said shortly. "Your day has not been idle either. I'll give you a receipt for this money, Miss Hilliard —"

"I don't want a receipt! It's not mine. I've got nothing to do with it!" I cried.

Garrity went on. "We may be able to get some fingerprints. I doubt it. But we'll do what we can to trace the bills. Also that money you put away for Miss Hilliard, Amberly. You can let me have that tomorrow. As to the time when this money was put in your coat pocket, Miss Hilliard, I'm inclined to think that it hasn't been there very long. A person puts his hand in his coat pocket and doesn't remember it. I feel sure you'd have found it if it had been put there more than a week ago — even more than a day or two ago. Oh, yes, I think that's a quite recent development. Here we are."

Andre's apartment house was like a thousand others; there was a narrow and snow-tracked foyer, a row of mailboxes and bells, an elevator which was automatic and bore a Christmas wreath at the back. We went to the third floor and along a narrow hall; we passed a few doors and nobody looked out to see who we were or what we were doing. "We got the key from the superintendent," Garrity said and unlocked the door.

Andre's apartment was unexpectedly big and comfortable-looking, which in an odd way comforted me; at least he had had a comfortable kind of life. It was also, however, impersonal; Andre had not been the kind to collect sentimental knickknacks. There were heaps of papers, some of them bound, others in filing envelopes, everywhere in curiously hit-or-miss stacks, which was not like Andre who was fanatically neat.

Garrity had brought us there, however, for only one purpose, which at once became evident. He turned to Richard.

"Take a look at those stacks of papers. Were they left like that when you and Bersche stopped your search?"

"No!" Richard stared at the sliding, confused heaps. "Not at all! Every time we'd look at anything Bersche would replace it carefully where he thought it belonged. Somebody has been here —"

"Well, of course," Garrity said rather wearily. "Somebody got Bersche's key. Somebody got his address from his billfold, likely, before he threw it away. Somebody was here, searching for the diary."

"When?" Richard said.

I thought of the bridge games, the night before; nobody had gone, nobody who belonged in that tight little circle of those close to Cecile had secretly left the house and come to this paper-stacked room and searched.

Garrity said with a shrug, "There was plenty of time. Bersche was killed in the afternoon, probably quite early, day before yesterday. It looked as if whoever killed him, thinking he had the diary, didn't find the diary in Bersche's possession and came here to look for it. Whether he found it or not — well, that will have to wait. But the autopsy report is positive as to the approximate time of Bersche's murder. The murderer had a good twenty-four hours to come here and search." He turned to me. "He had reason to believe that Bersche had the diary,

Miss Hilliard. I've gone over and over every word you could remember of your telephone conversation with Bersche. When he said he had these papers you said, 'You do have it.' Didn't you?"

"Yes. I said it was important. I had to have it."

"So if somebody listening heard only your end of the conversation he had every reason to believe that Bersche had the diary and would bring it to you. And Bersche was killed."

"How?" Richard said.

Garrity nodded to the two policemen who had accompanied us and they began stacking all the files into three big cartons which stood empty near the sofa. Garrity said, "My guess is that he had your housekey, Miss Hilliard. He had removed it from your handbag —"

"Mr. Benni!" I cried.

"Maybe." Garrity went on. "He let himself into your house. Bersche was in your father's room — perhaps he hadn't found the diary and was searching there for it. Sounds possible. In any event whoever killed him took him by surprise. Perhaps they had talked. Certainly the murderer shot him because Bersche could have identified him. Bersche may have made some effort to defend himself because he was knocked out before he was shot. At least that's the way it looks. All right?" he asked the policemen. They signified that they had packed up all the papers.

Garrity said to me, "Your property. We'll take them to your house and wait while you go through them yourself. We've fingerprinted this place. Found your fingerprints, Amberly, and of course Bersche's and a cleaning woman's — nothing else. Ready?"

We trooped out into the narrow hall, went down in the elevator crowded now with the cartons, through the clean but rather dreary foyer and into the police car again. Somehow they managed to wedge the cartons into it. Garrity said, "We'll never find Bersche's wallet. There seem to be two keys to your house, Miss Hilliard, missing. One from your handbag, one from Bersche's pockets. I expect both keys and Bersche's wallet will be scooped up by the street cleaners when they get to work on this." He waved at the masses of soot-flecked snow along the curbs. "Probably our murderer has got rid of both keys by now."

"You searched me last night," Richard said quietly. "You know that I didn't have the key to Fran's house or the key to Bersche's apartment."

"Not then," Garrity said agreeably.

Not much else was said during that ride downtown. The house on Pennyroyal Street was lighted. A policeman was there and opened the door. The other two policemen lugged the cartons into the library. Garrity shed his handsome overcoat in the hall. He eyed the marble Venus, got a kind of gleam in his eye, and went to drape his overcoat over one of her dimpled white shoulders. He stood off and looked at it; the effect was shockingly nude, her whiteness emerging so abruptly from the decorous folds of his overcoat. He shuddered and removed the coat to a chair.

We went into the library. We turned on every light. We looked through the cartons. The two policemen helped. We sorted out stacks, we sorted out bundles, we sorted out files. Everybody worked and we got nowhere. But Andre's murderer had had, as Garrity said, twenty-four hours' start of us.

We did find an address book. It was a loose-leaf notebook, with some of the names and addresses typed in, others written sometimes in my father's handwriting, sometimes in Andre's. Certainly the entries had been made over a long period of years. I looked at it, holding it under the light on the desk in the library.

"Take your time," Garrity said. "Don't try too hard. Just see if any of these names ring a bell." His voice was easy; his green eyes very intent upon me.

I took my time, reading a page and then another; some of the names rang a bell but not the kind of bell Garrity meant; I recognized some names connected with long-ago cases, a few firm names, my own school addresses and the telephone numbers. It seemed to me both a business and a personal address book. It was so old that some of the pages were yellowed and soiled; indeed only a few pages seemed to be fairly new additions. In a way it could have been a record of my father's life. But there was no Delia Clabbering; there was a Benson, not Benni, and even that part of a firm name; there was an Amberly but merely that and the address. I handed the address book back to Garrity. He looked disappointed but said philosophically that he hadn't hoped for much.

"Looks as if he trusted his memory for the special names and addresses of those letters. Not many. He'd have remembered Sisley Todd's club address. He had your address, Amberly. There was only Mrs. Clabbering's address and Benni's address to remember."

"And the address for the fifth letter," Richard said.

Garrity said, "In any event, this office address book seems no more helpful than the small one in his briefcase. Well, let's go on."

We went on and the only fact which began to emerge which might have some significance was actually what we didn't find. We found no reference at all to the Mr. Benni affair. We found no reference at all to Mrs. Delia Clabbering. We found no reference to Uncle Sisley Todd. We found no reference to Amberly, any Amberly.

Yet my father had saved a smeary blotter; he had saved a brown button; he had saved newspaper clippings about Cecile's murder; he had saved Uncle Sisley's ill-advised letters.

By nine o'clock we had scarcely made a dent in the heaped-up files, envelopes, masses of papers, receipts, the accumulation of many years. As on the night before, a policeman struggled into his overcoat, disappeared and presently returned with sandwiches, hot coffee and two packages of cigarettes, which he handed over to Garrity.

My hands were so dusty that I went into the little washroom off the hall, under the stairs. It was antiquated, as was all the plumbing in the house. It was dusty with a black, gritty little film over everything. The mirror over the washbowl was filmed over and it had a red mouth drawn on it, curved eyebrows and hair, nothing else. The mouth was done with lipstick and the lipstick itself lay on the ledge. The curving eyebrows and hair were suggested simply by wiping off the dust in two thin strokes for eyebrows and by a cleared surface which followed the outlines of a woman's hair, widely bouffant and parted in the middle. It was a ghostly Cecile. It could only suggest Cecile. It was terribly like her picture with that neat part up the middle and the wide curving sweeps outward.

I heard my own steps, running back to the library. Richard came to meet me. Garrity came to meet me. Everybody, even Richard, went to look. Richard came back first.

He said, "I'm sorry —"

I didn't understand him. He said, "I'm sorry you had such a shock."

"It's like her."

"Oh yes." He looked sick and white. "Oh yes. It's like her."

Garrity came in. I heard one of the policemen pounding through the hall, and then the outside door banged. "They'll take fingerprints, examine the washroom, everything," Garrity said. "Is this your lipstick?" He held out the small metal tube.

"I suppose so. It could have been in my room. I've used that kind and color."

Richard said, "So we've got this kind of murderer —" and stopped.

Garrity said cautiously, "It's possible. Yes. Your fake alibi puts you back as you were in the beginning, Amberly, as prime suspect. You can't evade that. We can't. As I expect you know, you've never been quite crossed off as suspect. But if you didn't kill her —"

I think Richard started to say, "I didn't," for his lips moved, but he checked so obvious and indeed worthless a denial. Garrity went on, "— if you didn't kill her, then this kind of murderer has always been a possibility. The struggle in her room, the — everything suggests a certain kind of personality. Doesn't make it easier. Can be anybody. I wonder when this — this drawing" — he too looked sick, revolted, even surprised, and I had thought that nothing could surprise him — "I wonder when this drawing," he repeated after clearing his throat, "was made. Have you been in the washroom since you got back from France?" he asked me.

"No —"

"You?" He turned to Richard.

"No."

He looked at the stacks of files and papers.

Someone had apparently examined the clothes from my father's baggage and then neatly folded everything on a sofa at the end of the room. A dark blue cashmere coat lay on top. He had been very dashing and debonair in that coat. I looked away.

Garrity nodded at the second policeman who stood in the doorway, his eyes bulging and his face faintly green. "Take some sandwiches and coffee for yourself and Brien. Get busy on that washroom as soon as they get here with equipment."

The policeman scooped up some paper-wrapped sandwiches, gave them a sickened glance as if he couldn't possibly eat anything, gathered up a carton of coffee and two paper cups and vanished. Garrity closed the door after him and stood for a long moment or two, looking down apparently at his neat brown shoes. Then he said with an effect of determined briskness, "We'll find out if the fingerprint men went through that washroom last night. I'm inclined to think they didn't. It's hidden under the stairs. They wouldn't have fingerprinted every closet and every cupboard in the house. We'll wait and see."

"It does look like — like Cecile," Richard

said. "Yes, I know."

"Why?" Richard said.

Garrity's face looked a little green, too, but he shrugged. "That kind of murderer," he said as Richard had said. "No reason, probably. One of those ugly things. Now then —" He approached the desk and glanced around at the heaps of papers. "We've done about as much here as we can do tonight. We haven't found any reference at all to your wife's murder. We haven't found anything which indicates a hold Orle Hilliard had over anybody else — as you say, Amberly, the person who received that fifth letter." He sat down and looked at me. "You did send five letters —"

"Of course I did. I told you —"

"Yes but — in any event this fifth letter must have gone to somebody who is willing to pay you for the diary. And somebody who thinks you have the diary. If it's Bersche's murderer, then he didn't find the diary — that is, if he put that money in your pocket in the past thirty-six hours, as I think it likely he did. Now then, your coat has been either here in this house, at the Amberly house or on your back during this time. Amberly didn't put it there, he wouldn't have paid you to keep you quiet about something we already know — that is, his false alibi, the alibi your father gave him."

Richard gave a short kind of laugh. I said no.

"Sisley Todd wouldn't have put it there for much the same reason. You have removed yourself as a threat to him; you gave him back his letters. Benni now, I believe, has the button. We've talked to Mrs. Clabbering. She knows you do not threaten her in any way. I think we must find out who got that fifth letter."

"If it was Cecile's murderer," Richard began, and Garrity said flatly, "Oh yes. It has a certain argumentative logic. Only a very grave accusation would result in Andre Bersche's murder." He shoved a heap of papers from a chair to the floor, where they fell with a swish and a little cloud of dust, and sat down, crossing one knee over the other and carefully adjusting the knife-edge creases of his trousers. "Yes," he said to Richard, "your wife's murderer. Have you any ideas at all about that, Amberly?"

Richard shook his head. "Nothing except — that horrible sketch — the lipstick — the curve and the part of the hair —"

"Yes, well —" Garrity cleared his throat again. "I've been going over our files about the case, of course. Every detail. Some of this is going to be painful to you, Amberly —"

Richard said, in a kind of weary but matter-of-fact way, "It was, in the beginning. Horrible. But now — go ahead."

"Do you mind if Miss Hilliard hears all this?" Garrity said. His green eyes looked friendly but also watchful.

Richard shook his head. "She's seen the papers. It was all in the papers anyway."

"Not quite all," Garrity said.

Richard gave him a quick look, frowned and rose; he walked to the window. He said over his shoulder, "I see. No, Fran doesn't know that."

It reminded me flashingly of just such a gesture, just such a movement across the room, just such a comment over his shoulder. That had been in Nice, on Christmas Day. He had said then that there was a certain amount of evidence.

Garrity said, "You knew, of course, that we found three men she had picked up in bars. All of them had firm alibis. We checked them out thoroughly."

Richard nodded. "We took care of her — I mean, we tried to take care of her. We couldn't always. We didn't that night she was murdered."

Garrity said, "Yes — it was a pitiful thing, of course. Hard for the family. Very hard for you. According to the file, you got your wife into sanatoriums twice and both times she managed to get away."

"Yes." Richard sounded very far away and very tired.

"It was only when she was —" Garrity cleared his throat again; he was having a difficult time with his throat. I stared at the rug and felt my toes curling in as if I were about to step into an icy pool and dreaded it, but I had to listen. Garrity went on. "It was only when she had had too much to drink that she was likely to get away from the house, pick up anybody she took a fancy to. You quarreled about that."

"I suppose so. Oh, the answer is yes. I felt that she didn't try hard enough to help herself. I think I was wrong. Yet I did what I could. I'm sure she tried to stop. I felt sorry for her, of course."

"The night she was murdered you'd quarreled."

"Yes."

"She was already dressed, you came into the room, and found her drinking, staggering, hardly able to talk."

Richard whirled around. I looked at him once and looked back at the rug and memorized the pattern, which was like interlacing diamonds. Richard said harshly, "You know all this. You've always known it. Why talk about it now?"

"I'm sorry," Garrity said and from his voice I thought he meant it. "But as I told you, I've been going over and over the files in the hope of finding something new. I'd like to go on."

"Go on," Richard said after a moment.

"Well, then, there she was all dressed in her pink dress and her jewelry and — well, drunk. She couldn't go anywhere, not in that condition. So you thought."

"So I thought," Richard said. "And I left her alone. I left her to be murdered. I left her —"

"Amberly!" Garrity said a little too softly, a little too disarmingly. "There comes a time when anybody's patience is used up, when he's not really responsible for what he does. There's a name for it —"

"I know," Richard said, "intolerable provocation."

"Intolerable provocation," Garrity said, still too softly so his gentleness was like a trap. "That's right. Any jury would probably sympathize with you. You did kill her — didn't you, Amberly?"

I had known it was coming. I had expected it ever since I knew of the false alibi.

"No," Richard said almost as softly.

There was a little pause. Garrity slowly

lighted a cigarette; he reached for an ash-tray. He leaned back, adjusting the crease in his trousers, and said in the same mild, horribly disarming voice, so it seemed to promise friendship and support, "Did you love your wife?"

I rose. I didn't know that I was going to move but I did and I went to stand beside Richard. I put my hand on his arm. Richard put his own hand over mine. He didn't look at me; he looked at Garrity.

"I don't know," he said.

Garrity's green eyes studied me and studied Richard. "Yes, you both feel the same. Your wife, Amberly. Your father, Miss Hilliard. You've had your troubles. It makes a bond. Sure I'll admit that."

But he had perception, this trimly tailored man with his green eyes. He had too much perception. He said, "You don't know whether or not you loved your wife, Amberly. Is that because you can't remember or because" — his eyes touched me — "you have a new interest?"

I jerked my hand away from Richard's arm but he caught it and held it firmly.

"I say that I don't know whether or not I loved Cecile because I really don't know," Richard began, and we heard the hall door open and the sound of heavy footsteps and men's voices in the hall.

Garrity said, "Whoever made that face in the mirror hated your wife. Whoever killed your wife hated her. You really must have hated her. How could you have helped it! Think it over —" He went into the hall and closed the door behind him.

Richard held my hand tightly. I said to myself, yes, it's true. Yes, I'm in love with him.

It was a perfectly natural kind of realization, nothing overwhelming about it, mere fact. There was nothing surprising about it; it was as if I'd known it for a very long time. I didn't even wonder how or when it had come about.

Richard released my hand. "I didn't hate her," he said. "I didn't kill her. . . . The coffee's still hot. You'd better have some."

He went to the table and poured coffee into a paper cup. The door opened and Garrity came back in.

15

He seemed to think the coffee was a welcome idea, looked in the container to make sure there was more, and poured some for himself.

He then sat down and sipped and looked at his brown oxfords and finally said to Richard, “Why don’t you know whether or not you loved your wife?”

“That isn’t what I meant,” Richard said flatly. “I meant that too much has happened. It was too soon after we were married that the — the trouble began. And then — everything seems obscured. It’s like a wall. I can’t see back, on the other side of the wall.”

“You married her,” Garrity said, sipping his coffee. “You must have loved her then. But you grew to hate her. Didn’t you?”

“Not hate,” Richard said wearily. “It wasn’t hate.”

“Disappointment, certainly.”

“It was hell,” Richard said, still in that flat and weary voice. “What else could you think it was?”

"But never hate?"

"No — no —"

"She went to a lawyer and talked of divorce. Why didn't you let her go through with it? Why didn't you take the opportunity to get rid of her?"

"She changed her mind."

"Then you'd have consented to the divorce? Happily, I expect."

"The police went over all this when she was killed. Over it and over it. My answer is the same. I don't know whether I'd have consented to the divorce or not. I suppose I would have. But she wasn't responsible. Somebody would have had to take care of her. Not that I did such a good job of it," Richard said, looking very tired.

Garrity had seemed friendly; he had seemed to believe everything we told him of the diary and of the letters; he had almost seemed to place himself on our side, willing to believe and help us. But all the same, all the time, he was the hunter.

He said, "You say now that you walked out of the house that night, walked along the park — just where was it?"

Richard's shoulders squared. "I've told you. A few streets south. I really don't know exactly how far. I sat on a bench and smoked."

"Didn't go near the ball?"

I knew, of course, that Garrity and perhaps others must have questioned Richard minutely at the time, after the discovery of Andre's murder, when Richard told them of his false alibi. I had waited a long time in the bare little room of the precinct station. But Garrity's question now seemed new to Richard. He frowned, puzzled. "No."

"Didn't stroll over to the Waldorf at all?"

"No."

"Didn't happen to see Orle Hilliard at the Waldorf?"

"No! I wasn't there —"

"But Orle Hilliard was there," Garrity said.

He went over to the desk and sorted out the clippings which still lay there, under a stack of files. He took up one clipping and turned it over. "Here you are. Society notes. The murder story ran off the front page and into one of the back pages; see. Here. The front-page story breaks off with a reference to another page and on the other side of that page we have society notes. It was the day after the murder. The photographer who got that picture of your sister-in-law and her brother must have been surprised to find Hilliard's photograph turn up in a murder story instead of on the society page. But here's a report of the ball. Your father was one of the patrons and was at the ball, Miss Hilliard. Hatever was a patron, too. Want to look?"

It had not occurred to me or to Richard to look at the reverse sides of the clippings. I did then and, of course, Garrity was right. There was part of the account of the ball, not all of it. But there was a list of patronesses and patrons and Orle Hilliard was one of the patrons. Mr. Hatever's name did not surprise me; he was a frequent patron for worthy causes. But my father had been very short of money for charity. A further note at the bottom of the clipping mentioned my father's presence, along with many other names.

Garrity said, "Costs money to float one of these balls and still have something left over for charity. But I guess your father would call it investment; at least it kept him in circulation as a name. But he was at the ball, no question of that."

"You know now that he wasn't sitting in an apartment-house foyer at Ninety-second Street," Richard said.

Garrity's green eyes had an ugly flash. "Sure, we should have known it then. Somebody goofed. We don't read the society pages. But that's in the past. Today I got hold of a woman who was one of the patronesses, who remembers that he was there around eleven, white tie and tails. Dancing some. Says she saw him once or twice, thinks he left early. She doesn't know. There were over eleven hundred people at the ball."

"I wasn't there," Richard said. "I don't see what difference it makes but I wasn't."

"I was only thinking that maybe — just maybe you saw Hilliard at the ball and you cooked up the alibi then."

I didn't think that Garrity really thought that; it seemed to me that he threw out the suggestion merely as one throws out bait, hoping some unwary fish will come along. Richard shook his head. "It would have been a better alibi than the one we really did cook up. It would have been fact. I wish I had been there but I wasn't."

"No, well —" Garrity looked at his watch and said abruptly, "I'm sending you back to the Amberly house now. It'll take the men a while to get through with that washroom —" He turned to me. "I think we'll leave all these records here, if it's all the same with you. They're your property. We'll take care of them."

"I want the address book," I said.

Garrity's eyes turned greener. "Sure, take

it. Do your best —"

I didn't hope for anything but I wanted to go over every single name in the book, slowly; perhaps, just perhaps one of them would suddenly spring into memory as Uncle Sisley's name had presented itself. I took the book. Richard said, "When do you want it back?"

"Give her time. Long as she likes. Here, take the diary Hatever brought you, too. Hunt through it. See if anything at all strikes you as — oh, unusual." He gave me the diary, which was no diary at all, but I took it. "I'll take care of the money." He scribbled something quickly on a pad he took from his pocket. "Here's a receipt. We'll work on these bills and also the five thousand you got in Nice. You can give that to me tomorrow, Amberly."

"Garrity," Richard said, "that ball. Mr. Hilliard was taking quite a chance, stating that he went to see somebody at Ninety-second Street, when in fact he *was* at the ball. Somebody might have come forward and said he was there."

"Maybe," Garrity said, "and maybe not. He'd have had some way of covering himself if that happened."

A huge floodlight was set up in the hall just outside the tiny washroom. It cast queer lights and shadows upon the marble Venus so she seemed to lean forward, curious and listening. Men were shuffling around.

I hurried into my coat. Again a police car took us home. It was very late. There was a light in the hall and in the library. The house had a depth of night stillness which somehow induced us to lower our voices and go very quietly up the stairs to the library. The lamp on a table was still lighted; the usual tray of decanters and glasses and ice bucket stood on its usual table. The fire had burned down to blue and gray embers.

Richard looked in the brass coal bucket which stood on the hearth, found a supply of coal, stirred the embers to a red glow and made up the fire. It began to crackle and snap. There were doors to the library, wide doors which met in the center of the doorway into the hall. I had never seen them closed. Richard closed them then, and went to the table. "Nightcap?"

I said no, and stood before the fire. I half expected Miffy to open those doors and peer in. I thought about Richard, too. He settled down in a lounge chair, stretched out his long legs and looked absently at nothing and I was very much in love with him. It seemed to me that there should have been some moment, indeed some instant, when I ought to have known that I was falling in love, but there wasn't.

The only thing I knew was that it must have happened to me sometime in the last five days. It didn't matter when or how it had happened. I wondered what he was going to say. I thought that he must have something in mind that he wanted to say to me; otherwise he wouldn't have closed the doors. Still, perhaps he only wished to be sure that our voices, or the crackle of the fire, didn't wake the household.

He said at last, slowly, "I really don't know how I felt about Cecile."

Cecile. I said, "Oh" in a whisper. There was a big footstool near me and I sat down.

Richard whirled the glass in his hand absently. "It's all obscured by the thing that happened. I only know that I was desperately sorry for her. Sorry when she was killed so horribly. It was tragic. She was so young and — it was tragic."

I said yes and hugged my knees.

"Sometime I must have loved her or thought I loved her or — but then it began to seem as if that might have been in a different life, a different world. I can't even remember it. It's all blotted out. Except the sadness of it. She was so young," Richard said again.

"You can't blame yourself."

"Well, I do. If I hadn't left the house that night, if I hadn't left her alone — But I know, too, that there wasn't much hope for her. Ever. Some people are born like that. Under the wrong star, the evil star, something like that. Doomed." He lifted his glass. "I've never talked much of it. At first I couldn't. Then later it didn't seem to matter. You felt sorry for me tonight. You came and stood by me."

Of course I did, I thought; I'm in love with you; can't you see it? It seemed rather unmaidenly to say it! I turned around and looked at the fire. "I — I knew that Garrity was going to say you killed Cecile. He asked you if you killed her —"

"My dear, I've been asked that so many times and in so many different ways that I can sense a trap a mile off. I can even smell one. Which reminds me, I wonder what exactly has happened to our smelly friend, Benni."

"I hope he's gone forever."

"He's got that button. I think that's all he wanted."

There was a little silence except for the crackle of the coals. I watched the darting blue and golden flames and suddenly was overtaken by a kind of dream; suppose I was sitting there beside Richard, in some roseate future with no fears, no dread, no doubts, no questions to be answered.

Richard put down his glass and I could hear the tiny click of it on the table. He rose and came to me. "It's late," he said, looking down into the crackling blue and red of the fire. "You'd better get some sleep. God knows what tomorrow holds."

I looked up at him. "But they haven't arrested you yet, I was afraid they'd arrest you as soon as they heard about that fake alibi."

He said thoughtfully, "I think Garrity wants to be sure I get a fair deal. He's a good officer."

I lowered my head and made a fold of my skirt between my fingers; yet my voice shook just a little, betrayingly. "I think they're only waiting for some kind of further evidence — the smallest thing —" I stopped. But he had heard the slight unsteadiness of my voice. I could feel him looking down at me, closely. There was a moment's utter silence, except for the fire crackling. It seemed like an instant suspended in eternity.

Then I felt his hands on mine, drawing me up to him. Then I felt his arms around me. I felt his cheek warm and hard on mine and then he kissed me. It was as if the whole world stopped; as if the room, the house, everybody in it dropped away into space. It was as if nothing else existed but his mouth on mine and his arms holding me — and then he gave a jerky kind of laugh, and put me away from him, at arm's length. The lights of the fire seemed to reflect themselves in his eyes. "I'm sorry. I didn't mean to — No —" He put his head up and his eyes held mine. "No, I'm not sorry. But you must know that —" It was hard for him to find words. He took my hands again but lightly this time. "Dear, I'm older than you — I feel as if I'm a hundred years older. You've known me — really only five days. I'm nobody's prize. I'm a man with a past. And the fact is I may be a man with no future. I'm not the man for you."

I tightened my own hands and couldn't think of a word to say. He smiled a little and said, "Forget that. Will you?" I would never forget it and was about to say so — I think he saw my intention in my eyes — when that miserable Miffy opened the door and came in.

She was wrapped in a pink dressing gown. She couldn't have failed to see the way we were standing, not in each other's arms which I swiftly regretted, but certainly very close to each other. Yet she looked for a moment merely puzzled. "I heard you come in and go to bed an hour ago," she said to me.

"We've just got home," Richard said and released my hands.

"Oh. Is there any news?"

"No," Richard said and looked at the clock on the mantel. "It's late. You girls go to bed." He went to adjust the fire screen.

Miffy followed me up the stairs as if to make sure that I did not return to the library and Richard. I opened my door, sailed in, closed the door and stopped, for Mr. Benni was there. I couldn't see him but I could smell him. I took a great gasp of air and clutched for the doorknob as Mr. Benni stepped out of the bathroom and said softly, "Don't scream. I warn you. Don't make a sound."

When you know that somebody who tells you not to scream places as light a value upon human life as Mr. Benni was purported to place, you don't scream. In fact I don't think I could have so much as squeaked. I could have opened the door though. He said, "Don't touch that door. Move over here by the window."

I did. I couldn't have stopped myself. He came closer. His face was sallow in the light of the bedside lamp; he wore a beige overcoat, turned up around his ears; he wore a hat. He said, "I'm not going to hurt you! Didn't I send you an orchid?"

"Oh —"

"That was to show you that I want to be friendly. Don't scream now because I'm not going to hurt you. Why I could have smothered you, easy as not, the night I got into your hotel suite at Nice. But I didn't, now did I?"

Obviously he hadn't smothered me. I shook my head. He said, "I didn't take anything either. I only looked for the diary. I'm not a thief —"

I swallowed hard and said huskily, "My housekey. You took my housekey —"

"Huh!" His eyebrows went up in surprise; he seemed then to understand me and looked merely scornful. "You mean the key for that old wreck of a house near the park? I didn't need a key for that. This house was a little harder. Had to find a back window and back stairs and even then some woman was on the prowl and poked her head out."

Miffy. "She saw you — an hour ago."

"Oh no, she didn't see me. I was too quick for her. May have heard me shut a door though. But that old house of yours," he said almost as an admonition, "is easy. Too easy. You'll have to get some new and better locks. Easy. What do you think I am to need a key for that?" he asked in a hurt way, which really sounded quite sincere and rather indignant.

"You — Andre Bersche —"

"No!" His sallow face and dark eyes grew hard. "Don't get me wrong. I was in that house, sure. I got what I wanted —"

"A button —" I whispered.

"Never mind that. I got it. But I didn't kill that guy, Bersche. I read about it in the papers. I didn't kill him and I don't know who did. Now I want my money back."

I was vaguely surprised to hear myself speak. "When were you in the house? When did you take that button?"

He eyed me for a moment, as if debating about how much of the truth he could safely tell. Then he said, "Okay, that button's in the bottom of the East River. I'm on my way back home to Italy as soon as — never mind that either, but soon. Sure, I was in that house. Early in the morning. Searched the desk and all the baggage that was heaped up in the hall. Took my time to do it. The button was on top of the desk all along but I didn't find it right away. Some newspaper clippings were on top of it. But I was out and gone long before that guy could have been killed. Believe me, I wouldn't go back to that house —"

I said, "How did you find my room? This room?"

He grinned slyly. "Saw your baggage. Remembered it. What do you take me for? I tell you I'm an expert. Now let's have the money I gave you."

"Did you take the diary?"

He looked scornful again. "No diary can hurt me now. Nothing can hurt me now. Do what you please with that diary. Although — matter of fact, I don't believe there is any diary. Old Orle Hilliard — that is, I mean your father, was a sly old crocodile. I don't think he had any diary at all. I think he was just trying to scare me into giving you some money."

I said in a small voice that it was a mistake; I hadn't known about the letters. He eyed me skeptically. "Maybe not. But I couldn't take a chance. Now then, the money —"

"I can't. I don't have it. It's in a safety deposit box."

His eyes turned cold. His sallow face set itself and seemed to shine a little. "When can you get it out?"

"I can't. I mean, the police want it."

"They're going to try to trace the bills.

They can't," he said with decision. He eyed me for a long moment and then said philosophically, "Well, so I kiss good-bye to five thousand dollars. Can't be helped. Neither can this —" He came lightly toward me. "I really do beg your pardon. It won't hurt much but you can see for yourself I can't have you screaming."

I didn't see any motion of his arm, not really; I had only a confused sense of a kind of flick, a thump somewhere in my consciousness, and of falling and then being caught by something and then nothing at all.

It was really more efficacious than any sleeping pill. Sometime later I had a misty notion of light in my eyes and roused a little. I was decorously placed on the bed and an eiderdown was pulled over me. I did realize that but not how I got there. It was only when I awoke thoroughly and the light was still burning and daylight was coming in the windows that I discovered the sore aching spot on my jaw where Mr. Benni had neatly and ever efficiently silenced me. Mr. Benni had also as neatly, as efficiently disappeared. There was only a trace of his perfume in the room.

It was a perfectly preposterous occurrence. If it hadn't been for that lingering whiff of perfume — and my sore jaw — I couldn't have believed that it had happened. Although the eiderdown, carefully put over me, seemed consistent with Mr. Benni's peculiarly inconsistent character, by rights I should have awakened with a white orchid in my hand. I hoped and believed that I had seen the last of Mr. Benni. His tenacity, and his skill in entering a strange house, literally full of people, talking to me and getting away again without discovery, seemed to me more formidable abilities than I wished to encounter again. I rubbed my eyes and sat up feeling frowzy and wrinkled and was then aware of an odd quality of silence.

It was everywhere. I scarcely needed to go to the windows to see that the snow had begun again, with great white flakes which suggested an enormous reservoir of supply. But the silence was within the house, too. It was as if I were the only person in it, which was, I thought, quite impossible. I hurriedly got out of the clothing in which I had slept. I couldn't remember whether it was hot water or cold water which should be applied to bruises, so I applied both alternately under the shower. When I wrapped my bathrobe around me and emerged into the bedroom, Miffy was there. She had neatly folded up my clothes and hung up the skirt in which I'd slept and she had a newspaper in one hand. As quiet and composed as a beautiful doll, she said, "Richard was arrested. It's in the paper," and handed me the paper.

There it was. The storm usurped the big headlines, which gave me the oddest instant of comfort. There was a picture of Richard and smaller headlines below. There were only a few, brief paragraphs, as if the news of his arrest had barely made this edition of the paper; there would be more later, I knew. But the fact was clear; he had been arrested on suspicion of murder. There was a concise reference to the false alibi.

The police had known the facts of that false alibi for nearly two days; I did not believe that they would have made up their minds to arrest Richard on that score, suddenly, in the middle of night.

Miffy said, "Didn't you hear the police last night?"

"No. When?"

"They came not very long after you'd gone to bed. Half an hour. I heard them and went down. Richard had answered the doorbell. They wanted to search his pockets and he laughed and said go ahead — told me to go back to bed. So I went back up around the corner of the stairs. But I heard them leave and they arrested Richard and took him away."

They must have barely missed Mr. Benni, which did not just then seem to matter. Besides, I hadn't a doubt that Mr. Benni would have made himself invisible somehow.

"But what did they find?"

"I don't know. I couldn't hear much."

"Didn't you hear them say why they were arresting him?"

"No. But it's that false alibi your father gave him, of course. You saw it there in the paper."

"Miffy, did you know about that alibi at the time? I mean that it wasn't true?"

"Why of course. Your father was at the ball long before midnight. I saw him. He couldn't have seen Richard when he said he did."

"Did you — tell anybody at all that the alibi was false?"

"Why, I don't remember really. It wasn't exactly a secret in the family. I'm sure Mother Amberly knew of it. Stella. Wilbur. Why?"

Yes, why? It made no difference really; it seemed to me that Miffy's shining eyes were too flatly blue, too enigmatic, but that didn't make any difference either. I said,

"What are they doing about Richard? Has he got a lawyer?"

"That's why Mother Amberly and Uncle Sisley are out. They've gone to see the family lawyer. But it's New Year's Eve. I mean tonight is New Year's Eve. I don't think he'll be in his office —"

After a moment I said, "Didn't you do anything at all last night? Did you just go back to sleep again without telling anybody about Richard's being arrested?"

"Oh, no! I was very upset. I didn't want to wake Mother Amberly. But I woke up Slade and told him about it. He was very sorry." She leaned forward. "What happened to your jaw? It's all red and blue."

For once I allowed myself to speak the flat truth to Miffy. "I ran into a man's fist."

But she didn't believe me. She merely looked slightly annoyed as if I'd made a silly joke. "I really don't see that anybody can do much for Richard today. New Year's Eve. Snow —" She walked out of the room.

I sat on the edge of the bed and read the newspaper, every word concerning Richard's arrest, and was no wiser. There must have been some development of which I knew nothing; there had to be something new, something to tip the scales against him, which had been very dangerously balanced all along. They had searched his pockets — why? What had they found? There was no hint of it in the terse columns of newsprint.

I knew, of course, what I was going to do and that was see Richard. I didn't know what I could accomplish. I got into clothes and brushed my hair. Looking into the mirror suddenly, I didn't see myself at all but instead saw that dreadful smear of lipstick and shining surface in the little washroom under the stairs of the Pennyroyal Street house. Garrity had seemed to think it indicated that a very cruel and malevolent hand had drawn it there. I didn't see how Garrity could have arrested Richard. But he had.

I went downstairs and Miffy was in the library at Mrs. Amberly's writing desk, calmly and quite openly reading Mrs. Amberly's Christmas cards. She lifted her head. "This is funny. Somebody's been cutting out a word. . . . Coffee's in the kitchen."

I was halfway down to the hall before her mild comment took on meaning and then I ran back up to the library. "Miffy! What card? Where —"

"What are you talking about?"

"The word — the word somebody cut out of it. Where is the card?"

She lifted her eyebrows and waved at the heap of cards and it was, as we might have suspected, the first word of the Christmas carol that everybody, sometime during the Christmas season, sang and listened to over and over again. I wondered why it hadn't occurred to any of us. "Silent night" the card read, but there was a neat space cut out which had contained the word *silent*, the word in the message enclosed with two thousand dollars and slid into the pocket of my coat. "Silent more to came."

Miffy said, "What's the matter with you? You look queer."

I took the card and ran to the telephone and then stopped, feeling as if I'd managed to stop myself just before I plunged off a cliff, for this wasn't evidence which would help Richard. It was very much more likely to hurt him; Richard had access to those Christmas cards. So had Slade. So had Uncle Sisley. So had — why, Wilbur, of course. And Stella and Mrs. Amberly and Miffy. I had access to them myself.

16

I put the mutilated card in the pocket of my skirt and went downstairs. I got myself coffee, which was still hot. Slade — why? Uncle Sisley — why? Wilbur — why? Each could have put the money in my coat pocket. But they all had had alibis for the time of Cecile's murder. Certainly the police had cleared each of them — Stella and Mrs. Amberly and Miffy, too.

And there was the gun, which must have been safely hidden all those months since Cecile's murder. The house had been searched. Stella's house had been searched; the police had searched minutely for that gun. Yet it had remained hidden until Andre had to be killed. So where had it been? Snow was covering with new whiteness the soot-flecked shapes in the garden outside the French doors, and Wilbur came plowing through them.

Whoever had cut the word "silent" out of that card was afraid of me and afraid of the diary. Was it Wilbur? I drank some more coffee and went to unlatch one of the doors as Wilbur pounded on the glass. He surged into the room, bringing cold and snow with him. "I've got a job for you. Just heard about it. They want an interview. I'll take you now. Bank closes at noon today so hurry up and get your coat on." He seized my arm and hoisted me along into the hall, talking at the top of his enormous lungs as he went. "Chance of a lifetime for you. Girl who had this job got married last night — one of those drunken Christmas parties, if you ask me — anyway she phoned this morning and there's the vacant job. Right up your alley. Foreign languages — Stella said your French is all right. How's your Italian? Come on, where's your coat? We've got to get there before that department closes —"

I didn't dig in my heels — the floor was too hard — but I skidded to a stop. "What about Richard? Why did they arrest him?"

Wilbur glared down at me as if I myself had arrested Richard. "Don't you know?"

"Only what's in the paper."

"I haven't had time to see the paper." He adjusted his neat gray scarf below his neat gray overcoat, so a rim of white collar showed. "I heard it over the early radio news. Went right away to see Richard — he was still at the precinct station where he was booked —"

"Why did they arrest him?"

He jerked open the closet door and shouted. Wilbur never spoke in a normal voice. "Jewelry. Some of Cecile's jewelry turned up last night. Pawnbroker reported it. One of his clerks had taken it in. They've all had the description ever since Cecile was killed — the pawnbrokers, I mean. This pawnbroker was out at a party, stopped in at his shop late just to check on the safe and locks, and found the jewelry. Diamond bracelet. Clerk had loaned two thousand on it —"

"Two thousand —"

Wilbur dug out my coat. "This one yours? The police came to talk to Richard, found the pawnbroker's ticket on him —"

"They couldn't have!"

"In his overcoat pocket. Same thing."

And the same trick, I thought. The roll of bills in my coat pocket; a pawnbroker's ticket in Richard's coat. A word cut from a Christmas card. All of it in that house. Slade? Wilbur? Uncle Sisley?

Wilbur boomed. "They haven't got a description of whoever pawned that bracelet from the clerk yet. He's gone up in the country somewhere, likely snowed in. Here, put your coat on —"

"Is that all the evidence they have?"

"Good God, it's enough! I talked to Richard for only a few minutes. Mrs. Amberly is getting their lawyer for him. He'll be arraigned this morning. That's all I know. Come on. You'll have to have a job, you know, no matter what happens."

Well, that was right. It was indeed a solid fact in a world that seemed to spin out of orbit. Miffy came softly down the stairs and Wilbur looked up at her. "Police been here yet this morning?" He shouted as if she were a mile or two away.

Miffy shook her head. "They were here last night. They arrested Richard —"

Wilbur turned purple. "Don't I know it! Well, anyway the police will be here with a search warrant. Sure to. The rest of that jewelry's got to be somewhere and they've got to find it. They seem to think that gun has been right here in the house, all the time —"

"Why?" I cried. "Why here in the house? Who —"

"Richard hid it, of course. That's what they think. Bracelet — gun — that darn diary of your father's. Oh, well, come on, if you want that job. I may be out of a job myself any minute. Banks don't like murder."

We banged out the door and into the

snow. We plowed through the snow, or rather Wilbur's enormous hand lifted me along through it. We took the subway. On the stairs going down to the platform it occurred to me how very easy it would be for Wilbur to knock me in the head or throttle me or even shoot me — where was the gun by now? — and nobody would be the wiser, for there were almost no other people on the stairs, and only one or two on the platform. There was a handful of passengers in the car we entered; melted puddles of snow on the floor gave evidence of earlier passengers.

Wilbur? Uncle Sisley? Slade? I was beginning to cross Wilbur off that dreadful little list, mainly because his behavior was so perfectly natural, so very Wilburish.

He had certainly offered me neither blood money — assuming that the fifth letter had gone to him — or any sort of harm. Not yet. But I wasn't afraid of Wilbur. Surely I would have been afraid of him, some sense would have warned me, if he had been in fact a murderer. Of course, that had no logic, no value whatever as a basis of proof of anything at all.

Miffy wouldn't have shown me that card if she had cut out the word *silent* and stuck it to a note and put the note in with two thousand dollars. Two thousand dollars for Cecile's diamond bracelet, I recalled.

And then I said to Wilbur, "When is Richard supposed to have gone to the pawn-broker's?"

"Huh?" He turned a startled face toward me. "I don't know." His eyes narrowed. "Why?"

"I was with him almost all day yesterday. He couldn't have gone then."

He thought it over; the train shot on through darkness and lights of stations and glimmering pale tunnel lights and jerked to a stop. He got up, tugging me after him. "Our station. We'll tell the police that. I'll take you to see Garrity after you've had your interview."

We argued all the way up the steps. Wilbur went like a demon and I was out of breath trying to keep up, although he had his huge hand gripped around my arm, pulling me with him. I wanted to see Richard — to see Garrity — at once. Wilbur said no, I had to have a job, didn't I?

I had a notion he would have taken my hair and dragged me if I had put up further resistance. We went into a vast, new building, crossed a deeply carpeted space and entered an elevator which moved so gently that I scarcely knew it had moved until the doors slid open and we were in another corridor, also deeply carpeted. Wilbur looked down at me, told me in a gusty whisper to straighten my beret and led me into a huge office. A man who called Wilbur by his first name said how do you do to me, and called somebody else, who began to speak to me in rapid French about New Year's customs in New York and France; he then spoke to me in Italian, engaging me in conversation about the mosaics in Italian churches, of which I knew nothing; however, I must have replied lucidly enough, for he then nodded at the man behind the desk and I was hired. The man behind the desk told me what my salary would be and I said thank you; this man walked to the elevator with us and told Wilbur in a funereal tone that he was terribly sorry to read the papers that morning and Wilbur turned scarlet and said of course it was all a mistake, the lawyers were working on it. We got into the elevator.

Wilbur said, "Well, now you've got a job. Good salary, too."

I had no recollection what the salary was to be but I didn't dare tell Wilbur that. I said, "Now we'll see Richard."

By chance we got a taxi outside the great revolving door. He took me to the precinct station, not the one where I had spent hours the night Andre was found but another one, uptown. "Richard was arrested on suspicion of Cecile's murder," he said shortly. "It was in this precinct —"

Lieutenant Garrity was not there; the man at the desk, whom Wilbur called Sergeant, said he didn't know when Lieutenant Garrity would be in but he'd try to reach him. After some other talk Wilbur came back to me where I stood near the door and another hot and hissing radiator. "Can you wait for him?"

"Richard —"

"Richard isn't here. They took him to Criminal Court. If you want to see Garrity, he'll be here. Wait for him. Tell him what you told me. He may not believe you," said Wilbur encouragingly, "but tell him." At which he departed, wrapping his neat gray scarf closely around his neat white collar again, and took the taxi which I then realized he had prudently kept waiting, for I could see him from the window above the radiator.

I wanted to see Richard. But I must talk to Garrity. So I waited and the snow fell in utter white silence and people came in and out again, letting gusts of cold air drift through the room; the sergeant talked over the telephone constantly in a low and rather monotonous voice.

There was a clock above the desk; noon came and the sergeant shouted "Happy New Year" to somebody on the telephone.

And of course when the hands of that big clock had crawled around another twelve hours it would be the New Year, with parties and champagne bottles popping and dance orchestras playing Auld Lang Syne and everybody kissing everybody else — and a murderer who had got off free, who had contrived to put Richard in his place. It was someone who knew where the rest of that jewelry was, someone who had had — and still had perhaps — the gun that killed Cecile, someone who could come and go in the Amberly house.

It was too hot near the radiator and when I slid out of my coat I was too cold. When Garrity came at last, his face red from the cold, swishing through the door, I did what I had determined not to do, I showed him the mutilated Christmas card.

He had been expecting me; when he entered he said to the desk sergeant, "Where is the young lady?" and the desk sergeant nodded at me, so one of those telephone conversations in that dull monotone had related to me. Garrity nodded briskly and led me into a small room, again with a table and some straight chairs. And I pulled out the card then and there, gave it to him and told him all about it; I told him all about Mr. Benni's visit; I told him that Mr. Benni had said he needed, and had, no key with which to effect an entrance into the Gramercy Park house; I reminded him that the message with the word *silent* cut from the Christmas card in it had accompanied the two thousand dollars and I told him that Richard could not have gone to a pawnbroker the day before because there hadn't been time.

He muttered rather bitterly at this point that Amberly seemed to have an alibi whenever he wanted one. He did admit, however, that he did not have a firm identification of Richard from the pawnbroker's clerk and since they had not yet succeeded in finding the clerk they would simply have to wait for an identification until they could find him. He muttered again then, rather bitterly, saying that everybody in the city seemed to have a holiday, everybody except policemen.

When I asked how they could hold Richard — when the clerk failed to identify him, that would constitute false arrest — he looked at me and shook his head. "We've got a pawnbroker's ticket for a piece of jewelry which was connected with a murder. The ticket was in Amberly's pocket. It was Amberly's wife who was murdered. He had plenty of time that night to hide that jewelry and the gun somewhere. He knew that Bersche could have found the diary. He also lied; he deliberately gave false evidence and obstructed investigation. What else could I do but arrest him?"

"What has he been charged with?"

He looked a little tired. "He was arraigned in Criminal Court this morning. I gave a short affidavit to the effect that I had arrested him on suspicion of murder. The judge ordered him held on a hundred thousand dollars' bail. He's now in the Tombs."

"Oh — no —"

"He'll have legal representation, don't worry about that. It's been held up a little owing to the storm, too. I gather that the family lawyer lives over in New Jersey and is there with the flu today. The roads are all but impassable. Amberly will be treated fairly, don't think he won't be. The point is that somebody suddenly got hold of that bracelet and pawned it. Somebody put money and a note in your coat pocket. Somebody turned up with a gun that's been missing since Cecile's murder. Doesn't it look to you as if that somebody is free to come and go in the Amberly house? How many people can do that?" He didn't wait for an answer. He put the mutilated Christmas card in his pocket and said the experts would take a look at it. He then took some time to tell me of the investigation of Cecile's murder and the search for the jewelry and the gun. "Amberly didn't have the gun or the jewelry that night when he reported the murder. I want to know where he hid them —"

"Where someone hid them," I said.

"All right — someone. Neither gun nor jewelry was in that house after the murder, believe me. It was searched minutely. Sisley Todd did not arrive until we had things organized; he was searched on entering; same with young Slade Bell. He really was at the ball — he could have left it, so could your father or anyone else have left the ball for a long enough time to go to the Amberly house and kill Cecile and then return to the ball — but nobody could find any proof that anybody had done that. Slade was searched when he returned to the Amberly house; no gun, no jewelry, and no opportunity to dispose of them. He went straight from the ball with a couple of his friends to a bar. Both of the men he was with swore that Slade had gone to the washroom and taken off his coat; he simply did not have either gun or jewelry; they'd have made quite a bulge in any pocket."

I said, "He could have left them in a checkroom. Grand Central — somewhere."

The flicker of a rather tired smile touched his eyes. "You don't like Slade."

"No, I don't. But still there's Uncle Sisley and —"

"Sisley Todd has his letters. I think that's your father's only threat to him. Of course, Wilbur Cullen has access to the house, too. We covered him at the time. We covered everybody minutely, believe me we did. The gun and the jewelry were not in the house immediately after Cecile's murder. But we've now got a notion as to where they were hidden."

"*Where?*" I cried. "*Where?*"

He seemed to feel that he had said too much. He did not reply; he rose as if to suggest that I leave but then said abruptly, "I'd like to know what happened at that ball, though. Your father saved only that one day's clippings. There were hundreds of clippings he could have saved but he saved only the clippings with an account of the ball on the other side of the paper. So why? What happened at the ball which suggested to your father that false alibi? I think he learned something, saw something, talked to somebody —"

"He talked to Miffy. She said so."

"What did she say about it?"

"Well, only that. Nothing else really."

He thought that over and said he'd get me a taxi. I tried a sort of last-ditch argument. "But don't you see? Richard wouldn't have had to sell some of the jewelry to get that two thousand dollars. All he had to do was write a check —"

Garrity shook his head a little pityingly. "And have the canceled check turn up to be explained. Better fasten your coat."

He took me kindly to a taxi.

"Where is the Tombs?" I asked him.

"Centre Street with the Criminal Courts Building. You're going to see Amberly."

"If they'll let me see him."

"Oh, you can see him."

"But you don't want me to."

"Not just now — no."

"Why not?"

His green eyes flickered once but his reply was candid. "For one thing, if they've managed to dig his lawyer out of a snowbank, the lawyer is with him now. They'll have to talk. They'll try to dig up bail, too. I just think it would be better for you to wait a little. But if you've got to see him now, go ahead."

Garrity could be very convincing; perhaps it was the Irish in him. He also had a fund of common sense and kindness. He said firmly, "There is nothing you can do now," gave the taxidriver the Amberly address and ushered me into the taxi. Then he leaned into it and said, "By the way, where is the sister-in-law? Young Mrs. Amberly. My men said she had gone out this morning before they got to the house with a search warrant. Do you know anything about it?"

"She was there when I left," I said. He closed the taxi door and I had accomplished nothing. But Garrity was right; I could have accomplished nothing by hurtling off to the Tombs, either.

When I reached the Amberly house Stella came to the door. "Oh, it's you. Did you get the job? Oh, Fran, what are we going to do! Mother's not home yet. Miffy's gone, too. The police have been here —" The snow was sifting in; I closed the door and Stella went on, "Nobody was here. They had to come to my house and they asked me to let them in here. They had a search warrant. I looked at it and that was really what it was. So I had to come here — I've got a key of course — and I had to let them search the house. And I really — oh, I hope Wilbur will say it was all right for me to let the police search the house."

"Wilbur couldn't have stopped them." Stella was pink-cheeked and her eyes were dark with distress. "Besides, he said something to me about the police probably getting a search warrant to look for the jewels again. He'll think it's all right." I wondered privately whether or not Wilbur beat Stella; yet I was sure he wouldn't do that for if he wasn't restrained from such vigorous measures by affection for Stella, his business position would restrain him. Then I felt ashamed for Wilbur had been indeed very kind to me only that morning.

Stella said, "You'd better take off your coat. I fixed some sandwiches. Just in case somebody came home to eat them. They're on the dining-room table. But I've really got to go home. It does seem silly of Miffy to go off like that without telling anybody. We were all going to a fancy-dress ball tonight. New Year's Eve, you know. Of course, I phoned yesterday and regretted for all of us. It wouldn't have done for any of us to go to a ball as things are. So Miffy must have simply gone somewhere for the whole week end."

It was not news to me that Miffy wasn't at home; Garrity had told me that, but it did seem remarkable that she'd gone for a festive week end.

I said, "Don't you know where she went?"

Stella shrugged. "Not the faintest idea. But she took some clothes. I went through the house with the police, you know. Some of her clothes are gone. So she must have taken a bag —"

"Stella!" A really dreadful notion seemed to fly out from the silent and empty house like a bat which had been hovering there for many months. "Stella, I've got to ask you. It's dreadful, but do you think that Miffy — I mean Cecile —"

"You don't have to explain," Stella said, white-faced all at once but steady. "We thought of everything at the time. Wilbur thought of that. Miffy didn't like Cecile. She wanted to marry Richard, you see. After Henry died. She still wants to but — no, she couldn't have killed Cecile. She wouldn't have, not like that. And she couldn't have got Slade to do it for her," Stella said, still white-faced and still steady. "Wilbur thought of that, too. There's a good reason. Miffy would do anything for Slade. But Slade wouldn't do anything for Miffy."

I believed her. I believed her so thoroughly that the ugly fancy which had come to me was quite dispelled.

She said, "Miffy should have left a note though. She just forgot. It's like her. Perhaps she told Mother she was going away and Mother didn't happen to speak about it to me. But then Miffy is — well, that's the way she is."

We were still in a kind of stream of frankness. "She showed me the room where it happened," I said. "Cecile's room. I didn't really want to see it, yet — yet I suppose I did —"

"Well, of course, you must know that Miffy doesn't like you. She's afraid of you," Stella said with devastating simplicity. "She thinks Richard likes you too well." She looked steadily at me for a moment and added, "So she showed you Cecile's room. She was trying to frighten you. Scare you away."

"No, Stella, she couldn't have thought that *that* would" — I used Stella's words — "scare me away from Richard."

Stella nodded firmly. "Oh, yes she could. She's very childish in some ways, you know. The fact is — you must have seen it — Miffy is a very stupid woman. She's beautiful and that's it. Henry knew; he always covered for her, treated her like an indulged child. She's just plain dumb," said Stella in an exasperated way. "That's the trouble. She can't see anything but something she wants. She knows what she wants all right and she goes after it. She thought that you'd think how horrible Cecile's murder was — and it was horrible. She'd show you the very room where it happened and talk about it until you couldn't stand the thought of it or the house or Richard even and you'd leave. That's why she did it," Stella said again with convincing simplicity. "That's the way she — I can't say thinks, she doesn't think, she simply acts. It makes her," said Stella unexpectedly, "a rather dangerous person."

I suddenly remembered Miffy saying, in a curiously threatening yet very soft and gentle way, that Stella meddled. I said, "Have you ever quarreled with Miffy?"

"Oh no." Stella did not resent the question, which I had no right to ask. "No. Not a quarrel exactly. I just don't want her to marry Rich and she knows it." She glanced around as if the silence of the house troubled her and said to me, "It's perfectly — well, you know, safe. I mean, there's nobody at all in the house. The police went all over it. They even looked — searched everything in Cecile's room. They were there a long time. I think they took pictures of something. It was like the night she was killed," Stella said steadily, but with an effort, and got into her coat. I went with her to the French doors and watched her plunge through the snow; it was snowing so hard by then that her figure became indistinct even before she reached her own gate. I then sat down and ate some sandwiches.

The house began to assert its character, and perhaps its memories, the way a house does when it is empty. Murder had walked in that house. It had crept down from Cecile's room upstairs. I wouldn't think about that; I'd build up the fire so when Mrs. Amberly and Uncle Sisley returned there'd be at least some warmth and cheer. I went back into the hall, and heard my footsteps, light and clear on the black and white marble squares. The door of the elevator stood open; a small light inside it showed the empty cage. I had a dim impression that the elevator had stood there, its door open, while Stella and I talked with such desperate candor of Miffy and Cecile.

A little bench covered with red leather stood at the back of the small cage, below a large mirror. In the dusky corner, there was a package. It was a large package wrapped in white paper. It was far too big to hold any more money intended to keep me quiet. Yet I remembered the deceiving white orchid on the package Mr. Benni had sent me and I had to see. I went into the elevator and bent over the far corner, peering through the dim light. It was a dress box, long and wide. It was addressed to Mrs. Henry Amberly. I took a long breath. So it was merely some dress which Miffy had ordered and it had been delivered probably after she had gone.

As I straightened up I felt a swish of movement behind me. By the time I could whirl around, the door of the elevator was closing and I was too late to stop it. It closed completely and the elevator started slyly upward.

It hadn't gone far when it stopped with a quiet but determined little lurch. There it stayed. Somebody was in the house; somebody had leaned into the elevator and punched one of the buttons set in the little panel. I couldn't have done it myself.

Somebody was in the house — yet Richard had told me that sometimes the elevator stuck. It obviously had its whims. Perhaps I had somehow jolted some connection. It didn't seem likely. But it didn't seem likely, either, that anybody could have crept up so close to me without my sensing it.

Besides, why would anybody do just that? An answer came to me; if anyone wanted to search my handbag or my room in the hope of finding the diary, an elevator known for getting stuck might give an opportunity for holding me a prisoner until someone came to release me.

There was a button painted red, which was an alarm button. There was nothing to be gained by punching that alarm button; whoever was in the house and stealthily shut me in the elevator was not at all likely to pay any attention to an alarm button — if anybody was in the house.

I then began to feel that in fact I was safer there than I could have been anywhere else. It is not nice to be caught in an elevator; I had an uneasy feeling that it might suddenly give up and plunge to the bottom of the shaft — or, for that matter, get a new lease on life and shoot to the roof. But at least for the moment it seemed quite steady and safe. I only had to wait and listen for Mrs. Amberly or Uncle Sisley to return. I couldn't hear a thing except the loud thudding of my own pulses. I was there an hour before Slade came and released me.

17

During that hour my thoughts naturally had raced but had raced in circles. The only sensible course that suggested itself was not sensible at all and that concerned the diary. The diary was still elusive; if the murderer still did not have the diary, he still wanted it. So suppose I made myself a target. Suppose I made myself a bait, rather on the principle of staking out some small animal to draw a tiger out of the jungle. Suppose, in short, I proclaimed to everybody that I had the diary and then waited to find out who would try to get that diary.

It seemed a very sensible thing to do, one which assured success although it took some courage. I felt a wave of triumphant excitement almost as if it had been done, before I flattened down again. The truth was that I did not have that kind of courage. My mouth was already dry from nothing else than fear at the very idea that someone might have crept up behind me and shut me in the elevator; it was plain, humiliating, devastating fear which made me prickle and feel hot and cold at the same time. I wished I had a cigarette. There still was not a sound in the house.

It occurred to me then that in fact nobody had tried to search me or my room for the diary. So, I reasoned, it seemed likely that Andre's murderer had taken it. Therefore, I told myself, I was in no real danger. Perhaps I had imagined a whisper of movement and a flick of the elevator button. Once I was sure that I heard the telephone ring; if so, it stopped.

Sometime during that hour, waiting, my eyes fell upon the label of the dress box. I puzzled over it a little, for it wasn't any Fifth Avenue store that I knew; it didn't have the label of any famous couturier, which somehow I'd have expected it to have, for Miffy's dresses were never bought off a hanger. Costumier. I looked at the word absently for some time before I remembered the fancy-dress ball. This then was in all probability the costume Miffy had intended to wear; somehow I thought of enormous skirts and a white wig, perhaps of the period of high, wide and handsome days of the French court; I could see how Miffy's beauty would bloom in such a costume; it was a very large dress box; it had to hold enormously wide skirts.

I thought of Richard, too, of course during that long hour, and the moment in the library, with the fire crackling and all the rest of the world vanished into limbo. It seemed to me that perhaps something very important to me and to Richard had been about to happen, something that might have lasted for the rest of our lives. But Miffy had stopped it. Now, with Richard arrested and perhaps to be charged with murder, anything could happen; things could change; there might be a barrier between us always.

Slade released me. I heard the outside door bang and it was the only sound I had heard for that entire hour, apart from the phone. I heard his footsteps, loud on the marble floor of the hall only a little below me. I heard him whistling Auld Lang Syne, rather ahead of time, for it was nowhere near midnight. Then there was a kind of genteel click and buzz from the bell, the elevator tamely recovered from its indisposition, gave a little sigh and moved down again. The door opened and Slade saw me.

We stared. "What are you doing there?"

I got out of the cage as fast as I could. "It stuck."

"Oh." His eyes weren't dancing as I'd have somehow expected. He said, "Why, it must have given you a scare. It does that sometimes."

He was wearing an overcoat and a scarf, which he unwrapped. "You should have pushed the alarm button. It rings in the basement. Somebody would have heard it and got you out. But sometimes it works, as it did just now, when somebody pushes the hall button beside the elevator."

Of all the people in the house who might have sent me up in that elevator, hoping it would stick and merely as a childish but malicious kind of joke, I would have chosen Slade as being the most likely to do just such a thing. I remembered a martini spilled on my skirt and a cigarette burn in my sleeve. Accident? Or a basically malicious intent to annoy me, the stranger, who had arrived with Richard? Miffy considered Richard her own exclusive property. Slade would have defended Miffy's claims in his own interests, if for no other reason, for obviously he depended upon Miffy's financial help. Yet if someone had pressed the elevator button for an uglier purpose than a joke, then there had been no further effort to carry out his plan.

Slade said, "Were you just going to sit there until somebody came?"

"Yes —"

His eyes then began to dance. "Didn't you even try to get out?"

"There's nobody here. They've gone to talk to the lawyer about Richard."

"Oh. Well, the family lawyer won't be in his office this afternoon. I think he lives in Maplewood. They've got a hard trip in this snow. Where's Miffy?"

"Gone. She took some clothes with her."

"Miffy!" He gave me a bright, blank look. "Oh, no, she can't have — look here, you'd better sit down for a minute. It's not much fun being stuck in an elevator. And in an empty house at that."

I sat down.

Slade said kindly, "Do you want a drink? Some brandy —"

"No, thank you. I'm just so glad to be out of that elevator."

He glanced inside it, frowned, and went to look at the dress box. His face under the dim light in the cage looked older and rather pallid. But then it occurred to me that he, like Miffy, must be older than he looked. He put up his head and came back and looked very young and boyish again. "It's the fancy dress Miffy ordered. There is to be a ball tonight. We were invited. Sure you don't want a drink of some kind? You look a little pale."

I shook my head. I would never have

thought that I'd be thankful to see Slade Bell and to talk to him but I was. He eyed me — for once it struck me — rather soberly and intently. "See here," he said suddenly, "why can't we be friends?"

That left me with no answer.

He said, "You haven't liked me — you've had reason not to like me — I'll admit —"

I had to be fair. "I don't think you meant to spill the martini. Or burn my dress with the cigarette."

"Oh," he said and thought for a moment, his eyes on mine. "Well — that's very nice of you. Why do you say that?"

"Why, because — because it would be so childish on your part. So —"

He interrupted. "I really want to be your friend, you know. I'd like to let bygones be bygones and I'll promise — oh," he laughed brightly, "anything you like. Just give me time," he said lightly and laughed again.

I made a rather stupid effort to be bright and light, too. I was thinking really of whether or not Slade had murdered Andre and had murdered Cecile and deciding that he hadn't. The same reason obtained which had convinced me that Wilbur was not the murderer; Slade had every opportunity in the world to choke the diary, or my life for that matter, out of me, and he made no attempt to do so. I said, "That sounds like a bribe."

It then occurred to me that that was exactly what it sounded like. Some other things occurred to me, too; flashing like beads stringing themselves swiftly together. My father could have seen Slade at the ball and for some reason had believed that Slade at least knew something of Cecile's murder; he therefore offered an alibi to Richard. It would be easy for somebody at the ball to leave it for a time and return; nobody can keep his eyes on anybody else all the time at a ball where there are hundreds of guests. A quarrel between Slade and Cecile, a motive for murder, was something I could make no guess about, but jewelry had been taken and Slade was living on a moderate salary and he had obviously expensive tastes.

Slade could have followed me from the Amberly house the night I went into the drugstore and telephoned to Andre; Slade could have listened from the next booth; Slade could have heard my words, which would certainly have convinced any listener that Andre had the diary; Slade could have heard me repeat the time and place of my appointment with Andre. Slade could have got the housekey from my handbag; nothing would have been easier than for somebody in the house to get that key.

Slade could have reached the Gramercy Park house before me; in time to see — and kill Andre — and then go through his pockets in search of the diary. Slade could have returned to the Amberly house, getting a chance taxi perhaps, in time to open the door later for me. I had lingered, in the Lexington Avenue drugstore, trying to telephone to Andre; I had walked to the subway; I had walked across from Lexington. Yes, he'd have had time to have been in the Gramercy Park house, to have started down the stairs when he was at last convinced that I must have gone, and then have arrived at the Amberly house before I arrived and opened the door — his cheeks red not from amusement at seeing me, struggling with the snow and cold, but from having been in the cold himself.

Slade, not Miffy, could have stealthily opened the door to the tiny study off the dining room — and have known that Mr. Hatever gave me a diary. He wouldn't have known that it was not the right diary; he'd have known only that it was a diary. He could have crept up behind me and pushed the elevator button and while I was in the cage he could have searched my room for the diary. That was supposition; no proof for it.

But Slade could have had the jewelry and the gun that killed Cecile in his possession all that time; Slade could have pawned the bracelet and Slade could have slid the two thousand dollars into my coat pocket, along with a message including a word cut from a Christmas card, which lay on the desk in the library.

Slade could have made that ugly ghost of a likeness to Cecile on the mirror in the washroom of the Pennyroyal Street house. Why? To incriminate Richard, I thought; he would have known that the slug from the gun would be identified as having come from the same gun that had killed Cecile. So he had made that ghostly picture, for only somebody who had hated Cecile could have made it. Only somebody who hated Cecile would have killed her. That was the logic behind the police interest in Richard; he had had cause to hate her.

It was like Slade, somehow, the drawing on the mirror; it was like the martini, spilled on my skirt; the cigarette burning my sleeve. Even the swiftness with which these speculations shot together was just then convincing to me. I don't think that more than a second or two had passed while I traveled that careening path of thought. Slade was watching me, half smiling.

He said pleasantly, "But I do want to be friends."

Mr. Benni had said that; he had said almost plaintively, "But I wanted to show you I was friendly; I sent you an orchid." I said to Slade, "The fifth letter went to you!"

And then I was terrified; I heard my own words and couldn't believe that I had said them. I was too frozen even to move, to try to cover them, to do anything but stare at Slade as if he were a snake and I some fool bird. I couldn't see anything in his blue eyes; his smile was just a smile and hadn't changed. He said, "What letter?"

I could not possibly have answered him, even if words had come into my mind, as they didn't. I realized only that I had done what, during that hour in the elevator, I had resolved not to do; I had staked myself out as a bait.

I hadn't said that I had the diary but I had accused Slade of receiving one of those letters; it amounted to the same thing. If Slade were the tiger, then he would spring as any prowling tiger would spring upon some tethered animal. The murderer of Cecile and the murderer of Andre wouldn't hesitate; Richard had said that; he would only be afraid of being caught. Slade would only be afraid of being caught and I was the threat. I had staked myself out, yes; but if Slade were the tiger no one would ever know.

I actually wondered, wildly, how he would do it. It seemed a pity that I couldn't make my mouth work and tell him — tell him what? Anything, I didn't care; tell him there was no diary, tell him anything.

Slade said, "See here, don't faint. I'll get you a drink —" He started for the kitchen.

This was my chance to get away, out the front door, anywhere. He turned at the dining-room door. "You do look very white. Being shut up in an elevator all that time was frightening. Relax."

I could see him in the dining room. I slid cautiously out of the chair and over to my coat and handbag which still lay on another chair. I kept an eye on the dining-room door while I plunged my hand into my handbag. The diary Mr. Hatever had given me was still there and so was the office address book. I clicked my handbag shut and slid back again into the chair. Slade had had all the opportunity there was to open my handbag and find the black book labeled diary if he had wanted it. He hadn't. I leaned out to watch Slade and I could see him at the buffet. He didn't get a thing, no knife, I thought wildly again, nothing. He came back with the small glass. "Better take it neat," he said and handed it to me and watched while I drank it and didn't make a move or say a word. My whole fabric of suspicion collapsed like a tent when the ropes are pulled away.

He said, "You'll feel better in a minute. What letter were you talking about?"

I said, never mind, I'd go upstairs and lie down. I said something, anything, and took my handbag with the diary that meant nothing and went up to the library. There I sat down and listened. Presently I heard the hum of the elevator; it passed the second floor and went on. If Slade had wanted the diary he had had a chance to get a diary, not the right one but a diary. If he'd decided to kill me, too, he had had a chance. Wilbur had had a chance that morning, on the subway stairs. I hadn't really meant to make a bait of myself but it had happened. Perhaps without knowing it I had made a bait of myself for someone else.

It seemed to me that I could hear Slade whistling again off in some room upstairs. There was not another sound in the house. I went down to the hall again, my knees still feeling a little unsteady. I had a notion that Slade was dressing to go out and Stella's house and Stella's company were infinitely preferable to that empty and echoing house where once, on an April night, murder had been done.

I snatched up my coat, forgot to put anything over my head, and went out through the dining room and the French doors. There was a light in Stella's house. I plunged through the drifted snow of the garden and through the gate and went to the back door. I found a bell and rang.

After a long time a woman peered out through the glass, saw me, and opened the door. "Why, you're the Madam's friend — the young lady at the Amberly house," she said. "Come in —" She shut the door behind me and I asked for Stella.

Stella was not at home; Mr. and Mrs. Cullen had gone to a New Year's cocktail party. "It's some sort of business party," she said. "They felt they had to go." Stella's house still seemed safer than the Amberly house. I asked if I could stay for a while in the hope that Mrs. Cullen would return and the cook said, well, yes, of course, except — the fact was that she herself had planned to go out to a New Year's party.

"But you'd better come in, Miss Hilliard, and I'll get you some hot soup. Madam told me that you had nobody to cook dinner at the Amberlys' tonight. Seems all the caterers are busy."

We went through an entry into a bright kitchen. She bustled around cheerfully; it hadn't occurred to me that that night the usual team of women had not arrived in the Amberly kitchen. The cook gave me soup and coffee and then, apologizing, bustled away.

After a while I got up and went to the back door again. From there I could see the Amberly house. At least I could see the fourth floor and Cecile's windows, which streamed out lights into the snow and darkness. The police were there, again! They had searched Cecile's room. They had taken more pictures of it. Now they had returned and I thought perhaps Richard was with them.

I flung my coat around me and went out into the snow. The lights from Cecile's windows shone more brightly as I stumbled and slid across the snowy garden. The French door was still unlocked as I had left it. The hall was quiet; nobody was there. They were all upstairs then, in the blue room where Cecile had struggled and died. The elevator stood, its door open.

It had stuck once that day; it wouldn't be likely to stick again so soon, I thought, as I entered it and pressed the fourth-floor button. The door slid across and this time the elevator rumbled gently but smoothly upward. The white dress box was gone. It then occurred to me that perhaps Miffy had returned. Perhaps it was Miffy in that fourth-floor room.

The elevator stopped and the door opened. No one at all was there. The light from the blue room came in to the hall and lay at my feet like a path. Something glimmered in that path. A tiny fleck of red lay on the floor; a tiny fleck of yellow lay close to it. A tiny trail of colored dots, yellow and green and red and blue, led into the room from which the lights streamed; they were confetti.

I bent over to look, puzzled. I went on, following the little spots of color, drawn by them and the light into Cecile's room, where there were only the blues of draperies and rug and the whiteness of dust sheets. There were no policemen there; Richard was not there. Nobody was there. Rather oddly the cushion for the little blue chair had been apparently hurled to the floor and it still lay there.

I picked up the small, drunken-looking cushion; I started to replace it in the chair and saw a peculiar thing, nothing much but peculiar, for it was a kind of depression, down in the chair between the covered spring seat and the padded arm of the chair. It looked as if something had lain there, pressing into the upholstery for rather a long time.

A small thing it must have been, about the size of a gun of small caliber. There was not a sharp outline. It was rather like the drawing of Cecile on the mirror; only the suggestion was there but it was a strong suggestion. The gun — and perhaps the jewels — would have made just such an impression.

They couldn't have been there in that chair, in that room, the night of Cecile's murder. The police had searched the house minutely, at once. They could have been put there later; something had been there and it had to have been there for some time, pressing into the padding and upholstery long enough to make that indelible mark.

The trail of confetti lay in tiny bright specks on the blue rug, beckoning me, as if it were trying to say, come and look, come and look. The trail led straight across the room to the balcony door, which was a little open, letting in wind and snow. I leaned over to scrutinize the confetti and that was what it was, no mistake about it.

There was a movement, the barest rustle of sound behind me and I whirled around. I had been mistaken about the disappearance of all the Santa Clauses on Christmas day. A Santa Claus, bulging in red and white, with a mass of white beard and white hair, stood in the doorway and looked at me.

He could have been anyone. Only the eyes twinkling out of that mass of curling white hair could have been identifiable but they twinkled so strangely that they were not. He wore huge white cotton gloves. The padding disguised his figure; the bulky red suit showed no identifying lines, not even of his height or breadth. He could have been Miffy, he could have been Wilbur, he could have been anybody. I could barely see the motion of lips behind the mass of white beard. "Where's the diary?"

I shook my head. That was all I could do. I was pressing close against the balcony door, instinctively trying to get away, but there was no escape, for the bulky red figure with its white hair and sparkling eyes stood in the doorway.

"I've searched your room. I did it while you were in the elevator. I couldn't find it. Where is it?"

The voice was a kind of falsetto which gave me a flicker of courage because it indicated a desire to keep the identity of the Santa Claus a secret from me. The disguise itself argued a degree of safety for me, too, for if he had intended any harm, if he had intended to murder me, he wouldn't have cared whether or not I knew his identity. He'd have felt himself safe. So he only wished to bargain. Didn't he?

This was a poor argument though. Such a disguise, on New Year's Eve, would arouse no question in anybody who happened to see him. It argued safety for him — not for me. And, besides things might have gone wrong; I might have been in a position to accuse him. Yes, fancy-dress costume made it far safer for him. This murderer was not one to overlook that patent fact.

He said in that shrill falsetto, "Your father's letter said there was a diary. You told Bersche to bring it to you. He didn't have it. Hatever had a diary and gave it to you, so I gave you two thousand dollars to keep your mouth shut about it. But I can't get rid of any more of the jewelry. I pawned that bracelet but I can't sell any more jewelry, it's too dangerous. I can't pay you —"

Because he said Hatever, it occurred to me flashingly and contrarily that the Santa Claus might be Hatever himself, using his own name to confuse me. Mr. Hatever had had the power of attorney; Mr. Hatever was respected in his profession, but my father had shared his offices for a long time; suppose sometime Mr. Hatever had stepped aside from his respected and respectable path and my father had known it. I could tell nothing from the voice that issued from the mass of curling white beard; the twinkling eyes were merely eyes, very bright and knowing and determined.

I said, "It was a mistake! I don't want money! I didn't know about my father's letters."

There was a moment's pause. I thought of flinging open the door behind me and screaming out into the night. Nobody could possibly hear me.

He said — she said — I still didn't know whose face was behind that fleece of whiteness, "But you know now. You know me. I can tell —"

There was a little movement. A white-gloved hand came out of the red suit and I looked straight at a small black hole surrounded with the gleam of metal.

I knew it for what it was. It was preposterous. Things like that didn't happen. This was happening. I caught at the draperies near me and knew that Cecile had done just that.

"Besides," said the red figure with chilling calm, still in a horrible falsetto, "the jewels are gone. Somebody took them. They were all in that chair, shoved down, hidden. Nobody ever comes in this room." The red figure was advancing toward me, quite deliberately, aiming the gun. "This gun — and the jewelry — they've been hidden here for months. Cecile had to be killed. She asked for it. There wasn't anything else to do. She knew me and she struggled and — I thought she'd be out cold but she wasn't. She woke up and fought me and — But the jewels are gone now. I got out the gun. It was here, too."

The falsetto was hard to keep up; it cracked a little. He wouldn't feel quite safe, I thought coldly, until he had touched the trigger of that gun — and then escaped, only another Santa Claus, on New Year's Eve, going to a fancy-dress ball.

He said, "I had to get out the gun. I didn't want to kill Bersche, either. But I had to. He made me. He said that I must have had one of those letters. I offered him the jewels to keep his mouth shut. Of course I wouldn't have given him all the jewels but — but then he wouldn't bargain. He wouldn't give me the diary. He knew me. I had to shoot him. He didn't think I would. He just stared at me —" There was almost a chilling kind of giggle behind the white beard. "He looked just the way you look now. But then he hit at me and I hit him and then — this gun was still loaded, after all that time. Five shots still in it. Four shots left. But you'd make it easier for yourself if you'd just drop yourself over the balcony. They'll call it suicide, too. But first, where is the real diary?"

I knew then who it was. He had looked in my handbag while I was trapped in the elevator; perhaps he had trapped me there for that purpose; he knew that the diary in my handbag was not a diary which could threaten anybody; so he said, now, where is the real diary?

I knew who had taken that enormous dress box from the elevator; I knew why the dress box was so big. It was because it had held two costumes and one of them was a Santa Claus costume, wig, beard, padding, gloves, even confetti.

I knew why there had been a trail of confetti leading into the room, beckoning me to follow; it had roused my curiosity, it had led me closer to the balcony door and the balcony and the long drop into darkness and snow and then nothing.

I edged back and the gun steadied. There was a movement behind the Santa Claus. I tried not to look, not to show that I had seen that movement. Uncle Sisley's wizened face, red-cheeked from the cold, bright-eyed, a green woolen scarf still around his throat, showed for a second beyond the Santa Claus's red shoulder. It was only a second, for Uncle Sisley shot upon the Santa Claus and flailed wildly at the white bearded face.

It nearly cost him his life, that idea of Uncle Sisley's to the effect that I knew something of Richard's false alibi and therefore something about Cecile's murder and that, therefore, he must keep a close eye on me even though he trusted me. For he had come to look for me, he had listened at the door. There was within him a blend of chivalry for me and caution about Richard's alibi. Chivalry won, for he launched himself at the Santa Claus and the Santa Claus fired the gun but not very coolly, taken by surprise. Uncle Sisley yelled and clapped one hand at an ear and fell down behind a chair in a scrambling heap and Richard came running from the hall, shouting at Garrity. The gun went off several times but Richard had the Santa Claus by the arm so the shots only hit the ceiling. Garrity had his other arm while a couple of policemen came pounding up the stairs and into the room. The gun slid across the rug and a policeman picked it up.

A little pale man, still in an overcoat, his hat in his hand, was thrust forward. Uncle Sisley jumped up and snatched off the Santa Claus's big white beard, which came off with the red cap and white wig, all in one piece. Uncle Sisley yelled something.

Garrity said, "Did you hear him admit murder?"

Uncle Sisley cried, "I heard it all! I heard it! That's the man. He murdered Cecile. He murdered that man, the secretary, Bersche. He did it for the jewels. He's your man."

Somebody thrust the little pale man forward. Everybody then looked at Santa Claus's face, which was now bare of white beard. He was young, yet he couldn't be as young as he looked. He was very like Miffy somehow standing there; but of course it wasn't Miffy, it was Slade.

The little pale man proved to be the pawnbroker's clerk but he was a disappointment. He couldn't identify Slade. He leaned over and peered and cleared his throat and shook his head and said he was sorry. "I can't be sure. This is a murder case, isn't it? Very serious. No, I can't be sure. The man who pawned the bracelet — that is, I think it was a man, had on dark glasses and — and you see it was a holiday and perhaps I'd had a drink or two at lunch, just a drink or two and —" He gave Garrity a despairing but dogged look. "I can't say it wasn't this one — this Mr. Amberly. I can't say it was this one — this — this Santa Claus. I can't say."

He never did say. But Uncle Sisley shot his cuffs and with a trickle of blood down his cheek from a neat nick on his ear said that he would swear to Slade's guilt. "I heard it all. I heard somebody up here. I — the girl — Miss Hilliard — anyway, there were reasons why I felt I ought to keep an eye on her, so I crept up the stairs and sure enough she was here and he — Slade — told it all. I heard it, every word. Come on, Fran. This is no place for you."

It was a moment of triumph for Uncle Sisley. He showed real nobility in cutting it off. He took me by the arm and hoisted me gently down the stairs for I really wasn't walking with any degree of steadiness. Mrs. Amberly looked at his ear and got a Band-Aid for it. He told Mrs. Amberly all about it.

She was a different woman, all at once, as if she'd dropped not only years but a crushing burden. "It's horrible," she said once while we waited. "Horrible. But it proves Richard didn't kill her. He's a free man now, really free. He never has been — not really since Cecile was murdered."

Uncle Sisley put coal on the fire; he told me that they had barely got home, he and Mrs. Amberly; he said that they had had to hire a car and go out to New Jersey because the damn fool lawyer had managed to get the flu and wasn't in his office and that the roads had been so bad that it had taken hours to get home again. The lawyer had come with them, temperature and all, and gone to his town apartment intending to see Richard the next morning. The police and Richard had come in only a moment after Mrs. Amberly and Uncle Sisley. They would have been too late.

Uncle Sisley patted his nicked ear gingerly but with pride and I couldn't even say thank you because he then eyed me and said, "Now — now! It's all over. Can't have you crying or anything —"

We heard them go down the stairs.

I thought of Slade, in the fancy-dress costume which had arrived in the same dress box with the costume Miffy must have ordered. Miffy must have known that Slade killed Cecile. She had almost defended Cecile's murderer; she had told me that perhaps Cecile had given him cause to murder her. I wondered where Miffy had gone and why. I thought of Slade, opening the heavy front door after he had searched my handbag and my room, pretending so convincingly that he had that instant come home, whistling, crossing to the elevator and releasing me — and then making his offer of friendship so much in the same way and for the same disarming purpose that Mr. Benni had sent me the white orchid. He had even said, almost in so many words, that he would pay me if I gave him time.

Richard came slowly into the library and Garrity came with him. Garrity came to me. "It's all right," he said. "I took the new evidence to the judge. He vacated the order for Amberly's arrest. It's all right."

I think I held Garrity's hand, rather to his embarrassment, while I listened to the new evidence. The police, that morning, had found the slight indentation in the little blue chair and had discussed it and measured it and taken pictures of it. Miffy had gone; so they looked for her, for somebody, Garrity reasoned, had recently removed the jewels, somebody had recently used the gun which, too, could have been hidden in that chair, in a room which was closed, which had its dreadful memories, which was never used.

"We started with the luxury hotels. She was in the third one we tried," Garrity said. "The police in the house this morning reported that she had gone. I phoned here thinking she might have returned. Nobody answered the phone."

Because I was trapped in the elevator, I thought. Then, discovering that I was still clutching Garrity's hand, I let go. He looked rather relieved and went on. "I simply tried hotels. It seemed to me that she might have gone so hurriedly this morning because she knew that we had a search warrant and were going to take a look again through the house for the gun and the rest of the jewels. She was quite likely to go to a hotel. Travel is so difficult in the storm that — well, it seemed worth a try. She was in the third one we tried." He turned to Richard who was standing at the mantel, his elbow on it, his hair still disheveled from his struggle with Slade. "The gun and the jewelry had to be hidden in some accessible place. It looked as if they had been hidden in that chair. But they weren't there or in the house when you reported your — Cecile's murder. We searched the house within the hour. So if they had actually been hidden in that chair, later, they had to have been brought back to the house at some time. We'd kept a close watch on everybody concerned for several days after Cecile was murdered. I didn't see how anybody could have gone to a checkroom or even to a safety deposit box without our knowledge. If the jewels and the gun were here they had to have been taken out of the house immediately following the murder and returned sometime later. And then," Garrity said, "I was studying over the accounts of the murder again and looking at the pictures and there was one showing Mrs. Henry Amberly — Miffy — returning from the ball. She was getting out of a car and you could see that she had taken off her dancing slippers. She carried a stole over one arm and I thought she must have had the slippers under her arm, too. I wondered if by any chance she had the gun and the jewels and if so how she got them."

Uncle Sisley said, "How?"

Garrity went on. "One of the men on duty here that night remembered Miffy because she was so pretty and he had hated to tell her what had happened. He said she had a brown paper bag under her stole and he looked at it, just a glance because the slippers were sticking out of it. That's all he saw. Slippers. But the jewels and the gun must have been in the bag too, below the slippers. She brought the jewels and the gun back here — *after* the house had been searched. She hasn't admitted it yet but my guess is that she kept the gun and jewels near her, perhaps in her own room until Cecile's room was closed. Nobody went into Cecile's room so Miffy simply shoved them into the chair, thinking they'd be safe, as they were."

I whispered, "Miffy had a key."

Uncle Sisley nodded vigorously. "Wait till I tell you! But go on —"

Garrity said, "Well, that's all. She had to get them out this morning before the police came to search. They would of course search the closed room. Slade knew where they had been."

I think I whispered, "Yes —"

"He had already got out the gun and killed Bersche."

I thought, yes; yes, he did. Uncle Sisley nodded again. "Go on. Go on."

"I think Miffy wanted out. Maybe she was getting to be afraid of Slade. Maybe she didn't have any plan except to get away — and take the jewels with her. But she had the fifth letter. She hadn't tried to dispose of it. Maybe she kept it as a hold over Slade. Maybe she just — kept it. I don't know. But the fifth letter was stuffed down in a pocket of one of her bags." Garrity squinted up his green eyes in a puzzled way. "She's very — childish, isn't she? A little naïve?"

"Naïve like a rattlesnake," said Uncle

Sisley waspishly but then he seemed to consider it and added, almost to himself, "But she's dumb. Always said so."

Richard said, "Let her see the letter," and looked at me.

Garrity showed me the letter. It was of course in my father's handwriting. There was an envelope directed to Mr. Slade Bell with the Amberly address. I read, "My dear Slade: I saw you check a paper bag about twelve o'clock the night of the ball, *after* Cecile had been killed. I spoke to you and I guessed from your manner that there was something odd about that paper bag; you didn't want me to see it. So I waited around near the check stand. I waited until Miffy came along and presented the claim check and took the paper bag. Miffy, not you, so I knew you had told Miffy to take it. I heard the news of the murder over a radio news report early that morning. I was sure there was something wrong and I gave Richard an alibi. No gun, no jewelry have turned up; I've watched the papers, I'd know. Now we'll forget all this — but it is in my diary which I am leaving to my daughter."

He ended with almost the same words with which he had ended his letter to Richard, which gave me the uncanny feeling of having lived through this before, at another time. "Almost the only thing my daughter has in the way of inheritance is my diary. With my gratitude in the measure that I must have had your gratitude for telling nobody that I saw you check a paper bag and Miffy carry it away." Yes, my father had sent the letters only to people who, he believed, had money — or the means to obtain it. Slade, he knew, had had the jewels.

There was a long silence. Then remotely in the distance through the snow we heard the sounds of automobile horns. A burst of shouts came up from some New Year's celebrants, going probably from one party to another.

Uncle Sisley reached out and turned on a radio; we heard shouts of Happy New Year and a burst of music and at that moment Wilbur and Stella came. Wilbur put his head in his hands when he heard and moaned. "And I got him a job! He's been away from the office half the time this week. I warned him, I told him, but I never thought of this —"

Perhaps all of us except Garrity stared at him and remembered. Wilbur had warned Slade, he had told Slade angrily that he'd better get on the job and keep regular hours; none of us had paid any attention to it. Not one of us had said, where was Slade if he wasn't at the office; was he at the house near Gramercy Park? Was he using Andre's key and searching the papers in Andre's apartment?

The key to that apartment and the missing keys to the Gramercy Park house were never found. Probably the keys, as well as Andre's wallet, were scooped up sometime into the maw of a truck clearing away snow.

Stella came to me and put her arms around me and kissed me quietly. Garrity looked at me and looked at Richard and said, "Happy New Year to you both."

Last New Year's Eve seems now a long time ago. The days that followed seem remote, too. They were never able to induce Miffy to admit taking the jewelry from the blue room after she had heard from Wilbur that the police were coming with a search warrant; yet the jewels had been found in her possession. She would never admit having known anything about the gun. She refused to say what her plan was — if she had a plan. She refused point-blank to explain how the fifth letter came into her possession, too, or why, knowing what it meant, she kept it.

It is possible that she took it, as Miffy

would, calmly, out of curiosity; that she kept it because she thought she might sometime want it. She wouldn't admit having taken the paper bag from the checkroom either. Yet Slade must have asked her to do it and he must have told her why. She must have seen my father there; she must have spoken to him briefly, and he knew, as he said in his letter, that there was something wrong. She had certainly brought the gun and the jewelry back into the house, after it had been searched, in the simplest, most open manner in the world. She had certainly concealed them, perhaps in one place and then another, like a grisly game of hide-and-seek during the days of the police inquiry. When at last Cecile's room was closed and locked and never visited by anybody, the little blue chair must have seemed a safe hiding place for at least several months. What she or Slade were going to do with them eventually remained a matter of conjecture; Slade would sell the jewels almost certainly, but only when and how it was safe to do so.

The only thing that was certain was that Miffy had prudently decided at last to jettison Slade, taking the jewels merely because she liked them and perhaps had grudged Cecile their possession. But Miffy never explained herself; she was childishly direct, as when she tried to frighten me away from the house and Richard, showing me the dreadful blue room, urging me into an elevator which had a habit of sticking; at the same time she was complex and stubborn. She always knew what she wanted.

She also knew what Slade had done; she couldn't have helped knowing. He had made it clear that he had gone from the ball to Cecile, believing that she'd be in a stupor, but she awoke and recognized him and they struggled over her jewelry and he shot her; he put the jewels and the gun in a paper bag from the kitchen and went back to the ball. He had told Miffy something or everything; Miffy had known; she had protected Slade.

The trial is over, though, and Miffy's gentleness, her beauty perhaps, something went far to exonerate her; her defense claimed that she had acted under duress, in fear of Slade, unwillingly, and the jury decided to believe it. The jury did not hesitate about Slade; and the case against him was so strong that he did not even appeal. Uncle Sisley was a star witness and wore a different waistcoat every day.

For some weeks the only thing approaching a diary was the hit-or-miss notebook which Mr. Hatever had so conscientiously and so dangerously returned to me and which meant nothing so far as a record was concerned but which Slade believed was the real diary. This was the diary for which he had searched while he kept me a prisoner in the elevator; which stuck as he hoped it would. Disappointed, he had then opened and closed the outside door with a bang and whistled and pretended that he had only then returned to the house instead of earlier, stealthily, at some time when neither Stella nor I heard his return.

But then the real diary was found. It came by mail to Mr. Hatever; the wrappings were battered and loose; the address was blurred and incorrect; the handwriting was spiky and French. Apparently my father had had one of his nurses wrap and address the small package and it had not only required some research on the part of the post office but it had got itself confused in the great volume of Christmas mail; it seemed remarkable that it ever reached Mr. Hatever at all.

The diary itself was in an enclosure marked "Hold for Fran if she ever asks about it." There was no way of knowing my father's motive except it seemed clear that he could not give the diary directly to me for he could not have told me of his scheme, yet he had felt he couldn't destroy the diary either. There was no solution for him so he had taken the only course that occurred to him.

The diary was not actually a diary; it was a specific recording of the facts of the Amberly case as he had known them. It came too late but it bore out the facts as the police then knew them. Mr. Benni appeared in it also; Mrs. Clabbering appeared; Uncle Sisley did not appear. There were some other entries which Lieutenant Garrity read with a gleam in his green eyes but shook his head over, and during the trial it seemed to me that everybody went to some pains to keep these odd entries from being read in public. After the trial I burned the diary myself; Garrity and Richard watched me.

Tonight is New Year's Eve again. The blue Mediterranean, stretching to the sky outside the windows, is beginning to turn purple and wine-colored as the sun sinks. There will be festive dinners tonight, all up and down the Côte d'Azur. The dress I'll wear is already across the bed waiting for me; it is white and lacy; it was my wedding gown.

Yes, it was inevitable, this return to Nice. But Richard and I can go now, anywhere we choose; we can return home when we like and there will be no whispers, no lingering doubts, no danger. We'll dance tonight and have champagne but pause for a moment when the New Year comes in and perhaps remember. Then the lights and the music will come up again.

The employees of Thorndike Press hope you have enjoyed this Large Print book. All our Large Print titles are designed for easy reading, and all our books are made to last. Other Thorndike Press Large Print books are available at your library, through selected bookstores, or directly from the publishers.

For more information about titles, please call:

(800) 223-1244
(800) 223-6121

To share your comments, please write:

Publisher
Thorndike Press
295 Kennedy Memorial Drive
Waterville, Maine 04901